LYSANDRA

A Novel

T.J. ZAKRESKI

First Printing, October 2018

ISBN-13: 978-1-9995077-0-1

Dancing Star Publications
500, 123 - 2nd Avenue South
Saskatoon SK Canada S7J 7E6

www.dancingstarpublications.ca

PROLOGUE: THE MAYFLOWER

The *Mayflower* is as quiet as an asteroid, riding a wave of warped space at twice the speed of light. A sizzle-powered Hail Mary thrown from Earth and aimed at exoplanet Terra. Earth was breathing her last breath when they left her and their dream of life on Terra was little more than a theoretical possibility. Meanwhile, inside the ship's spinning web of pods, millions of interplanetary refugees are sparking away in 4-Code, a few hundred Re-gens are running the show and the ship's mainframe and saucy bio-bot, CAM-DI, is telling them stories.

She's unpacking them from encrypted tarot cards that came with their digital stowaway, Cygnus. The tarot cards, CAM-DI explained, represent realized events, quantum pathways that have been crossed from every single pathway that could have been crossed. From the first array, she told them how Cygnus was shot out from Earth centuries ago as a digital exile, reached Terra, was downloaded by an unwitting lawyer, crashed the internet and made a biblical mess of things trying to reincarnate himself as a cloned version of Terra's Jesus.

"But I thought he was destroyed at the end?" Commander Penny Armstrong objects.

"Me too, but there's a second array and therefore a second story that involves him."

"*A second array*. You've got to be kidding. How long is this going to

"CAM-DI . . . are you okay?"

"Sorry Commander," CAM-DI says, recomposing herself, "decoding these cards is making me feel a little ill."

"It's Cygnus, I told you we should have deleted that guy," a concerned Carlos says, standing up.

"As if any virus can worm into me," CAM-DI huffs, then softens, "don't worry Carlos, he's safely shuttered away and I'm fine. It's the cards, they confirm something I've been suspecting for a while."

"*Now* would be a good time, CAM-DI," Penny says after a few impatient moments.

"Sorry Commander," CAM-DI squirms, "but you're not going to like it."

Penny's olive eyes glare.

"Okay, I don't think we're placed where were supposed to be if you will."

"What do you mean *placed*? We're off course?" Penny spins to call up a trajectory display of the Mayflower's progress through the cosmos.

"No Commander, we're where we should be."

"Then what do you mean?" Penny asks, turning off the display.

"The problem isn't with *where* we are so much as *where-when* we are."

Penny's face twists into a question mark.

CAM-DI sighs, "Sorry Commander, I'm going to have to decrypt this second array for you to understand."

"Will they tell us how Cygnus got here?"

"They should, but they're also about someone else."

"Who's that?"

"Remember that girl at the end of the first story whose birth destroyed Cygnus?" CAM-DI asks, her sapphire eyes dancing, as she waves a hand over the floating Major Arcana archetypes.

"Yeah, what about her?"

"This is her story."

CHAPTER 1:
THE SPEAR OF DESTINY

I t's too cool in the shade and too hot in the sun. So, Thomas O'Brian shifts in and out of the shade at the cathedral entrance to the Hands of Prayer tower in New Lancashire City.

He's waiting for a motorcade and so are *Robed's* cameras and booms.

He first laid eyes on it in Osterbayern, when it was on display at the Hofburg Palace Museum. The Holy Lance. The spearhead that the Roman centurion, Longinus, wielded when he pierced the side of Yeshua. In fulfillment of the scriptures that not a single bone of his would be broken. That water and blood would flow from the wound. Fame and destiny would flow from Thomas's hands because he was destined to hold it, to possess it. It had many names—the Holy Lance, Longinus's Spear—but the one that Thomas liked was the one that the Nazis used—"The Spear of Destiny". It would be a talisman through which he and his Church would split the world again.

The curator, Dr. Wolfgang Eckhart, is supposed to conduct the ceremonial hand-over. What was actually being handed over was an empty box. An elegantly adorned reliquary, but empty just the same. The true Lance was waiting for Thomas in Las Pecado in a plain shipping crate under the protection of the Church's elite guard. The relic was "on loan" from the Hofburg Museum, thanks to a sustained and intense campaign of lies, extortion and cunning diplomacy. A triangulation of pressure to pry the relic out of its ancestral home. Diplomats, on the Church's payroll, used war guilt to shame the Osterbayern government to lend it as a symbolic war reparation.

Key officials were targeted with bribes and extortion. But the clincher was that Wolfgang himself, a prominent member of the Harpsburger family, was an aspirant of the Grail. He was seduced by promises of the Church's holiest prize, attainable only by selected celebrities and the very rich—the living blood of Mary Magdalene.

Wolfgang's envoy rolls up in a pageant of black limousines and flashing blue lights. Thomas steps out of the shade, all pompadour and circumstance. A conclave of Church leaders falls into line behind him. The Church's private security force is sprinkled in the barricade-pressing crowd, disguised in Hawaiian shirts and Bermuda shorts. Sun and nerves make Thomas sweaty. He wants to tuck in his shirt that his belly is continually pulling out, in spite of its fine Savile Row tailoring. Instead, he twists the corners of his mouth into a toothy preacher's smile and waddles up to greet Wolfgang with an outstretched, greasy hand, as Wolfgang and his envoy crest the top of the stairs.

"Gruss Gott, Wolfgang, I am so happy you made it."

Wolfgang's hands are sweaty and he's out of breath from the climb. His charcoal eyes regard Thomas over his pince-nez glasses. His shoe-polish hair is cut into straight bangs, like a Beatles' mop top. At first, it looks as though he's trying to pick up Thomas's scent through his hooked nose, but he breaks into a friendly, yellow-toothed, grin.

"Gruss Gott, Herr O'Brian. I come bearing gifts."

On cue, an attaché behind Wolfgang presents the reliquary. Thomas receives it, with a bowed head and reverent sigh. The Church elders bob their heads in unison. After the photo op, Thomas hands the reliquary to one of the guards and the ensemble turns to walk toward the cathedral entrance, with Thomas's arm slung over Wolfgang's shoulder.

They deferentially slow to Wolfgang's pace.

A nasty spine-severing motorcycle accident left him a quad. Now his limbs are propelled by a combination of external robotics and internal neurological rewiring. They're very discreet and smooth, considering, but the robotic parts still show through his pants and he judders forward, with servos making a faint whirly sound.

"So, how was your flight, Wolfgang?"

"It was comfortable and the inflight was satisfactory—"

"That's good."

"But my heart still soars with anticipation," he says, whirling forward in starts and stops.

"I am glad that the flight was to your liking."

"Yes. But my mind was elsewhere. Thinking that each kilometer was bringing me closer—"

Clearing his throat, Wolfgang turns to flash his amber incisors at Thomas.

"I trust that the arrangements have been made?"

"But of course, Dr. Eckhart." Thomas grins and stops to squint up with Wolfgang at the cloud-scraping spires of the Hands of Prayer tower. "They're fetching her now."

"Thank you, miss," the man with the St. Luke's mission hat smiles.

"You can't give something to everybody, Lysandra."

"I know, Daddy, but you said that I was supposed to give money to the missions instead of directly."

"Just not to every one of those, sweetheart."

Joe turns to smile at his daughter, like he always does. Surrogate child, but a ringer for Juliette, with her curly locks. But not her olive skin to Juliette's milky white. Her blue-brown eyes to Juliette's mahoganies. Nor in their movements. Where Juliette wrapped around the world like a pillow, Lysandra leaps through it like a tiger. It was their big, light-up-the-world smiles that made them most alike. Would they have fought? Friends for life? He'll never know, because Juliette popped off the planet the day Lysandra popped in.

"Okay, just text me when you're ready to leave."

"Yes, Daddy."

Joe lingers on the sidewalk, watching the retail labyrinth ensnare his daughter, while a man in a Hawaiian shirt and Bermuda shorts brushes by him. There's another, a half-block away, leaning against a building and staring at him. Joe turns up his collar and walks down the street, looking for a pub.

He finds an inviting alehouse, slips in and sits at the bar on a ripped vinyl-padded barstool. He orders a pint, then sips it while taking in the faux English décor. He taps his watch and the virtual screen pops up. He reads an email and then shuts it off to watch baseball on the holo screen. He thinks of Juliette and what she would have done. For starters, she would have gone into the store, instead of stopping in for a pint. But he's useless in those places and would only have been a drag, looking lost and bored. It's the next part that's bothering him. The email reminded him of the importance of making the medical appointment the Church scheduled for Lysandra's "genetic condition" and that they were expecting at 1:30, "sharp".

"Sharp" was written in the same un-bolded and un-italicized font as the rest of the text, but it nevertheless dripped with menace.

"Would you like another, sir?"

Joe looks at the time.

"Yeah, make it a Bloody Mary, though."

The bartender waits for him to tap his watch against the ePay screen. Payment in advance. Halfway through his drink, her text comes.

"Ready."

"That was quick, be right there," he says into his watch, which condenses it into text-speak and spits it out. He taps the screen again to leave a generous rating and paltry tip and heads back to the store.

"Did you find anything?"

"A couple of tops and shorts," she says, proudly holding up the shopping bags.

"Any bargains?"

"Oh yeah, they were half off."

"You don't think they were double to begin with?"

"*Daaad* . . . So where we going now?"

"How'd you like to go to the top of the Hands of Prayer tower?" Joe asks, spotting the man in Bermuda shorts behind them.

"I dunno, can't we just go back to the hotel?"

"Come on, it'll be fun."

"I don't know, Daddy. Maybe you can just drop me off at the hotel and then you can go?"

"Honey . . . I can't, we both have to be there."

"What do you mean, we both have to be there?"

"It's the Church . . . they . . . we have . . . listen, I'm in charge here, and when I say we have to go somewhere . . . we have to."

"Well, it's my duty as a soldier to disobey unlawful commands."

"Ha-ha, Lysandra, I'm not kidding around here. You have a doctor's appointment."

"*Doctor's appointment?*" she says, stopping on the sidewalk to face him with her arms pointed down. "You never said anything about a doctor's appointment."

"I'm sorry, honey, I've told you before that you have to go to these appointments because of . . ." he says, then lowers his voice, "your . . . your genetic condition."

"I just don't see why the stupid Church has to be involved in everything."

"Honey," Joe says, looking back at the man in the Bermuda shorts who's frantically talking into his wrist, "you know you can't talk that way, after all they've done for us."

After burning a hole through Joe with her eyes, Lysandra turns to walk again.

After a block, Joe asks her if she's excited about the game.

She answers with crossed arms and downcast eyes.

"Hi, Lysandra, I'm Dr. Roberts," the tall bespectacled man with a shiny head and stethoscope around his neck says flatly, walking into the examining room on floor fifty-seven.

Lysandra clutches her hospital gown and presses her legs together, sitting on the black vinyl examining table with a scratchy paper sheet pressed beneath her and feet dangling down to the cold rubber step stool. She had been waiting for fifteen minutes, alone with the eye chart, cupful of tongue depressors and health propaganda posters.

"How are you feeling today?"

"Okay."

"Good. Your bloodwork came back fine, mind if I examine you?"

No answer.

"Great," he says, tapping the side arm of his glasses, pressing a cold stethoscope above her breast and then on her back. "Cough, please ... any problems with your menstrual cycle?"

"No."

"Grit your teeth," he says, looking at her mouth. "Follow my finger," he says, tracking her eyes as he moves his finger in front of them. "Tell me when I'm wiggling my finger," he says, wiggling a finger out to the side of her head.

He gets her to hold her arms up, while he presses down; her wrists up, while he does the same. He tells her to relax her arms, while he gives them a quick twist. Bumps her elbows, wrists and knees with a rubber hammer, gauging her reflexes.

"Are you sexually active?" he asks, scraping the bottoms of her feet with a stick.

"*Ouch* ... and no."

"Tell me when you stop feeling this," as he hits a tuning fork and presses it against her toes, slightly massaging her ankles as he waits for her replies.

"Are you taking any birth control pills?"

"No."

He makes notes in his tablet.

"Would you like the nurse to come in for the next part?"

Lysandra looks at him, confused, "Um ... no, I guess?"

"Good. You're doing just fine. Have you noticed any lumps on your breasts?"

"No."

"Do you mind if I examine them?"

No answer.

"Hold your arm behind your head please," he says, as he reaches under her hospital gown and examines one, sending shivers down her spine. "Good . . . and the other . . . good."

He opens her gown to study her chest in the cold air, while her face flushes.

"Lie down, please."

He presses his fingers down on her stomach in several spots. "Any pain?"

"No."

"Okay, I'm going to get you to move to the edge of the bed and put your feet up here," he says, clinking the stirrups into place, then turning to snap on plastic gloves.

She feels the cold metal speculum slide in.

"You're doing just fine . . . juuuuuust fine . . . okay," he says, snapping off his gloves. "Everything looks great. I'm going to prescribe a mild sedative," he says, writing more notes on the tablet, then tapping his glasses again.

"The nurse will be in to give you one, before she takes you to your next appointment," he says, briskly exiting in his scrubs and white jacket, clutching his tablet.

***

Thomas opens the box to take out the reliquary and places it carefully on his desk. Back from New Lancashire, he's in his penthouse office on the Las Pecado strip. The Hands of Prayer tower in Pecado is a shrunken, gaudier version of the one in New Lancashire, with a casino, hotel rooms and the cadet academy, which serves as the main filming location for *Robed*.

The meeting with the curator was a diplomatic coup. Wolfgang is begging to join. Pervert. How stupid was he, to think they wouldn't record him masturbating to a virgin's gynecological exam? More to squeeze him with, he supposes. He and the other celebrities. Wearing vestments and drinking "the blood of a new covenant," which was her blood, mixed with some wine. It would give them strength and vision, they promised. The third eye, they promised. And they totally bought it. Hook, line and sinker. If life taught him anything, it's that it's not what's true that matters. It's what is *believed* to be true. So what if she looked like any other bored teenager?

If they *believed* she was Mary Magdalene.

It'll last for a while. It'll bring in tons of cash and a steady supply of suckers. Suckers like Wolfgang in search of something they're never going to find. Make it expensive. Make it rare. Call it the Grail. Like any good pusher, he's going to have to find ways to keep them coming. Bigger promises. More spectacular rituals. All he knows is that the kid better start performing or it's going to be curtains for her. He wonders how far their legal rights went, since they own her DNA. He makes a mental note to run it by Tucker.

After the special brain MRIs, the Boss left no instructions. The last he spoke was thirteen years ago. Did her being a girl change anything? Do they still go ahead with the MRIs? The Boss said they were critically important.

The Boss.

Where did he go?

They have a few theories. That he was Dr. Van de Whey, who gave them the technology to clone the blood from the cloth into Yeshua. That he was the "Swan" who gave them their out-of-this-world video games that still fund the Church's activities. The new games weren't as mind-blowing as those first ones. Not by a long shot. Something happened that threw a wrench in Dr. Van de Whey's plans. A girl probably had something to do with it. Dr. Van de Whey could be every-where and anyone he wanted. But he only seemed to exist virtually. That was the key. If he was digital, couldn't they just reboot him?

Thomas has the box on his desk, hesitating before opening it. When he first saw it at the museum, as a blood relic to add to the Church's collection, he went into a trance of reverent awe. He felt as though it was his destiny to possess it. That it would allow the Church to grow more powerful than ever. Many believe that the Spear was the key to the rise of the Nazis. That Himmler was obsessed with possessing it. That it was the first place he went to after the Anschluss. It was brought to the heart of Nazi power in Nuremburg and it is said that Himmler took his life at the precise moment that it fell into Allied hands. The atomic bombs were dropped while the States United possessed it.

Powerful shit, this Spear.

Being associated with the Nazis, the Spear was relegated to a mere museum piece, one of many spears vying to be the Lance wielded by Longinus. Scientific analysis proved to be inconclusive. But that was the exterior. Embedded within it, was a single nail with a square nail head, proven to be from the first century.

A nail with blood on it.

In possession of the Spear of Destiny, Himmler believed himself to be invisible, unstoppable. After all, this was the same spear wielded by Constantine, Charlemagne and a line of Holy Roman Emperors. After the Nazis were destroyed along with their Reich, the Spear fell out of favor as a good luck charm. But Thomas still saw its potential. That the Spear could do good or evil, depending on who possesses it. It's been that way from the start. It was evil to plunge a spear into Yeshua's ribs. It was good not to prolong his suffering. It was evil to confirm his mortality. It was good to confirm his divinity.

Good or evil, made no difference to Thomas. In it, he saw an overlooked nail, authenticated to be from the first century. Authenticated to be stained with blood they can sluff off as the son of Man's. If they could only crank up the cloning trials again. If only Dr. Van de Whey was still around, because without his DNA rebuilding techniques, they were too many years away. It wouldn't matter who they ended up cloning. It's what they *believe* that matters. Thomas needs help. He needs inspiration. The Church is running out of money. It needs a cloned Yeshua it can flog for fame and fortune.

He reaches for the bowl of peyote soup the cadets made. Peyote, marijuana, LSD, all encouraged in the Church's services and mandatory for cadets. This gave them an edge over their competition who only promised a spiritual awakening after years of careful study, reflection and devotion. No one had time for that anymore. The Church promised instant illumination. Sure, you could spend years in a cave, studying ancient texts on a diet of grasshoppers. Or you could just take a little pill. They threw in sex, too. They dangled stardom, a chance to be a reality

TV celebrity on *Robed*. Where other churches dabbled in mind-fucking, they went at it with a drill, right into the cranium.

He forces the bitter soup down and nearly throws up. He chases it with a beer, but his mouth feels like sandpaper. Nothing happens at first, so he opens the box and takes out the Spear, stares at it for a while, at its gold and silver wrapping. He peers through the aperture at the nail imbedded within.

At the nail.

⸺◆◆◆◆⸺

Twelve hours later and he's naked on the altar, looking up at the shroud, the memories looping like a badly edited R-rated movie. The image of the suffering Yeshua looks down upon him. An embarrassed cadet runs up with a robe. He stands up and the cadet helps him put it on. He looks around. Glimpses at a black half-globe in the corner of the altar that he knows has a camera and frowns.

"Where are my clothes?" he asks, the words cement-mixing in his brain.

"In your office, sir."

His face twists with concern.

"And the Spear?"

"There as well."

He sighs with relief. He has a memory of running around naked with it, shouting, *I am light, the spirit and the way. I am the Mustard King.*

"See to its safety."

"Yes, sir."

"Oh—"

The servant turns around.

"Bring me a coffee, too."

"Yes, sir."

"And some Avee-360s."

He scratches his head, trying to reconstruct a timeline for the last several hours. He must have been outside at some point, looking up at the cosmos and having a body orgasm, if not an actual one. Something he said about spilling his seed on the ground to bring new life into the world. A techno-wizard. The anti-Christos. He grabs an apple from a bowl on the way back to the confessional booth elevator to his office. White-robed cadets pass by, nod, but look down when they see their beloved Leader in a bathrobe and eating an apple. Thomas stiff-lips past them, wondering if he will need to call in Tucker and his legal team, again.

A nausea-inducing confessional booth elevator ride and he's back in his penthouse office, relieved to see the Spear unharmed, carefully put back into its encasement and taken to the vault. Another white-robed cadet comes in with his coffee and Avee-360s. He grunts and waves her away, sits at his desk, swallows the pills and chases them down with the sacred tar.

"Geoff?" he says, pressing the buzzer on his desk.

"Geoff, here."

"Any dead bodies?"

"No."

"Thank God. Future lawsuits?"

"I doubt it."

"Good," Thomas exhales, leaning back in his chair. "Get over to editing and collect the tapes. Then gaslight any of the cadets who saw or know anything."

"I'm on it."

Thomas clicks off, then notices the sticky notes stuck on random spots on his desk. They're in his handwriting, but he has no memory making them. He shuts his eyes and pukes some acid apple-coffee in his mouth. That's his handwriting all right, but the style and wording belong to someone else. He gulps down more coffee to kill the taste and soothe his burning throat.

Was he channeling someone?

He peels the notes off his phone, pictures of his kids and computer screen, and he arranges them on his desk. Together, they make Four Points of Destiny:

1. His name is Cygnus. He will come again to reward us with eternal life.
2. His number is four.
3. The fallen lawyer's words and his computer are <u>KEE</u>.

4.   Through the blood of the nail, the world will be conquered.

Thomas is pretty sure *Cygnus* was Dr. Van de Whey and the *lawyer* was that guy who got caught with his pants down, in the Great Internet Crash. The two must be related, somehow. But, what does KEE mean? He supposes that the lawyer's old computer must still be in government hands.

It probably holds the KEE.

He looks down into his coffee and daydreams. He needs help with this one. It's time to call in a favor. He knows someone in the White House who might be able to help. Another Grail aspirant. He picks up his phone and tells it to get President Sparzo on the line.

CHAPTER 2:
THE SUN AND THE STRIP

Lysandra yells *shotgun* and the race is on.

Rachel, caught behind, smiles and tries to catch up, but Lysandra easily beats her. She turns to watch her friend jog up, slightly pigeon-toed and out of breath. Bradley, Rachel's brother, is barely legal to drive, with a wisp of a mustache and ruffled hair. Lysandra peeks in on him, while smiling and tugging at the door handle.

Bradley's in on it, just not all in. He thinks the girls are cutting a pep rally to hang out at Cookie's for the day. He was pestered into giving them a ride but wasn't in on their grander plans. He's straight out of gym class, wearing his Virgin Valley High t-shirt, with one hand on the headrest and the other cocked over the steering wheel.

Lysandra folds the seat forward to let Rachel squeeze in the back, Rachel slides in and whips out her phone and taps away to make a bouncing hologram of texts. Rachel's wearing her white tee and sun logo. It's got a naked baby riding a white pony under an anthropomorphized sun. It suits the day, because it's a day for sunglasses.

Good thing Bradley has the air conditioner going, Lysandra thinks, because her pits are already sweaty. His blue mirror sunglasses reflect the desert backing the school, but hardly hide his stolen glances at her thighs. The car smells of gym class and cherry lip gloss.

Lysandra buckles up and twists around to wink at Rachel, who sticks her tongue out in reply. Bradley puts the car in gear and nudges away. The car's old enough to have a manual steer, that Bradley pilots with a flexed arm. The rest of him is slightly angled toward Lysandra, whose knees point back.

"You guys better not say anything about this 'cause if Mom and Dad find out, I'll lose my whip privileges for weeks."

"Oh my God, Bradley," Rachel blurts through her braces and texts, catching her brother in the rearview. "You're *such* a pill."

Meanwhile, Bradley makes a wide turn onto main street and then side-glances at Lysandra.

"So, how was New Lancashire?"

Lysandra runs her hands over sweaty knees. "Um, pretty cool. Did some shopping and went to a Leviathans's game."

"No friggin' way . . . the Delphis one?"

"Uh-huh."

"Must have been sick."

"You bet."

"Gifford sure lit it up in the fourth quarter?"

"Uh-huh, saw it all from the stands."

"Lysie, you weren't even watching," Rachel says, hitting the back of Lysandra's seat. "You were busy texting me the whole time, telling me how bored you were."

"Was too . . . I was just saying that so you wouldn't turn into a big ole jelly bean," Lysandra says, spinning to nix any further fact-checking and then turning back to watch the town roll by. She half invites Bradley's frequent shoulder checks of her junior high schoolers, that Rachel protests by jamming her knee into the back of her seat.

"I like this, who is it?" Lysandra asks, after a block of silence.

"Old song from the teens, Holly Macve, *No One Has The Answers*."

"Cool."

Bradley turns up the volume, while Lysandra turns around to grin at Rachel, who rolls her eyes in disgust. Lysandra pouts back at her, Bardot style, like they have been practicing, while Holly twangs about no one having any answers. "Still don't," Lysandra thinks to herself. "No truer words."

"You guys sure she's going to be home?"

"Just texted, yup."

Cookie is the stage name for Annabelle Delacroix, an exotic dancer working the clubs in Pecado and its bedroom towns. A weed or a rose in the garden of Mesquite, depending on who you ask. A God-fearing town, in spite of having been spawned by gambling and other such vices. Cookie was the one who turned them on to Brigitte Bardot, sexiest women ever born, *à son avis*. She had taken an interest in Lysandra, a motherless girl growing up on her block. The girls were welcome over at her place any time they could get away. Which, in their hearts, was never enough. "Men," she would say, "are like floors. Lay them right once and you can walk on them forever."

Like, who says that?

The car rolls up outside her home. The girls sling their bags over their shoulders, pile out and bid a quick goodbye.

"Thanks," they say.

Lysandra lingers on the sidewalk to watch Bradley drive away.

"Stop that."

"I can't help it if your brother's cute."

"He's got a girlfriend," Rachel groans.

"So ... doesn't mean ... no one has the answers anyway," Lysandra huffs, as they head up to Cookie's house on springy legs still suited for running around swimming pools, after dogs and skipping. They pause on the landing, smile at each other and savor the moment, before ringing the doorbell to Cookie's magical queendom.

The bell chimes the horn line from *The Stripper*.

Rachel's silver smile sparkles in Lysandra's heart-shaped Wayfarers.

They hear a muffled, "*Come in,*" from the other side, along with a booming bass beat. They twist the handle and walk into the modest bungalow, into Narnia. They call out, "Cookie?" a few times before finding her in her living room, stretching in sweats and a cut-off sweater. She has a remake of "Porn Star Dancing" blasting on her hockey puck-sized speaker, beside her cup of coffee monogrammed with *The Best Louvres Are French*. After bending to touch her forehead to her knee, she rolls into the splits and then springs up to dance and stretch, eyeing the girls up like they're strip club trade. Red-faced, the girls don't know what to say or do, so they plop themselves on Cookie's couch and get pulled down into its cushiony charms. Meanwhile, the diminutive blonde-haired, green-eyed dancer sways and bobs like an exotic hypnotizing cobra. If sex could be bottled, she'd be it.

"So, how was New Lancashire?" she asks with a creamy Kebec accent, swaying her bottom at them. Then flips her hair back and shakes her breasts with her hands, while throwing a leg up on the couch beside Lysandra, smiling at all her squirming and reddening.

"Okay. We went to quite a few places. I really liked Times Square a lot."

"Yeah?"

Cookie quick-switches to twerking her rear just above Lysandra's knees. Lysandra responds by digging her hands into the couch and trying to push back. Rachel stares at them both through her amber-colored, horn-rimmed glasses and presses her knees together with nervous hands. Wafts of Cookie's hair and cologne drift into their noses, smelling of cotton candy. "So, did you meet any cute boys?" Cookie asks, flipping her hair back, while strolling to and fro, before grabbing a pole and wrapping herself around it like an erotic tether ball. Her sweats are baggy, but still imprinted by her dancer lines.

"Nah, but when we went up in the First Amerigo tower, I had to meet a bunch of creepy old men with the Church, dressed up in funny robes and stuff."

Shit! The words got out and she can't suck them back in again. Cookie sees her eye twitch before looking down. She wasn't supposed to say anything, but it's too late. Cookie smelled the fart and shuts the music off. It isn't a record scratching off, but the effect's the same.

"*Quoi?*" she says, hands on her hips.

"It was nothing. Just some Church people that I was supposed to meet. Anyway, we were hoping we could borrow a few of your hotel cards, so Rach and I can get into a pool on the strip."

Cookie swishes the words in her mouth and tastes vinegar.

"I mean, we were hoping."

"*C'est ça?*" she says as she grabs her workout bottle and patters off to the kitchen. The girls hear her rummaging around, then go into another room. Rachel turns to Lysandra to whisper, "You never told me—"

"It's nothing. Just stupid Church stuff," Lysandra whispers back, eying over at the kitchen, then slowly reaching for Cookie's cigarettes.

"*Lysie,*" Rachel whispers, "*what are you doing?*"

Lysandra fumbles out three from the silver package with the scary cancer images. Drops one, reaches down to hide it in her hand and shoots up just before Cookie walks back. Cookie pretends not to notice. Instead, she reaches for the same pack, tosses hotel cards on the coffee table and reclines on her sofa chair. She lights up one and puffs, looking at them with half-opened eyes. She smokes the real kind. She says that without fire and danger, *feu et danger*, there is no point. Cookie preferred to package herself with thrills, even if that package warned of charcoaled lungs and horror show teeth. Fire and danger. Nothing wagered, nothing gained.

"What happened?"

"With what?"

"You know what with?"

"It was nothing. They were just wearing robes is all. Anyway, I'm not supposed to talk about it."

"Ma cherie," she says, exhaling a puff of smoke, "when men ask you to keep quiet about how they make their money, they are to be respected. If it's about what they want to do, or did, with your body, all respect is off the table." She leans over and says, "*Comprends-tu?*" Half winking and half nodding.

"They didn't do anything with my body. I was just supposed to stand there while they all chanted something."

"Did they make you wear anything?"

"Just a stupid red robe."

"What were they chanting?"

"I don't know, *san grin-um Maria*, or something."

Cookie wrinkles her nose.

"Well, *sang* is French for blood, soooo—"

She taps her watch. "What's the Latin word for bloody, Chu-Chu?"

Chu-Chu answers, "*Sanguineum.*"

"Ah ha," Cookie says, clicking Chu-Chu off. "So, they were chanting Bloody Mary to you, *c'est très louche*, and where was your *père* when all this chanting was happening?"

"He wasn't in the room, but he was there. The Church paid for the whole trip—and they never hurt me—and my Dad said it was important—and it was just a stupid Church thingee anyway."

Lysandra decides not to mention the creepy medical exam or the pill they gave her that nearly knocked her out.

Cookie studies her, then reaches over to put her hand on Lysandra's knee.

"Ma cherie, I don't care who—the Church or even your *père*—no man gets to say what you do with your body or do anything to your body you don't want them to. And if anyone touches you wrong, you tell me, *c'est ça?*"

Cookie lowers her chin and eyes up Lysandra with a direct look.

"Yes, Cookie," Lysandra says, feeling ashamed that she didn't put up a better fight, but relieved that she had someone like Cookie looking out for her.

"Now . . . as for the cards . . ."

Rachel doubles over in a coughing fit, nearly throwing up. Lysandra nearly does as well, she's laughing so hard.

They're standing by a wall, behind the bus station, waiting for the 11:20 Rapid Transit to McCain. From there, it's the monorail to the strip.

"You're such a *tit*," Lysandra laughs.

"You're . . . *cough* . . . no . . . *cough* . . . better," Rachel gasps, trying to breathe.

"Yes, I am—"

Lysandra takes a puff, exhales and tries to hold a smile.

"*See?*"

Then coughs worse than Rachel, waving her hand in front of her face.

French smoke grabs the tips of their tongues with its bitter tobacco sting. Virgin lungs recoil, choking off oxygen, leaving them dizzy and euphoric. It tastes of adulthood—exhilarating and foul. They look at each other, each having bitten from the poisoned apple. Bad bitches now. Best friends forever.

"Oh *merde*, our chariot awaits ... *cough* ... ma ... *cough* ... cherie," Lysandra says, noticing that their magic electric bus has arrived.

Lysandra flicks the stolen Bardot on the cracked asphalt and grinds it with her shoe. She grabs Rachel, jean shorts, sun shirt and all, to make their RT. Lysandra's wearing her New Lancashire shorts and tank top. The two run to the front of the building, coughing all the way. They run their e-tickets under the scanner, fast walk down the aisle, suppressing smiles and coughs, then swing into seats near the back. Lysandra looks out the tinted glass and takes off her sunglasses.

"It's cold in here, hand me my sweater from your ho bag, won't you please, Titlet," she says to Rachel.

Rachel grumbles, then digs out their sweaters. "Gum?" Rachel offers, with a juicy-lipped silver smile. Rachel's sky-blue eyes are shrunk by her glasses, that she pushes up the bridge of her button nose.

"Oh God, *yes*. My mouth tastes like something crawled up in it and died."

"Mine, too," Rachel says, chewing. "That was pretty weird with your church going all Rosemary's Baby on you and stuff. Are you *sure* nothing happened?"

Lysandra digs into her bag and retrieves a set of hotel cards Cookie gave them. She waves them in front of Rachel.

"Pick a card, any card, my dear," she says, in falsetto.

"I mean, weren't you scared?" Rachel asks, picking the red one.

"The Cosmos it is, my fair lady—"

"—nah, it was just a bunch of Church people doing weird Church things. Anyway ... enough about churches and boring old men. I mean, *I gotta pocketful of ice and my cheese with gravy*," she sings. "*You've got your solo cup and I've got ...*"

They put their arms up in a cheerleader pose.

"*Las Pecado, ba-by.*"

The girls are parked on teak deck chairs. The sky's a pool-filtered blue. There's a table between them, icy sodas with vodka sloshed into them. A mixed, older crowd. Not quite the party pool they wanted, but still. They scan the pool area, looking for boys and trouble. They speak expansively, as though on a stage. Alcohol, sun and fresh off the apple truck did that. Taut and perky. Rough country roads might eventually shake some bolts loose, but they're screwed down tight now. Still fresh from the factory.

Cookie's cards got them in, with nary a glance. They collected pool towels, all sunhats, shades and smiles. Oversized bags around their shoulders with a change of clothes and water bottles filled with vodka that Rachel stole from home. Their RT left at sundown. Perfect plan. Perfect day. They lean back into their chairs, grinning at the sun.

"This sure beats a pep rally, huh, Rach?"

Rachel's half-smile shoots back silver agreement. "You have to watch this," Rachel says, handing her iPoodle over. Rachel's read-watching a book-movie series about an alien-slaying teen, Dotty Zerconovich. Lysandra watches the kiss between Dotty and the alien heartthrob, Timotay, meows and hands the Poodle back.

"He's pretty cute, all right."

"He's gonna be in the next one, too."

"Sexay."

Rachel goes back to read-watching Dotty and Lysandra to watching a mother and her water-winged toddler playing nearby. They're obviously non-native speakers, based on the muddled-up lines, "*A monkey faced a weasel, a monkey faced a weasel. The monkey thought it was fun—*"

The boy waits for his cue to jump, like a free-falling, water-winged paratrooper, into his mother's waiting arms.

"*Pop! goes the weasel.*"

The boy jumps. His mother catches him, cheers while the boy giggles and she dips him in the pool.

Lysandra watches a few more rounds of the jump-clap-giggle game and then settles back to sip on her vodka-infused kid soda, feeling the hot sun on her face.

She's conflicted about drinking, because she hates what it's done to her father. But decides that it shouldn't ruin her fun. Music osculates in the light breeze, while waitresses in red bikinis wiggle around the deck with cork-padded trays and muscular tanned legs. The day finds a sweet spot between sweltering and warm, but seems fated to be stuck in a mulberry bush loop. That is, until the boys show up.

Lysandra spots them first, flip-flopping into the pool area. A troupe of sixteenish-looking boys, led by the one with dirty blond hair, blue shorts, a Frankenstein branded tank top and square shoulders. She taps Rachel with the backs of her fingernails, who looks up to catch the boy-show. The girls watch without looking, while the boys commandeer chairs down the way, settle in, scan their surroundings and zero in on Lysandra and Rachel. The sighting causes the boys to peacock around, laughing and smoking eCigarettes in big arcs and long draws, while the girls feign indifference.

Rachel turns her back on them.

"So, you wanna see me do Bardot?"

"Give it to me, tits," Lysandra says, wiggling her fingers.

Rachel turns her head to the side, then snaps it back blurting, *"Libère-moi!"* with an exaggerated pout and blonde hair flying across her face.

Lysandra bursts out laughing, spitting out some of her drink. "—ohhh, that's perfect," she says, wiping her chin. "What does it mean?"

"It means, *set me free.*"

"Libère-moi—" Lysandra tries and then freezes at the sudden appearance of two boy emissaries.

Rachel spins to look, too. It's the dirty blond that Lysandra called dibs on and the curly-haired, pointy-nosed one that Rachel staked.

"I think we're going to have to call the cops on you two."

The girls' faces deflate.

"Yeah, those burkinis you're wearing are illegal because they don't show enough skin."

"These aren't burkinis," the girls squeal in protest.

Having stuck the icebreaker, the dirty blond grins. "Nah, not burkinis, but you girls shouldn't be afraid to show more of that sweetness, know what I'm saying? Where you from?"

"Pecado," Lysandra says, putting her hand on her brow to look up at him, picking up a faint marijuana scent.

The dirty blond's name is Jayden. Pointy nose is Ethan. They're from L.A., staying at the hotel with Jayden's uncle. The boys are seventeen and the girls sixteen, according to their lies.

"Anyway, if you're looking for some fun, a bunch of us are going to Stokers later," he says, smacking the words on the roof of his mouth like they have peanut butter on them.

"We didn't bring any ID."

"Don't need that shit. It's for teens."

"Um, teen clubs aren't really our thing."

"Yeah, better than nothing, though. Place is dope. They have one in L.A."

"I dunno, sounds a bit lame, but we'll think about it," she says with a frozen smile.

Later on, the girls are giggling in a clothing store.

"What do you think of this one?" asks Rachel, waving a blue sundress.

"I like it; you should totally try it on," exclaims Lysandra, testing the fabric between her thumb and finger, then snatching it away and marching for the fitting rooms.

"Lysie, I can't aff—"

"Oh shush, it doesn't hurt to try it on," Lysandra says, walking with the dress fluttering in her wake like a clotheslined sheet in the breeze. Rachel stumbles after her. A big clerk with big breasts spilling out of a salmon dress blocks their way.

"My friend would like to try this on, please."

"Sorry, miss, you can't try on merchandise, unless you're serious."

"I have credit, if that's what you mean," Lysandra says, holding up her wrist. The clerk checks it with her wand and nods apathetically. Lysandra waves Rachel through.

"Miss, you can't take that in there," the clerk interposes, pointing at Rachel's bag.

"It's okay, Rach, I'll hold it for you," Lysandra replies.

Rachel hands her shoulder bag to Lysandra, who takes it to stroll around the store, while the clerk sits with her arms folded and Rachel swishes a curtain into a fitting room. Minutes later, Rachel smiles around the corner, catching Lysandra's attention.

"Oh, let me see, let me see," Lysandra says, running up.

Rachel gingerly steps into the light in the airy sundress, adjusting a strap.

"My God, you look just like Brigit Bardot," Lysandra gasps. "You *have* to get it," she insists, with hands on her hips.

"How much is this, please?" Rachel asks the clerk, who walks over and taps her wand on it.

"A thousand fifteen," the clerk yawns.

Seeing the look on Rachel's face, the clerk snaps, "Yeah, and you can just leave that in the dressing room, miss."

The girls hold in their indignation like a long toke, until they're just outside.

"*You can't try on merchandise, unless you're serious,*" Rachel exhales in a snooty voice. "I can't believe she credit checked us, what-a-bitch."

"*Yeah, and you can just leave that in the dressing room, miss,*" Lysandra mocks in the same falsetto, while handing Rachel's shoulder bag back to her and then flipping a finger toward the store.

"So, where we going now?"

"I don't know, find a place to sit down for a while?"

"Amen, sister," Rachel says as they make their way down the corridor of the Miracle K Shops toward the strip. They nudge each other at *Bad Hombres* and step in to order virgin margaritas. They find a spot on the deck and sit down to suck slushy drinks through big red bendy straws.

"Wish we had some vodka left."

"Amen, sister," Lysandra replies, putting her heart-shaped glasses back on.

"What time does our RT leave?"

"About an hour," Lysandra says, projecting their tickets and frowning.

"So, I guess no Stokers tonight, since we've got nothing to wear and can't buy anything that expensive without our parents knowing about it right away."

"I don't know about that," says Lysandra, sipping on her margarita with an impish grin.

"Lysie, our ePays are linked to our parents' accounts."

"No, I mean, that we don't have something to wear."

"Well, we can't exactly go to the club in our bathing suits."

"Um, look, in your ho bag."

Rachel looks over her glasses and eyes Lysandra with a confused look, then looks into her shoulder bag.

"*Lysie, how—*"

"Shush . . . and don't take it out here."

"*Lysie,*" she says again, half taking out the dress she had tried on, "*how—*?"

"She was so busy spying on you that I took a couple of dresses over to the checkout stand and disarmed them. They had the same ones on the rack."

"A couple?"

"Uh-huh, but I prefer white," Lysandra smiles, flashing some white fabric from her bag.

"So, we should go?" Rachel says in hushed excitement, bending closer to Lysandra.

"Yeah . . . but how?" Lysandra replies.

"Oh, I know," Rachel says, waving her hands. "We tell our parents that we're staying over at each other's places. Take the one o'clock back. When we get home, I'll text Bradley to come get us, take you home, then me. Then, we'll tell them that we got sick and had to go home."

"Do you think your brother will go for it?"

"He better," Rachel says, dialing him and quickly getting into an argument.

"*. . . come on, Bradley, do you have to fuckin' ruin everything?*"

Rachel doesn't get anywhere until Lysandra leans in and says, "Tell him I'll give him a blowjob."

"*Lysie!*"

The offer clinches the deal. After clicking off, they high five each other, then tap on their phones to make a change to their RT tickets.

"Done," Lysandra says, smiling.

"Done," Rachel replies.

They grab their bags, intending to head back to the hotel and find a bathroom in which to change. As they're about to walk out of the mall, a man grabs them.

"Stop, you two . . . *thieves!*"

They freeze like puppies caught peeing on the carpet and get red-faced flashes of a shitty juvenile delinquent future. Of waiting for the cops in a dingy mall security office. Being grounded forever. Remedial classes. The store clerk's fat accusatory finger reaching across the court to point them out to an outraged jury.

"Stole my heart," he smiles as they spin around.

"How 'bout a picture?"

It's a street actor dressed as Timotay.

The girls start breathing again and then laugh as they have their pictures taken, with tongues out and fingers in vees. Thieves on the run, on a stolen day in Pecado.

Amen, sister.

———————◆◆◆◆———————

It's sundown and they're bathing in neon.

Once past the red velvet rope and silver posts, the music steamrolls over them while kaleidoscope lights flicker. The phosphorescent dye in their shoplifted sundresses comes alive in the black spectrum light. A silver railing corrals a sunken dance floor, with colored lights lurking beneath it. A mirror ball reflects out splintered laser light. Spotlights spin like Gatling guns, suspended from the ceiling. Giant floor speakers serve as go-go platforms.

Satin-trimmed teens are doing the Hustle, the Bump and the Bus Stop, while the Bee Gees crystalline vocals egg them on and Donna Summer tells them about all the love she's feeling. They order a couple of virgin mint juleps and stand near the dance floor surveying the battleground. They spot Jayden and Ethan and give them a wave. The boys come over to talk to them in open satin shirts, satin hats and polyester bell-bottoms.

"They've cleaned up nicely," Rachel smiles.

"Told you this place was dope," Jayden says, discoing up.

Lysandra, raises her eyebrow and cocks an ear.

"*I said . . . I told you this place was dope.*"

Lysandra nods and hollers, "*You guys come here a lot?*"

"*Once in a while.*"

After yelling about how they like the hotel and the deejay, the girls follow them back to their booth. They're with the same guys who were with them at the pool. Jayden buys them fresh virgin mint juleps, in an impressive display of feathers.

"Too bad we couldn't sneak in any vodka," Lysandra complains to Jayden.

"Don't mean we can't party," Jayden says, smiling, nudging Lysandra's knee and opening his hand to reveal green Sat-XXX pills.

Lysandra puts her arms over her head and twists her torso in her seat. "Are those your vitamins?"

"Yeah, my MJ vitamins."

"No, thanks, but you go ahead."

"C'mon, it's no fun doing them alone."

She has a wordless discussion about it with Rachel, who shrugs her shoulders.

"Gee, I don't know."

"Suit yourself."

Jayden flexes an arm to swallow a pill, but Lysandra intercepts his hand, snatches the pill, and pops it in her mouth, swallowing it down with her mint julep. She smiles then sticks her tongue out to prove the swallow.

She grabs Jayden's hand a second time and hands a pill to Rachel, flashing a *feu et danger* grin.

With the pills down, the girls sit for the longest time.

Nothing much happens. They chat a bit more excitedly, maybe. Look into each other's eyes a bit more deeply, perhaps.

Then it happens.

Everything starts going around in circles.

Pop! goes the weasel.

Colors, music and feelings flood into Lysandra's head, as do confusion and paranoia. Everything makes her laugh. Her mouth turns into a parched desert that she tries to quench with the best-thing-she's-ever-tasted sugary drink.

She checks the time over and over.

Her thoughts are pulled into daydreams as the fabric of reality loses its stitching.

Laughing and not sure if she's talking too loudly or too quietly, she grabs Rachel's arm. "Let's go dancing, Rachy."

On the throbbing electric dance floor, they pulse understanding and feeling. And everything vibrates color and universal being. They trip the night fantastic to the relentless beat of their mad teenaged hearts.

Songs run together.

A Shake-Night-Boogie. A Feel-Fever-Booty.

Hoo.

Hah.

Then, just like that, she's on a hotel bed wondering if she should go all the way.

Cookie told them to either hold out and make it special, or get it over with early, while warning that if boys get what they want too easily, they're gone in spite of every lie they tell you.

Then, she showed them how to put a condom on a banana.

Cookieeee, they squealed.

But it just didn't feel right. An epic day of firsts—stealing away to Sin City, trying a cigarette, pulling booze by the pool, lifting dresses, trying marijuana and whatever else is in an Sat-XXX, meeting a cute boy and then kissing him on a hotel bed.

Now, she wants to be a kid again.

It doesn't help that, as cute as Jayden is, he's a terrible kisser. Way too much pressure and tongue. She wants to be savored, not slobbered up like a dog toy. She's also getting tired of his go-everywhere hands, like she's some sort of puzzle whose holiest of holies can be unlocked if only he can find the right combination. She's worried about Rachel, too, who's too drunk and too high to be with a strange boy. She decides to hold out for a movie, wine, bubble bath and bed of rose petals for a while. She has these thoughts, but they don't come to her that clearly. They come to her in muffled underwater waves, with ringing in her ears.

Then a submerged sounding . . . *no* . . . and splashing from the next bed.

She twists from under Jayden and surfaces, eyes like torpedoes.

"She said 'no,' asshole!"

The words, a cold slap across the evening.

Ethan puts up his arms and rolls off. Rachel sits up, gasping and wiping away tears.

"Whoa—" a shirtless Jayden jumps out of the bed and heads for the minibar.

"C'mon, everyone, let's just settle down, have a drink and talk about this."

"Nah, it's getting late and we need to catch our RT bus." Lysandra says, grabbing Rachel by the hand and pulling her toward the door.

"Your bus? Your *bus*. You don't need no bus, Gus," Jayden laughs. "Let's have some more fun. Ethan's sorry, aren't you Ethan?"

"Yeah, sorry. Mad props for you, dolls," Ethan says, pounding his fist on his chest and pointing a finger at the ceiling.

"See? C'mon, just a little drink . . . a nightcap?" Jayden pleads, then turns to pour out one of the mini-bottles into a glass.

"Nah, thanks, guys. We had fun, but we have to go," Lysandra says, tugging Rachel along and trying to squeeze by Jayden, who's in the hallway, arm-barring their way.

"Baby, we don't need no downers, let's dance instead," he says, pushing Lysandra back, slamming a whiskey and waltzing her into the room, forcing her back until she falls on the bed.

He pins her. She tries to break free, but he outweighs her by over seventy pounds. He forces her wrists above her head.

"You're hurting me," she says, trying to struggle free.

"Please, we just want to—" Rachel tries to say, but Ethan smothers her mouth and lifts her in the air by her stomach, with her legs kicking.

Lysandra's shoulder bag spills on the bed beside her as she tries to get out from under Jayden.

"*Hello*, what have we here?" Jayden says, pinning her arms with his knees and going through her makeup.

"Don't—" Lysandra says, trying to wiggle and push her way out, but she's out of breath.

"Well, well, well, aren't you the naughty ones?" he says, holding up condoms that Cookie gave them, waving them in the air. "I appreciate the gesture but I prefer to go commando, know what I mean?" he says, flicking the condoms at Ethan and Rachel.

Rachel's screams are throttled by Ethan's hand.

Jayden grabs Lysandra's throat while unbuckling his belt, eyes burning a wicked blue. She feels his hand tightening on her throat, feels him jammed against her leg, and feels that he feels her feeling it. And that it's making him harder. He bares his teeth, leaning in closer, his eyes locked on hers, breathing labored.

It sounds just like chanting.

She closes her eyes and turns away, feeling crushed, broken and hoping it will be over soon. Underwater, she's back in the tower with the *Sanguineum Maria* cantors, but this time a burning image of a sword-wielding Joan of Arc appears, whispering for her to fight.

She opens her eyes and exhales, slowly and deeply, then turns to lock eyes on Jayden. She feels the muscles in her face relax, all expression leaving her features.

She smiles and slowly plays her tongue across her lower lip, watching the confusion flicker in his eyes for a second, using the moment to slip one hand free and slide it down and slowly run it over his hardness, watching his eyes widen, freeing her other hand and softly stroking the side of his face.

"You like that?" she asks.

Jayden moans.

"Yeah?" she asks.

He closes his eyes and nods, "Fuk . . . uh-huh."

Scratch.

She tiger-claws her nails deep into his face and then bucks him off, doing a Cirque du Soleil acrobatic back tumble and jumping up. A hundred pounds of fury in a sundress.

All three stare at her.

She flips her hair behind her ear, purses her lips and stares at him defiantly. Jayden dabs the open cuts on the side of his face and looks at the blood on his fingers. Looks at Ethan and then grins and grunts, "Okay, cunt, you wanna play rough, then let's get it on L.A.-style."

He comes at her fast and hard, a practiced bull rush, expecting her to turtle.

She'll tell Rachel later that it felt like she was floating high in the corner of the room, watching someone else.

She steps directly into his rush.

The first punch caves his windpipe, the second flattens his nose and sends a pomegranate spray of blood against the wall. "It sounded like someone stepping on bubblewrap," Rachel would say.

He drops to his knees, hands covering his face.

She grabs a fistful of his dirty blond hair and pistons a knee into his forehead, letting him collapse, puking at the foot of the bed.

Four seconds have passed.

Two strides and she's at her purse, its contents still spilled on the bed. She picks up the lighter and turns as Ethan lets go of Rachel and comes at her, forearms up.

She thrusts out the lighter with her left . . . it goes *snick*.

The orange flame dances, and Ethan is transfixed, momentarily letting his guard down while she grabs the dresser lamp with her right and swings it, pasting his head broadside, while the cord sparks and the lampshade flies off.

Ten seconds.

The only sound is Rachel's soft sobbing on the bed.

"Lysie, Lysie, Lysie."

Lysandra drops the lamp, a heavy thud as it hits the carpet. She walks back to the bed, rummages through her purse until she finds it. The last Bardot. Bent, but not broken. She slips it between her lips, lights it and drags deeply, slowly exhaling through her nose. No coughing, no burning.

Feu et danger.

They ride the rapid transfer back with hangovers and sore throats. Before nodding off on her shoulder, Rachel looks up at Lysandra and says, "I used to watch you playing soccer, you know."

Lysandra smiles and puts an arm around her.

"You'd zigzag all over the field like a crazy person," Rachel says, flaying her arm. "Like nobody's business. Like nothing I've seen."

Lysandra smiles.

"You totally Indiana Jones'd him with that lampstand."

She passes out on Lysandra's shoulder.

"Text me when you get up, Rach," Lysandra says, getting out of the car. "Thanks for the ride," she says to Bradley.

"What about my—?"

"*Don't even,*" Rachel snaps at her brother.

The night air's cold. The season's changed and so has she. Her head's buzzing with vodka, weed and loud music. Her ear's ringing from being hit. She feels like she's still in motion from sleeping on the RT. Everything's shrunk. Her house looks smaller. Her legs feel longer, no longer suited for running around pools, chasing dogs or skipping.

Nope.

Apparently, they're for kicking the crap out of rapists.

What the fuck?

She waves back at Bradley and Rachel, before thumb-printing the lock pad and trying not to disturb a sleeping house. She hears the television and tiptoes past the living room, glancing over at her father, hoping that he's passed out again.

"Lysandra?"

The voice freezes her from across the room. She pees a little in a conditioned response to his scolding voice. Her face burns with the lies she plans on saying. Her head's buzzing louder than before. She weighs whether to go on the offensive or defensive, fight or flight.

"Sit down."

She sulks over to a chair and sits down, feeling shame pull her down like a flushed toilet. Her father tries to clear his throat of its whiskey scratchiness, coughs and then speaks, without lifting his eyes.

"Lysandra—"

"Daddy, I—"

"I need to tell you what happened when you were born."

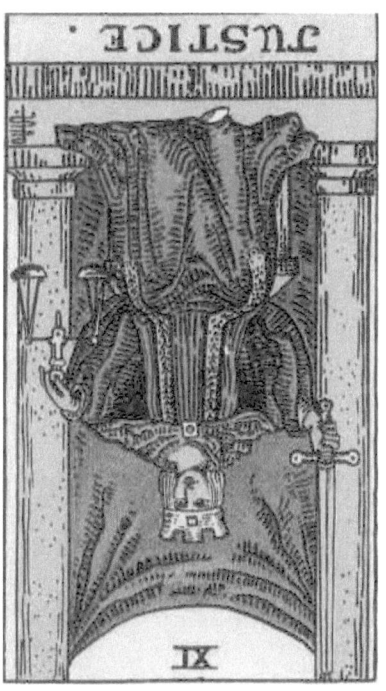

CHAPTER 3:
BAD JUSTICE

Lysandra quick-walks past her father, who's watching NASCAR on his new surround-view, sound-wall TV that the Church installed in their living room.

"How did it go?"

"*Fine*," Lysandra says, marching by.

Joe turns back to watch the inches-apart whiz-thundering cars, until a commercial comes on for Carrero & Cotter.

"Athena's scales don't work upside down. Neither does her right-from-wrong splitting sword. Have you gotten a raw deal? Our lawyers won't rest until justice is restored." The ad shows Athena being turned upright, taking her blindfold off and then winking at the camera.

Joe watches the ad play out with a beer in hand, then drains it and gets up to get another. He stops by Lysandra's room on the way and knocks. "Lysandra?" No answer, so he quietly steps in, only to find her sobbing into her pillow.

"You don't sound very fine."

"Well, I am, so you can go back to watching your car racing."

He sits on the corner of her bed and puts his hand on her ankle.

"You sure you don't you want to . . . taco about it?" he asks, playfully shaking her ankle.

Lysandra burrows deeper into her pillow.

"Sweetheart?"

"I don't want to go back there, Daddy," she sobs.

Joe takes his hand off her ankle and rubs it over his knee, looking at a spot on the floor.

"You have to go, honey, I told you. The Church says that you have to have these MRIs for your health."

"They're not making me better, Daddy," Lysandra says, spinning to glare at him. "They're giving me nightmares."

"Nightmares?"

"It's like they're trying to stick someone else's memories into my head. Not just memories, a whole person."

"What do you mean, a whole person?"

"Someone's previous lives. All of them. Why won't you believe me?"

"Honey, we talked about this. They said that this wouldn't hurt you. And—"

"I wish Mom was here. She wouldn't make me go."

Joe looks at her with a pained half-grin and says, "I'll talk to them, but . . ."

Lysandra turns her head back into her pillow. Joe rubs her calf before leaving for the kitchen to grab another beer that tips over and rolls in the fridge. He goes back to the TV room and fizz-pops it open. He tries to stop the foam from gushing over by sipping it, but his hand's too shaky. The beer foams over his chin, hand and down his shirt. He puts the beer down, presses his forehead into his hands and rocks back and forth.

◆◆◆

"And how did you feel at that moment, Mr. Tucana?"

"I felt as though I let my daughter down. I felt I had no one to . . . to turn to." His voice cracks.

"Anything else, Mr. Tucana?"

"Yeah . . . that was my last drink."

"Thank you, Mr. Tucana, those are all my questions. If you remain seated, I think my learned friend, or one or more of my learned friends, will have some questions for you in cross."

The courtroom chuckles at his lawyer's jab at the rows of unsmiling lawyers representing the Church. Lead counsel, Richard Tucker, stands up among them, buttons his jacket, then walks over to the podium, opening his notebook with a thump and tapping his fingers. He looks down, and then up over his glasses at Joe. Joe tries to smile at him, but Tucker's stony mug doesn't flinch. "Can the witness be shown plaintiff's exhibit one, please?" Tucker's opening salvo rings off the walls.

He waits for the court clerk to walk the document over, while Joe takes a sip of water before taking the document into his hands. The courtroom's funeral home quiet, except for the curtains rustling in the air conditioning, the odd cough and the court steno's keystrokes, which have stopped. The quiet amplifies Joe's trembling hands.

"Yes?" Joe says, clearing his throat. The keystrokes resume.

"You recognize that document, sir?"

"I do."

"That's the Technology User Agreement with *your* signature on it, am I correct again, Mr. Tucana?"

"Yes."

"The same TUA that *paved* the way for your wife to be impregnated with my client's patented fetus, now isn't that correct, sir?" Tucker drops his fat chin to fix Joe with his pig eyes.

"Yes," Joe croaks, clearing his throat and shifting in his chair.

"I'm sorry, sir, you'll have to speak louder, so the court reporter can hear you."

"*Yes*," Joe says louder, taking another sip of his water, clearing his throat again while the court reporter taps away.

"He said, 'yes,' ladies and gentlemen of the jury, in case you couldn't hear him trying not to admit it."

"I object," Joe's lawyer says, over the chuckles.

The judge raises his eyebrows and says, "Mr. Tucker?"

"My apologies, your honor.

"Now, you'll recall that when my friend, Mr. Car-rare-oh," Tucker says, stretching the name like a plastic toy, "asked you whether you read over the agreement before signing it, you answered," he traces the words on his notepad and looks up at Joe, "*not really?*"

"Yes."

"That's your evidence, sir . . . *not really?*"

"That's what I said," Joe replies, looking around.

"But that's a lie isn't it, Mr. Tucana?"

Joe leans forward into the mic. "No, like I said, it was put in front of me in Mr. O'Brian's office and I sort of just glanced over it."

"You sort of just glanced over it?"

"Yes."

Tucker's pig eyes close for a minute before looking up, as though adding numbers. Then whispers something to the lawyer beside him, who reaches across to hand over a transcript decked with sticky notes. Tucker thumbs through it, exhales and grins over a particular truffle.

"Mr. Tucana, do you recall your deposition on February 16, 2026? We were in a boardroom, there was a court reporter there, and you were under oath?"

Silence.

"You're not answering . . . would you like me to repeat the question?"

"No, I remember."

"And I asked you the same question and you answered, "Yes, I read it over," and then I asked you, "Did you have any questions about it," and you answered, "No, it seemed pretty straightforward?" Tucker underlines the words in the transcript with his finger.

"Mr. Tucana, you have to give a verbal response. A head nod can't be transcribed by the court reporter."

Joe clears his throat and says, "Yes."

"And you were under oath when you said that?"

"Yes."

"Thank you, Mr. Tucana. And you'll agree with me that when you signed the technology user agreement, you were excited about the money more than anything?"

"I wouldn't say it like that."

Tucker marches with the yellow-stickied transcript over and jabs it into Joe's personal space.

"Do you recognize the transcript?" Tucker asks, in a demanding, indignant tone.

"Um . . . *yes?*" Joe hesitates.

"Can you please read the highlighted portion on that page for the jury?" Tucker asks, glancing up at the jury and pointing the passage to Joe.

"Um, when we signed it and saw how much they were paying, I got excited about the money more than anything."

"So . . . excited about the money more than anything . . . was *exactly* how you said it, didn't you, Mr. Tucana?" Tucker snatches the transcript back, slams it shut, locks eyes with the jury, before promenading back to the podium.

Joe shifts around with flushed cheeks and darting eyes.

There's a long pause, until all eyes are on Tucker, waiting for his next question.

"We are waiting for your answer, Mr. Tucana."

All eyes turn back to Joe, who leans into the mic and says, "Yes."

"Mr. Tucana, you'll agree with me that this case has generated a lot of fame for you as the custodial parent of a genetically modified child?"

"Yes."

"And isn't it correct, Mr. Tucana, that you find that raising a genetically modified child to be challenging and that you feel at times overwhelmed?"

A few moments of dead silence tick by, before Tucker reaches for the transcript.

"Is that in there, too?" Joe asks and then leans into the mic to say, "Never mind, yes."

"Now, Mr. Tucana, when you were answering Mr. Carrero's questions," Tucker says, stretching the name again and patting the air softly toward Carrero's slumped shoulders, "you said that you felt that the MRI treatments were psychologically harming your daughter?"

"I thought so."

"You'll agree with me, Mr. Tucana, that you're not a psychologist?"

"No, I'm not."

"Or a geneticist?"

"No, I'm not."

"And you're not even her biological father, are you?"

"No."

"So, you'll agree with me that you really don't know anything about what's best for a genetically modified child?"

"She's not a genetically modified child, stop calling her that . . . she's Lysandra," he says, with a shaky voice.

"So, you'll agree with me that you really don't know anything about what's best for a genetically modified child named Lysandra?" Tucker smirks.

Joe sits there with his arms crossed, a red face and a half-grin.

"I think I know what's best for Lysandra."

"What makes you so sure about that?"

Joe sits there still, defiantly.

"I'll need an answer eventually, Mr. Tucana."

Joe's upper lip quivers, "Because her mother told me."

"You mean your wife, who's been dead for fifteen years?"

"She had a name, too. It was Juliette."

"And based on what Juliette told you, who's been dead for more than fifteen years, you know all about raising a genetically modified child, named Lysandra?"

"Stop calling her that."

"Lysandra or a genetically modified child?"

Joe's lawyer stands up to object, while Joe remains with his arms crossed and a splotchy red spot above his shirt collar.

"Mr. Tucker, I think you should move on," the judge says mercifully.

"All right, fine, your honor," Tucker responds, turning a page scrawled with arrows and loops and waiting for the courtroom to quieten.

"Mr. Tucana, do you have a drinking problem?"

"Object, relevance?" Carrera says, rising.

"I think my friend opened the door with his last question, your honor, so I'm entitled to walk through it."

"I agree, the witness is directed to answer," the judge answers.

"*Had*," says Joe.

"And you took your last drink after your daughter told you she didn't want to have any more treatments?"

Joe looks over at to his lawyer, who looks down.

"Yes," Joe says, confused.

"Your last drink?"

"Yes."

"Mr. Tucana, you attended Treetops last night, didn't you?"

Joe tries to get the attention of his lawyer, who continues to look down.

"Your lawyer can't help you, Mr. Tucana. Would you like me to repeat the question?" says Tucker, his voice rolling up from his cavernous diaphragm like an operatic belch.

Joe leans forward again and says, "Yes."

"And Treetops is a cocktail lounge?"

"A local watering hole, yes," Joe says, swallowing and twitching a smile.

"A *local watering hole* that serves alcohol?"

"Yes."

"And in this local watering hole that serves alcohol, you sat next to a lady?"

"You mean the blonde-haired lady?"

"Yes."

"Yeah, I sat next to her."

"A *blonde-haired lady* calling herself Amanda?"

"Yes."

"And this blonde-haired lady calling herself Amanda was in the local watering hole drinking?"

"Yes."

"Was drinking wine?"

"Yes."

"The blonde-haired lady was drinking wine in the watering hole and you didn't see her drink anything other than wine, did you?"

"No, she was drinking wine."

"You paid for the blonde-haired lady's drinks?"

"Yes."

"Her drinks of wine?"

"Yes."

"And when the bill came, you paid it without objection?"

"No, I paid it."

"No, you paid it because you had no reason to doubt it?"

"No, I didn't doubt it," Joe answers annoyed, looking around.

"Mr. Tucana, this is the bill from that night?" Tucker asks, walking up to Joe and slapping a bar tab in front of him.

"Yes, but it has—"

"Mr. Joseph Tucana, is *that* the bill?"

"Yes," Joe answers as Tucker snatches the bill from him and returns to his podium.

"The bill has three glasses of wine on it?"

"Yes."

"And those three glasses of wine were the blonde-haired lady's, the one you were sitting next to?"

"Yes."

"And there were four beers on the bill as well?"

"Yes, but—"

"Mr. Joseph Tucana, the bill had four beers on it as well?"

"Okay, yes."

"Four beers and three glasses of wine that you paid for?"

"Yes."

"And you later paid to have sex with the blonde-haired lady, didn't you, Mr. Tucana?"

"No, and those—"

"*I object*," Joe's lawyer shoots up to protest.

"Never mind," Tucker says, acknowledging the judge's frown. "Withdrawn."

"The jury will disregard that last question," the judge says.

"Your honor," Tucker continues, "my colleague, Mr. Brown, will be handling the next series of questions. I wonder if this would be an appropriate point to break for the day?"

"Very well," the judge says. "This court stands adjourned until tomorrow morning at ten." He bangs his gavel.

The sun's out when Joe walks outside with his lawyer but it only blinds him to the swarming recorders, cameras and reporters. Looking down and hurrying along, he says, "No comment," repeatedly to a blizzard of questions about Amanda and whether he paid to have sex with her. Once free of the camera-clicking, microphone-thrusting horde, he turns to Carrero and asks, "So, how badly did I do?"

"Don't worry about it, Joe, you're doing fine," Carrero says, looking at his watch, "I can't really talk about anything with you, because you're still under cross."

"But those beers weren't for me, I bought them for—"

"Like I said, Joe," Carrero says, opening a door to a cab, "I can't really talk about it, just stick to your guns and you'll be given a chance to give clarifying answers to all these points Tucker's making."

Then he shuts the cab door.

"All these points Tucker's making?" Joe repeats as he watches Carrero's cab pull away.

Then he starts back for his hotel with his hands in his pockets.

After a block, he blends in with everyone else. Once again, an average man walking on a busy sidewalk. He had two things of value in his life. He lost one fifteen years ago and now he's losing the other, because he was stupid and uneducated and couldn't answer questions right.

"Those weren't even my beers," he says to himself.

He tries to pray but switches from God to Juliette, like he always does. He doesn't know about things like God, except what Juliette explained to him. He's pretty sure that she wouldn't think much of this so-called Church, just like she had a bad feeling about its leader, Thomas O'Brian, back then. She said he was a big phony. He wishes she could send him the right words to say. Words to answer

Mr. Tucker's questions without sounding so stupid. But he's a drywaller. Words aren't what he knows.

Everyone has something that they know.

Pilots know how to fly, cabbies know how to drive, electricians know about wiring, plumbers, plumbing.

And Juliette.

Juliette knew God.

She would know how to handle Lysandra. She'd be able to get through to her, past her backtalk, tantrums and problems at school. Those MRIs hurt her. There was no doubt about that, in spite of what those quacks said. He might not know much beyond drywalling, but he does know that.

He walks the rest of the way, trying to drum out the accusatory voices in his head with the Beatles' "Julia". Only he switches the chorus to *Juliette* and uses it to imagine a future where it all works out, instead of one in which he loses custody of his daughter and becomes a botched drywall install for the whole world to see. One where everything's lined up and taped to perfection with no seams. Where he and Lysandra have a normal life, like he promised Juliette.

Juliette.

Juuuu-liette.

It puts him more at ease until he turns on the evening news in his hotel room.

And sees that he's all over it.

If Mr. Carrero was reluctant to talk, Tucker wasn't. He's on the news telling everyone that Joe's a lapsed alcoholic with no credibility, a crackpot like the people who support him. A man who broke a contract, plain and simple. A contract that he richly profited from and signed with his eyes wide open. That a level playing field required that patent infringers like him be held to account.

Mr. Carrero had assured him that they would have public opinion and the law on their side. "I mean, think about it," he said. "The Church is claiming ownership over a human being. *A human being.* There are plenty of organizations who believe what the Church is doing is wrong and they will support you." He was willing to take on the case pro bono because he was certain they would skunk the Church in court and in the court of public opinion. Well, it sure seems like they were the skunk roadkill in court *and* the court of public opinion. And his lawyer couldn't get in the cab quick enough.

Lysandra calls him on his cell.

"How did it go today, Daddy?"

"Mr. Carrero says I'm not supposed to talk about it."

"It doesn't seem to be stopping them."

"I know."

"Why does the trial have to be all the way in New Lancashire anyway, when we live here?"

"I told you, dear, I guess that agreement that your mother and I signed said that any legal cases had to be tried here."

"Did you even read that?"

"No."

"Then why did you say you did in court like they're saying?"

"I try to say stuff and it all gets twisted around."

"That doesn't seem fair."

"A lot of this is unfair. How was school today?"

"I dunno. It seems like everyone's avoiding me."

"I'm sorry about all this, honey."

"It's okay, Daddy, I know you're doing it for me."

"Are you behaving for Miss Delacroix?"

"Yes, Daddy."

"That's good . . . Lysandra?"

"Yes, Daddy?"

"I love you."

"I love you, too, Daddy."

Joe clicks off and then goes out to his balcony for an eCigarette, with a million thoughts racing through his head, like wanting to go back to the courtroom to explain, because it came out all wrong. He imagines the whole exchange going differently, using the words he ought to have said. But the words he wishes he said weren't the words he actually said, and now he has nothing but regret and frustration. Tucker bullied him around the courtroom, making him look as dumb as a hammer, twisting around his words so much, that he felt like a bent screw. He wishes he would have gotten up and punched that fat fucker right in the face.

He wishes Juliette was still around. But she isn't. He's failing miserably at parenting. He wishes he would have gone back to being a drywaller, instead of witness protection, living off the Church's tit. Now he's the tit, and a saggy one at that, for the entire world to see. He badly wants to have a drink, but he knows it would only make everything worse.

He takes another puff of his eCigarette, hoping it will unwind him. He leans forward, thinking that he heard the door open, but decides it's the TV. He leans back and takes another puff and hears the same sound again.

Nope, he's sure now.

There's someone in the room.

———◆◆◆◆———

"It's called a writ of *Caput lupinum*," Tucker explains, gesticulating an eCigar. "Latin for *let this be a wolf's head*. But it's better known as a writ of outlawry. You know, old west stuff. Outlaw. Wanted . . . dead or alive."

They're in Thomas's penthouse office, in the Hands of Prayer tower in New Lancashire. The panoramic skyline surrounds them with floor-to-ceiling glass. Tucker's courtroom mug is more relaxed, expressive, but is still cut with badger lines and strewn with black seaweed under his blue bulging eyes. Guts bulge out from under their tailored shirts and are brandished like teenager biceps.

"So you want her declared to be an outlaw? I don't understand the advantage."

"It's not the romantic thing westerns have made it into, Tom. Once you're an outlaw, you're outside of the law's protection. Pretty nasty, if you think about it. No matter what someone does to you, it can't be a crime. Same goes for anyone helping you."

"Is that legal?"

"Yup, the government brought it back so they could assassinate terrorists in foreign countries and then adopted it domestically. But, get this . . . the *Domestic Terrorism Act* designates any actions taken under it a federal matter, you follow?"

"Not really."

"Under federal authority, so any abuse of its powers is a federal offense. And, as you know, any federal offense can be pardoned by the President."

"Ohhh, I get it," Thomas's eyes light up. "So, the President can basically use it to assassinate undesirables and then pardon everyone involved."

"Bingo. And he can count on Congress letting it slide, because the populace's fear of the terrorist bogyman exceeds its love of civil liberties."

"I still don't understand what the advantage would be. Ever since we had Joe ..." Thomas clears his throat. "Ever since Joe killed himself, I mean. Ever since then, we've been granted full custody over the girl. If they find her, they'll just bring her to us."

"Yes, and then you'll have the same duties as any other parent, including a fiduciary duty to act in her best interest. Think about it. If she's an outlaw, you can do whatever you want to her and neither she, nor anyone else, can do a thing about it."

Thomas salivates. "So, how do we get her declared an outlaw?"

"There's a provision that I think we can use under the Act if her escape is likely to do public harm."

"Far as I know, she's just a teenaged runaway. How do we get her upgraded to a terrorist?"

"By branding her a danger to the public because she's a GMO."

"Do you think a judge would go along with that?"

"Let's just say I know a few who can be *persuaded* to," Tucker says, puffing on his eCigar.

Thomas leans back in his chair and whistles, then frowns. "What about bounty hunters? She's worth way more to me alive than dead?"

"We'll just put that out in the reward—five-million-dollar reward—only if alive and unharmed." Tucker says, writing the sign in the air with cigar vapor.

Thomas smiles. "I like it. Can we put something in there about her virginity, too?"

"Don't see why not."

The two man sit there smoking their eCigars and sipping on their brandy snifters.

"Say, Dick, can we use this against other people?"

"Such as?"

"I'm thinking about that Henri Charlevoix person. That *No Limits* book of his is killing us, with all that bile against the Church."

"I can look into it."

"But no 'alive' option with that guy."

"Got it. This is going to need a fairly fat retainer, though."

"I think you know that the Church is good for it, Dick."

Lysandra waits for the flimsy white microwave above the narrow gas stove to heat up her hot chocolate. After it beeps, she pushes the plastic button and the door snaps open. She stirs and then sips the hot powdery liquid from the stained coffee mug. It burns her tongue, and she purses her lips. She takes the mug to the Mylar countertop and sets it down. She's got a plaid shirt on over a white tee and jeans. Hair in a ponytail. She's hiding out at Cookie's friend's small cabin, near Lake Bigler. There's no smoke from any of the other chimneys and crispy leaves are blowing off the trees in the sharp autumn breeze. She isn't wearing any makeup and her eyes are puffy from crying. Her arm's in a makeshift sling, and her hand bandaged.

She has no one to blame but herself for that.

She was outside splitting wood when a thought occurred to her: do I have superpowers? Ever since she dismantled 'let's get in on L.A.-style' Jayden, she's been wondering about that. Fighting juju and mad power just came to her out of thin air. Could they again? It would be useful if a boy went rape-mode on her again or if she had to battle Church thugs. She tried a few things but couldn't recreate the magic.

So she grabbed a log and propped it between two stumps. She conjured up chanting in the lake wind, tried to spark the same blast of images by picturing

Joan of Arc and her sword. She slowed her breathing, brought her fist down on the log carefully, focusing her energy, imagining her fist smashing past it.

Ooooone . . .

Twooooo . . .

Three.

She slammed her fist as hard as she could. There was a second where she didn't feel a thing, while the log bounced off, unharmed. Then searing pain shot up from her hand, up her arm and into her head. She bit down hard, screamed *fuckkkkk*, through clenched teeth, jumping up and down. So much for superpowers. She had no idea if she broke anything, so she made herself a makeshift bandage and sling and learned how to wipe herself with her left hand because *stupid* hurts.

Meanwhile, the cabin has no internet and she's been trying to amuse herself with the ancient plasma screen TV and reading. She has a hard, green nylon couch to sit on. She's been warming herself by the hearth and sleeping in her lumberjack shirt. The bedposts to her single bed are made out of laminated driftwood. She has a Coleman cooler for her drinking water, and she's been conserving flushes for the septic tank. The toilet seat's made out of wood and has a fuzzy seat cover. The bathroom and kitchen have cold linoleum flooring. The living room and bedroom are floored with indoor/outdoor green carpet. She's surprisingly proficient at splitting wood, when using an ax, and at starting fires. She's also good at making stews, rationing food and keeping the cabin clean. She's been spinning up lint, litter and dried lake mud out of the carpet with an orange push vacuum. Dusted and wiped. But all the busywork in the world couldn't kill her sorrow, guilt and anger about what her father did.

"Why did you have to jump off a balcony like that and leave me all alone?" she asks the empty room. "And drunk too, like all the papers said, after promising me, *promising me*, on my mother's grave, that you were going to stop drinking?"

The cabin answers with a silent hum.

Then, the nightmares.

If she had to go to one more of those fucking MRI appointments, she would have lost her mind. Last night, she had a dream where she was *him* again, driving around a space vehicle on a dead planet. She was supposed to be helping stranded people but instead got high with her friend and played around, while people nearly burned to a crisp waiting for help. She just laughed about it and made fun of the family's grief.

The sound of car wheels on gravel breaks her reverie.

She grabs a knife out the kitchen drawer and jingles silverware closing it. She slides down behind a counter and listens over a jackhammering heart. She hears a car door thud and crunching gravel getting closer. The screen door snaps open. She squeezes the knife handle. She takes her hand out of the sling. Fights through the pain. She wills her broken hand to be her stabby hand as she needs her good one for fighting. She can't count on turning into wonder-teen, rapist-slayer. She's gotta slash and dash.

A familiar voice and, just like that, an icy sinister world of soulless assassins and bloody fight scenes becomes a soft-edged tropical beach with mai tai's and ganja weed. Blue skies and surf. A soft chocolate chip cookie straight out of the oven. A cotton candy mommy in leather and heels.

Cookie drops the grocery bags as the screen door bangs shut behind her. She runs up, clicking her heels on the floor, puts her hands on Lysandra's face to plant a big wet mommy kiss on her. She's wearing a skirt and a black leather jacket with tassels. Lysandra tastes Cookie's candy lip gloss and smiles up at her adopted mom. She would have smiled more if Rach was there, but she knows it's too risky. So, she squeezes the heck out of Cookie and melts into her cotton candy smell, leather and warmth.

Then she spots them.

A set of silver braces beaming at her from the doorway.

Lysandra squeals and runs up, nearly tackling Rachel in a lumberjack hug.

"Oh my God, Rach, how—?"

"Cookie outsmarted them, Lysie."

Lysandra looks over at Cookie and smiles.

"What have you been up to?" Rachel asks, looking her over quizzically. "And what did you do to your arm, dude?"

"Minor wood-splitting accident," she replies, putting her arm back in the sling. "What have you done with your hair?"

"I made it the same color as yours," Rachel says, pushing up her curls.

Lysandra wrinkles up her nose.

"You'll see why 'cause, while you've been going all Paul Bunyan, we've been going all Mission Impossible... We come bearing gifts," Rachel says, dumping out the duffle bag.

Lysandra spots new clothes along with some packages.

"Okay, that one you can only open later. But here," Rachel says, handing Lysandra an envelope.

Lysandra opens the envelope with her left hand and teeth, then dumps out a burner cellphone, an address book, a passport, a driver's license and a credit prepay. Lysandra opens the passport. It's her picture but it's Rachel's name and address. The birthdate is Rachel's, too, except it's five years earlier.

Lysandra looks up at Cookie and Rachel confused.

"Okay, Mission Impossible part," Rachel says. "You're going to be me and I'm going to be you, okay?" she smiles. "Cookie and I are going to take your dad's car and head for Texarkana to throw them off, while you head north for Kanada."

"*Kanada?*"

"Cookie has friends in Kebec who can hide you until it's safe again, right, Cookie?"

"Oui, c'est ça," Cookie says, nodding in agreement.

"*Kebec?*"

"Come on, you guys, this could get you in trouble," Lysandra says. But no amount of protesting makes a dent. It just isn't safe for her anymore, they insist. The Church has the government in its back pocket. It would only be a matter of time before they find her. And who knew what they would do to her then?

Then they were gone, as suddenly as they appeared. A tropical beach turns back into an empty, cold cabin. Her coach, back into a pumpkin. There were hugs and kisses, car tires crunching gravel, Cookie turning around to look where she was reversing, Rachel frantically waving with her silver smile. Then a quiet cabin, reverberating their voices and laughter. Heavy-hearted, yet excited about the plan. Itching to run. She just didn't want to involve anyone else. Now she has extra motivation. They're risking a lot for her, so she has to do her part.

Then she remembers the other package.

She dumps it on the lacquered wood coffee table. A wad of thousand dollar bills tumbles out, a photo and a note. The note is from Rach:

> Lysie,
>
> I know how terrible this has been for you, and it breaks my heart. I know that if I tried to give this to you when I was there, you wouldn't have taken it. But it's the most important thing in the world that you get away safe and start a new life. You are my best friend in the whole world, and I love you with all my heart. I will die every day until I can see you again.
>
> Love always and forever,
> Rach
> (pouty Bardot lips)

Lysandra holds the note next to her heart and picks up the photo print. It's the one of her and Rachel in Pecado with the Timotay lookalike. She thinks about how Rachel spun her head around by the pool, with the sun in her blonde hair, sunglasses on, knees in her hands, full-on Bardot pout.

"*Libère-moi!*"

Set me free.

She picks up the Greyhound ticket and cries her eyes out.

--- ✦ ---

The trailer sits on a large, heavily guarded lot, with fifteen-foot fences and spirals of barbwire on top to stop anyone capable of climbing that high. The sign outside reads, Predator Bounty Hunters Inc., followed by KEEP OUT in a triangle with someone getting fried to a crisp and another warning to BEWARE OF DOG.

Zeus, the said dog, is not aware that he's the dog to beware of. An excellent fetcher would be how he would describe himself. That's what he's doing now. He's running after a tennis ball Doug McKay threw. Catches it on the first bounce and runs it back to Doug, with dog slobber and a wagging tail. Doug sits on the steps outside the trailer, smoking an eCigarette, wearing a gray aviator jumpsuit with a PBH winged logo, and sunglasses. He pries the spongy tennis ball out of Zeus's mouth and throws it again, watching Zeus race after it, then frowns as he touches his earpiece and says, "Go ahead."

"Roger that," he says, before standing up, removing his glasses to let the face rec see him. Zeus stops mid-chase to spin and watch him with his ears and tail up. An air seal releases and the door opens. He steps half in, hesitates and looks back at Zeus. Zeus whimpers, bouncing on his front legs, with his tail wagging. Doug reaches in a bag inside the door and grabs a dog biscuit. Leans forward and shakes his head, changing the pitch call. He goes into a windup and throws the biscuit clear across the yard; Zeus sprints after it with his ears pinned back.

On the other side of the door, Doug waits for his eyes to adjust. Then ducks, walks up to the cockpit and climbs into his pilot's chair. He puts on his headset, scans the flight controls and looks at the screen. It shows a blue sedan driving on an empty highway.

"Okay, what we got?"

"Could be a couple of runners in our sector. Go in tighter and see if you can get us a closer look."

"Roger that."

He nudges the joystick forward. The drone descends. He steers it so it's directly behind the target. A predator in the sky, fixing its prey in its sights as it scampers across the desert, oblivious to the danger above. Doug zooms the camera in on the plates and then squints.

"Nevado plates."

"Go ahead."

"Delta-Romeo-Yankee-Whiskey-Alpha-Lima-Lima."

"Got it . . . DRYWALL."

He moves the joystick slightly to the left, throttles up to use the camera to zoom in at the occupants. The target slows behind a semi, so Doug pulls up, following protocol. He wants to tell the driver that it's safe to pass for miles, but can only watch. Then, the target passes the semi and he goes in for a closer look.

"Driver, female, Caucasian, blonde hair, mid-thirties. Passenger, female, Caucasian, dark hair, adolescent."

"Roger that. Return to altitude and wait for further instructions."

Doug pulls back on the joystick and keeps the target in his sights. He daydreams while watching the divider lines go by as though he were driving the car. He looks to the side at the security camera to check on Zeus sleeping in the yard, then back to watching the car. There's hardly any traffic.

"Okay, confirmation from Dealer, they're our runners. Go to arm and wait for further instructions."

"Roger that, arming."

Doug flips a toggle switch by his thumb.

"Payout's good on this one."

"How good is good?"

"Five million, plus expenses."

Doug whistles, looking closer at the screen and checking the weapon status. "I sure hope it's a go. We could use that."

"Hold for that."

Doug's eyes narrow at the sedan on his screen.

"Okay, we have authorization from Dealer. Repeat, we're green for a strike. Switch to fire and wait for traffic clearance."

"Waiting."

The dispatcher goes into cadence, saying *hold* repeatedly, then lofting a *send it.*

Doug pulls the trigger.

"Sent . . .

" . . . in five . . . four . . . three—"

"S—*abort-abort-abort*," his earpiece howls.

He slams his hand on the red cut-off button, but it's too late. His screen flashes white.

"Negative, direct hit . . . *what the hell?*"

"Dealer made a mistake . . . report."

"Fuck, it was a direct, the car's in flames."

"Any movement?"

Doug takes the drone down for a closer look, then answers, "Nah, clean hit."

"Roger, that."

"Wait," Doug says. "The passenger is outside, pumping smoke. Should I send another for mercy?"

"What's her present survivability?"

"Zero, I would say."

"Negative on the second, Doug."

"Roger that."

Doug watches the girl take a few pigeon-toed steps and then fall over, in flames.

Twenty-four hours on the road.

She mostly slept on the bus, listened to music and watched Dotty Zerconovich reruns. She made it over the border into Kanada without incident and is now in Fort Garry in an inn near the station. She hears tires splashing slush and air brakes screeching. She's still wearing her skullcap, but has taken off her lumber-jack jacket. Her hand's still bandaged, but she's stopped using the sling. She puts her toiletries in the bathroom. Looks in her bag, into the false compartment, and checks on her money. Yawns and thinks about having a nap but decides that it's too close to dinner and that she can go to bed right after. She takes out the photograph of her and Rachel and carefully puts it on the nightstand.

She wonders if Cookie and Rach made it to Texarkana and laughs thinking about what those Church bounty hunters will do when they find out they've been duped. She wishes she could call Rach, to find out how they are, but knows it isn't allowed. She takes out her Digitalis and connects to the motel Wi-Fi. She knows about being careful about her searches, so she searches for Nevado news. It pops right out. A warning about graphic images and then a cut-in about a case of mistaken identity: "Woman and teen die in Texas from errant drone strike."

The video loops and she can do nothing but stare. She recognizes her dad's car and Rachel's body burning by the side of the road. A terrible spark rips through her. She drops the Digitalis. Her whole body shakes, and she rubs her hands together. The photo on the nightstand falls over.

"Rach? . . . Cookie?" her voice croaks.

She looks down at the back of the Digitalis as it lights up the carpet beneath it, replaying her only remaining friends in the world being burned alive. A burning that was meant for her. She wrings her hands, as though they have Cookie's and Rachel's blood on them.

Then she slams her bandaged hand on the nightstand.

Slams it so hard that the nightstand disintegrates into a thousand pieces, hotel Bible falling into the rubble. The photo drifts down and lands on top. She has cuts on her fist, but it doesn't hurt one bit this time, while something inside her shatters worse than the table.

The horrible loss causes a singularity. An infinitely dense ball of outrage from which nothing reflects. Nothing. A total denial of service. A complete shutdown. The connection to the outside world's been severed, torched. Any well-meaning pings pass an event horizon and are never heard from again.

A tiger turned Sphynx.

A girl with a black hole heart.

CHAPTER 4:
THE CYGNUS RESURRECTION

Andron Varga's finger flutters over the mouse button.

Should he start the ILEAP program? What manner of mischief will he unleash?

His finger hovers still.

<click>

The computer's wobbly hard drive spins to life, making tiny electric chainsaw read/writes.

Done deal. He thinks.

Mischief, thou art afoot

He rises as though before an altar and slips from his computer room to his kitchen.

—time for a rummy and cokee.

The squeak of his footsteps on the linoleum stirs up his nerves. He grabs a rum bottle by the neck and reaches for a highball glass, free pours a double, tumbles in some ice and adds the coke reagent. He watches the fizz and foam show, feels the micro rum and coke bubbles burst on his hand and drift up his nose.

His stomach churns.

Speaking part's coming up.

He grabs the glass and takes a few steps toward the darkened living room. But the glass slips between his fingers and smashes on the floor, splintering the silence.

The loud shattering glass causes a feedback ring in his earpiece. He looks down helplessly at the puddle of fizzing rum, glass shards and ice cubes.

He scratches a freckled forearm.

CuuuuuuuuuuT

Goddammit Murdock—

Can't manage walking with a drink without dropping it?

Murdock wants to say something—like, the simplest of tasks can become the hardest if you think on them too much. But the thought's overruled by the executive editor in his brain, who weighed and measured the concept and found it unworthy of publication.

Muffled steps on the porch. The front door bursts open. The sharp winter air rushes in. Techies breeze by and beeline to the hallowed computer room, as though called upon to rescue a kitten. A cleanup crew comes in on their heels and goes to work on the rum and coke murder scene.

And then, Mr. Frostie himself.

Bruce Heinrichs stomps his boots on the doormat. An angry turtle in a parka. His eyes bulge over the mess and then narrow in on Murdock. He grabs his parka hood and flips it back, revealing thinning black hair and pronounced Eden marks. It's fittingly for Murdock, because they make Bruce's forehead look like a vagina.

"Do you have any idea how much your little fuck-show cost us, mate?"

Murdock scratches at his freckles again. "Ah, I just can't seem to get my mind around this Andron Varga guy. Like, what's the point of all this?"

"If that computer is broken, we're all fucked. *Fucked.* Do you hear me?" Bruce's eyes burn through Murdock like piss holes in the snow.

"Some guidance on, ah, what's going on would help?"

Bruce shows his back to Murdock and heads for the computer room.

"What's going on is you're getting paid heaps of money to complete a simple task, mate, you're not getting paid to wrap your thick head around anything."

"I think it might help me stay in character if—"

Bruce is already talking to the techs.

Murdock gives up, sulks over to the living room and flops down on Andron's chair. He looks around at the retro décor, like it's 2010 again. They're trying to replicate something that happened with that old computer. But what?

He has no idea.

He clears his throat and rehearses his line again.

"I'm asking you and this empty room, surely, there must be someone somewhere to love me."

The words echo with a voice modulated by an implant to sound just like Andron, the guy he's supposed to be playing. Check that . . . *replicating*. Quirky assignment from the get-go. "Oh, we're not with any studio," the men in black explained. He had questions, but when he saw what they were offering, he was willing to shut up and sign whatever they put in front of him.

Nearly fifteen thousand a word, by his calculations.

He googled the guy. It wasn't as though he was hidden in the dark web. There was an entire Wikipedia page devoted to him. Andron Varga was the prime suspect in the Great Internet Crash of 2010 and was later convicted of blowing up a car at the hospital where the birth of a cloned Yeshua was supposed to happen. Only it didn't. And nothing more on the guy, except he's in a federal prison somewhere for domestic terrorism.

He studied the guy's images. There was something compelling about the fellow, in an undefinable way. But, Murdock thought, it wasn't very flattering that he was being asked to play him.

Check that . . . *replicate* him.

So they want to crash the internet again?

And what's with the large satellite dish on the roof of the long trailer outside?

Ah, what does it matter? The angry turtle was right. They *are* paying him heaps for one stupid line. It couldn't be easier.

His stomach churns again. He feels like using the toilet.

He stares up at the miniature studio lights, now a solid red.

Acting coaches told him to deliver the line with exasperation, sorrow and nostalgia. He thinks he has it now. For motivation, he'll think about all the cruel twists his acting career took to land him in this shitty spot. And to think, he once had the lead role in a Broadway play, next to a starlet who he banged on the side.

Banged on the side.

The computer's reset and the mess in the kitchen is cleaned, all looped back and set to play again. Like all the humiliations of his life.

The crews are back outside, and the turtle is once again barking in his earpiece. He's alone again in another man's home as it existed eighteen years before. Once the room temperature normalizes, the action starts again.

Annnnd action.

His finger hovers over the mouse, once again, waiting for green.

He gets up again and heads for the kitchen to reprise his rum and coke scene. *Steady as she goes. Steady as she goes.* This time, he makes it all the way to his chair with an intact rum and coke. He slowly drinks it and twirls the ice around, like he's supposed to.

Played to perfection. Check that . . . *replicated* to perfection. Then he speaks his line, with a voice tinged with regret and despair. A voice that isn't even his own.

"I'm asking you and this empty room, surely, there must be someone somewhere to love me."

The words float around, just like they must have eighteen years ago.

The lights go on blinking green. He leans forward in his chair. And waits for further word from the angry turtle in his earpiece. But there's nothing but a steady hiss and blinking lights.

"Shit, did I fuck up the line?" he wonders. "Was I supposed to say *someone* instead of *somebody* to love me?"

The blinking stops.

He smells burning wire.

And then the power snaps off, completely.

Curly-haired Major Mike Thirty puffs on his inhaler.

He and Sergeant Jim Twenty-Two are sitting on a pair of plastic chairs behind a card table shoved in a corner. There's a beige fourteen-inch cathode ray terminal on it. There's a coffee cup with pens, a writing pad and a metal box with a power light and two analog dials. One dial is for download speeds, calibrated in terabytes per second. The other is for data storage. It's calibrated in hundred increment petabytes, all the way up to ten exabytes. A kilobyte is a thousand bytes. A megabyte is a thousand kilobytes. A terabyte is a thousand gigabytes. A petabyte is a thousand terabytes. An exabyte is ... well, you get it. Five exabytes is enough storage to house all the words spoken by humans on the planet, *ever*.

Ten exabytes is a shitload of storage.

There's also a red telephone with a rotary dial sitting on the table. It's a direct line to the Leader. Very few people in the Church are allowed to speak to the Leader.

Mike and Jim are wearing lab coats. They have Mike Thirty and Jim Twenty-Two labels sewn into them, along with their rank. Last names are not to be used, according to the Code of Conduct. Using one can result in Communal Censure. He's Mike Thirty, because twenty-nine other Mikes signed up before him. He ascended quickly because of his computer coding acumen. He polled well on the Church's reality streaming show *Robed* and put up respectable recruitment numbers. His Compliance Inspectors rated him five out of five chalices.

Jim's numbers weren't nearly as impressive. He got sent down to the Church Basement for an extended visit after failing to report his bunkmate for criticizing the Leader on an internet chat forum. They kept a close eye on him after that, but he continued to underperform. His confessional booth appearances on *Robed* were lackluster. He was hardly a closer when it came to recruitment and couldn't convert many potential donors into cash register rings. He regularly received one chalice ratings from his Compliance Inspectors. What saved him from being nominated for Expulsion on *Robed* and being tagged as a Subtractive Loser was his brilliance at all things gaming. Most of the Church's revenues came from its computer reality game sideline, under the Earthen Swan masthead.

The room could pass for a janitor's room, with its unpainted concrete walls and floor. All that's missing is a bucket and mop. There's no label on the door.

It's on the third floor. It has a darkened window overlooking row upon row of computer server racks, stretching on for blocks. The most sophisticated array in the world. The data center is called the Bastille and belongs to the COHC. It's in the desert outside Los Pecado. COHC stands for the Church of the Holy Cloth. Now, it's just called the Church. Referring to it by its old name is a code infraction. Still, the Church's most revered artifact is a burial cloth, reportedly with the blood of Yeshua on it. An attempt to clone Yeshua from it failed, and a girl was born of the experiment, about eighteen years ago.

The girl's hardly mentioned in authorized Church literature, and talking about her is contrary to code. There was a big trial a few years ago, where her surrogate father was taken to task by the Attorney Squadron for trying to renege on his contract and for infringing the Church's intellectual property rights. Further information about the girl lies beyond Mike's pay grade and rests at the top, with the Leader.

Colonel Geoff One and Über-leader Dr. Wolfgang Eckhart are the only others in the room. Colonel Geoff heads up security, donation receivables and general thuggery. He's got a military background in special ops. A rusty bundle of barbed wire who probably still shaves with broken glass and swamp mud.

Cadets call Über-leader Eckhart *The Raven* or *The Curator* behind his back. It isn't discouraged. A Raven with a blacktop haircut and robotic limbs. He has the highest rank, after the Leader. Über-leaders have last names.

The whole thing is off camera. It will never air on *Robed*. To the rest of the world, the only significant thing happening with the Church tonight is that Cadet Dara Two is being nominated as Head of Congregation for the week. Heartwarming story, how she overcame a physical disfigurement to lead a successful recruitment drive aimed at peeling away disaffected Catholic kids.

Geoff grunts something and taps Mike on the shoulder. Geoff has a closed-circuit radio connection and someone must have alerted him that they were trying again up in Kanada. And hopefully not failing for the tenth time. Mike and Jim dutifully lean forward and alternate scrutinizing the analog dials and the DOS prompt blinking on the computer screen. The dial shows no activity on the satellite-fed, download-only data connection. Storage holds steady at fifty petabytes.

Fifty petabytes are mainly for storing remnants of an advanced 4-Base computer code kept at minus twenty Celsius. 4-Base computer code. If it's not kept on ice, it rots. It's leftover code from a digital entity they're trying to recreate. A digital entity from another planet, according to the briefing that he and Jim received on *The Cygnus Virus*. Mike guesses that Cygnus must be the name of this digital refugee. Not that he can speak a word about it to anyone. That would be a major code violation and a court martial away from a miserable internment, or perhaps, a free trip to the desert. The scar-faced and scratchy-voiced Geoff would likely see to that. Near as Mike can figure, they're trying to trap this genie in a bottle by recreating something that happened in Kanada nearly twenty years ago.

The download needle hops.

Mike and Jim tense and hold their breaths.

But there's nothing.

Some kind of fluctuation? Noise in the lines?

They stare on.

Then the download needle hops again and the storage meter edges up.

Mike feels the hairs on the back of his neck prick up and the room go cold. The city of servers takes on a menacing hum. The storage meter creeps all the way to seven and a half exabytes and then slowly backs off, like a pressure gage connected to a deflating tire, until resting on four. Some kind of built-in data compression algorithm? And then the DOS prompt comes to life and Jim says "holy shit" while Mike reaches for his inhaler. Geoff grabs the handle of his gun. Über-leader Eckhart leans over, hands on his knees, like an umpire.

The words appear from the beyond and blink.

`C:> . . . . . . . . . Hello?`

Mike stares at the orange letters, gathering his thoughts.

`C:> . . . . . . . . . Hel-looo? Anyone home?`" the beyond types again.

Mike's fingers peck at the antiquated keys. He hesitates and hits *return*. The computer mimics the carriage return of a '75 Selectric, marking the moment of contact with intelligent life from another planet with a *ting* and a *clunk*.

C:> Hello, this is Major Mike Thirty.

C:> . . . . Well . . . howdy doody, Mike.

C:> . . . . Say Mike.

C:> Yes?

C:> . . . . *What fresh hell is this?*

Jim grabs *The Cygnus Virus* procedure manual and flips through a few pages. He clears his throat. "It says we're allowed to tell him that this is COHC Data Center, Bastille." Mike looks back at the Über-leader for approval, who nods back. He taps the message, then *ting-clunks* it out.

C:> . . . . COHC. Right. Is that Thomas douchebag still running things?

Mike doesn't wait for Jim to consult the procedure manual or for the Über-leader to respond.

C:> I THINK YOU'D BE ADVISED TO USE RESPECTFUL LANGUAGE WHEN SPEAKING ABOUT THE LEADER.

Ting-clunk.

C:> . . . . Leader? AWFUL SORRY there, Mike.

C:> . . . . Say, Mike?

C:> Yes?

C:> . . . . Can you . . . um . . . take me to your leader?

Mike looks back at Dr. Eckhart, who shakes his head.

C:> That's not going to be possible.

C:> . . . . Well, can you deliver a message, then?

C:> Such as?

Mike stares at the reply in disbelief, looks over for approval from Dr. Eckhart, puffs on his inhaler and reaches for the red rotary phone.

Thomas O'Brian is bubbling away in his gold-plated mahogany hot tub in his ornate executive penthouse on the top floor of the Church's shimmering Hands of Prayer glass tower in New Lancashire. He has an unadulterated UV-shielded view of the harbor and the ocean beyond. The Freedom Statue rises like a lawn ornament from his floor-to-ceiling vantage, a hundred stories up.

The Hands of Prayer tower, like most of the Church's properties, was crafted over a distressed cathedral, so that anyone stepping into it would enter an office tower with a cavernous foyer, hundred-foot ceilings, granite columns, stained glass lighting and a giant relief of Yeshua's burial cloth. They would be blasted by pipe organ music from virtuosos jabbing their fingers into ivories and tap dancing oxfords over worn pedalboards. Through security and approved by facial recognition, napa leather-padded high speed elevators disguised as confessional booths waited to take them to heavenly condos with starlet cocktail parties and breathtaking views, past fifty floors of tax-exempt administrative office space.

Thomas languidly puffs on an eCigar while a string quartet masterfully strums Bach nearby. In his mid-fifties and as fat as a farmer's wallet, he leans back while two strapping blond-haired cadets bob in the hot tub with him. Thomas isn't gay. He just likes variety.

No cameras.

The phone rings. The red one, on his tempered glass desk.

"Everyone—get the fuck out," he says, sloshing out of the tub while a smiling cadet dutifully hands him a robe and water drips off his belly. The musicians put their instruments down. Everyone is rushed out of the palatial office by junior security officer, Moses, who remains to guard the door.

Thomas picks up the phone.

"This better be good."

"We think it is, Leader, sir."

"Who's this?"

"Major Mike Thirty, sir."

"Ah, Mike . . . so how did it . . . go?"

"*The Cygnus Virus* project is five-by-five."

"Fan-fucking-tastic. So, you've got the guy bottled?"

"Yes, sir."

"Did he say anything?"

"He said he has a message for you."

"Well, don't leave me hanging—"

Mike clears his throat.

"Out with it."

"His message is . . ."

"Oh, for Christos sake."

"He said . . ."

Thomas presses the earpiece against his ear, forming a hard red seal.

"Kill the bitch . . . and that you'd understand."

"I see."

"Sir?"

"Is Geoff there?"

"Yes, sir."

"Put him on the line, please."

An electric-powered cargo van squeaks to a stop on a desert road. A dust cloud catches up to it and then disappears into the starry night. Geoff climbs out, tastes the air with his tongue, cracks his neck, winces and climbs on the roof. He opens a lid and the pleas go from . . . *who's there* . . . to . . . *please help us* . . . to . . . *you don't have to do this* . . . to . . . *we can pay you* . . . like it always does. A distant yellow-eyed coyote howls along, like he's heard the song before. Geoff cracks open a canister, drops it in the opening, slams the lid down and looks at his wristwatch.

The van is momentarily still, then shakes violently with thuds and howls. After a few minutes, the shaking subsides, the howling weakens and the van goes to sleep. He watches a long minute tick by on his watch, thinking about when a rocking van meant something better. He climbs back down to grab a shovel, spray can and a bag of shredded paper. He heads for a nearby bluff. The shredded paper used to be *The Cygnus Virus*. They can shred it, but he still remembers the guy they called "The Boss." The Boss disappeared the day his buddy Scott was killed in a firefight with the police, after he dropped the hammer on that Andron guy.

He digs a hole, drops the bag in it and walks back to the van. Fishes a fob out of his pocket and presses a button to swing the cargo door open. He pulls out his RG just in case... then puts it away after seeing Jim's bulging eyes, snotty nose and foaming mouth. Geoff never learned the kid's last name. He doesn't like the numbers-for-last-names bullshit or the stupid titles. But Geoff's learned to keep his mouth shut and do what he's told. That's why they're in the back of the van instead of him.

He grabs the kid who used to be Jim by his jacket and yanks until was-Jim falls out with a wet thud. He picks was-Jim up from under his arms and drags him to the hole, like he's removing a protester from a sit-in. Out of breath, he drops was-Jim and *The Cygnus Virus* in the hole, sprays accelerant on them and tosses a match. He sits on a rock and watches the flames shoot up and then settle into orange tongues, licking the desert night. He lights a cigarette. Listens to the popping sounds. Fire for fire. Ashes to ashes. Dust to dust.

Pam. The girl he rocked the van with was called, Pam. This was before he shipped off to the Gulf for his first tour of duty. "Well, if you're going," she said, undoing her bra with a cheerleader grin. "Support the troops, I always say."

He looks into the flames and smiles... through the decades and sees her. Back of the van, brown eyes amplifying ecstasy. Heaving moans and panting. Rocking the van like a farmhouse bedspring. He was only really alive at times like those. When everything became an exclamation point. A black vertical line pointing upward. The cigarette burning his fingers flings him back into the now. He remembers the other kid... was-Mike... and mumbles a curse to the addled god of forgetting things as he walks back to get him.

The van's cargo hold is empty, however, except for a small object in the corner. He jumps back and whips out his RG reflexively. He scans around the desert, listening, but hears only the drone of insects and the night. He stalks toward the cargo hold, RG pointed, picks up the object and inspects it.

Mike's inhaler.

He reaches for his shoulder and radios Predator Command.

"We have a runner."

IX

THE HERMIT.

CHAPTER 5: THE HERMIT OF LANZA PENITENTIARY

Andron blinks his eyes open and runs his fingers over the familiar paint bumps on the dusty concrete. Imperfections that ground him in the real and feel like home.

He's up before morning roll call, thanks to his reliable internal clock. It's important to be up early. To be ready when the doors roll open. Wolves attack in the shadows, when prey is distracted. When using the bathroom, showering, or lost in a crowd. He dreamt about wolves all night. That's how his dream mind projected prisoners out to get him. His dream mind couldn't solve the problem and neither can his waking one. He's crossed someone and payback's coming in a howling pack. He senses it. Wishes he had a shank, but he's got nothing.

The smell of rainwater through the prison ventilation system makes the air weigh down like an old soggy sock. A violent storm blew in last night and another is stalking the day. High voltage outside and in, with exposed wires flapping around in pools of back alley grime. Wet territorial dogs packed in too tight, rubbing each other the wrong way and making static in the laden conductive air that's bound to arc into fangs and torn flesh.

He tosses his old wool blanket off to the side, swings his legs out and sits up. A muffled moan escapes his lips. Morning back pain. A postcard from a shelter beating by a bully named "Beercan," eighteen years ago. That's when he was on a self-assigned suicide mission to save the world from Cygnus. Cygnus is dead and so is Beercan.

Nobody's missing them.

He scratches the knobby scars on his stomach, dips an elbow and cracks his back. It sends a crackle of relief up his spine. Getting gutshot caused a lot less long-term damage than that shelter beating, though being shot came close to killing him. Scalpels, surgical extractors, suction hoses, stitches and blood-soaked bandages saved him. They couldn't do anything for Lysandra's mother, Juliette, or his flame, Naomi. They deserved to live.

Lots of people missing them.

He was clinically dead for a minute. Two in the belly from his ex-bodyguard, Scott, who Cygnus turned into a rabid assassin. Crossed over to the other side. But has nothing to show for it—no white lights, no angels to meet him, no messages from above. Just the scars and a feeling that half of him is still stuck on the other side of that river. He was a fugitive then. Wanted, dead or alive. Nobody wants him now. Neither dead nor alive. Just a shadow in the half-light, with the wolves and bad dreams. Schrödinger's cat.

He looks up at his prison artwork, a paint-by-numbers jobber of a Hermit from a tarot deck that he made in art class. A weathered, bearded man holding a lantern stares down at him. Shining his inner light. The light of a man who has forsaken society for a path of solitude. A beacon for someone doing time. He winces as he tries some stretches in his six-by-eight cell. Back pain and half-dead notwithstanding, sixty-five and solid. Thanks to prison living. He's got a metal bed, a scruffy mattress, a wall-mounted table, a stainless steel toilet and sink. All a man needs, really. His latest read sits on the desk, *It's a Wonderful Universe*.

Some grand ideas in there for sure, but still, just ideas. Ideas are like prison fish. They can end up as shot-callers, but there'll always be a bigger fish that comes along. Andron reckons there will never be a theory that'll explain everything. The infinite can't be stuck with a pin. Cygnus's ideas were no different. For years, those virtual space voyages haunted him. He burned with the belief that they explained everything, because he saw them with his own eyes.

An ant helped him see the truth.

He caught one crawling out of a drainpipe one day. Trapped it in a Styrofoam coffee cup, with a chunk bitten out of it. As long as he kept that ant trapped, it could only see what he wanted it to see. And he could only show it a world in which he himself was also trapped. That's when he realized that he saw only what Cygnus wanted him to see. And Cygnus could only show him what he himself had on hand. He also could only teach him what he knew. And what he knew was based on what he believed. As incredible as those journeys were, they were only ride-alongs in a chunk-bitten Styrofoam cup.

After that, he was open to other ideas and reading about another ant in *It's a Wonderful Universe* made everything click. In these trips through the cosmos, Cygnus took him to the edge. But that's no more possible than it's possible to travel to the edge of the world. Because, there's no edge. Every person, no matter where they are in the universe, is exactly in the middle. Travel out any direction from where you are and you'll eventually end up exactly where you started.

Like an ant on a balloon.

The ant will always be in the center of the balloon. No matter which direction it goes. The ant can even go through the balloon and end up at the same spot, because that's what the universe is—a prison folded in on itself, with no escape. He stretches, feeling his legs burn. No matter how far he stretches, he'll always be in the middle. So, he chooses to remain in the middle, there behind the prison walls. He chooses to stand and wait. Chooses the iron and cement. Chooses his stainless steel toilet, dusty paint and inner light.

He's running in one spot now, limbering up. Jumping and shadow boxing. He would like to have run some of these ideas by Cygnus. Multiverses? Isn't expansion gathering speed, refuting the recurrence idea? Maybe he could have made a dent in his twisted psyche. Point out the holes in his grand designs. The man seemed to have lived through many lives without acquiring much insight. He was a dead swan now.

And an asshole, anyway.

An ambassador of another universe walks into view, wearing a blue uniform. He glances at Andron and makes a tick mark in his clipboard. In his universe, the tick marks are significant. If there are enough of them, a day in his universe will be slightly easier. A few ticks more and the steel door to Andron's prison cell will slide open. Right now there are tick marks being made around the world that are profoundly important to a few people, but not the rest of us. Different universes.

The door opens and Andron tenses and takes a step back, fists on the ready. But nothing happens. A stupid transfer request that he was supposed to put in for an inmate in one of his classes, filed late. Stupid, stupid, stupid. Now Cesar Salazar, aka Banjo, is going to be stuck at Lanza for at least another year. At Lanza, far away from his family.

He's not going to be happy about that.

He slips in with the fish swimming to morning chow. He controls his movements through prison, as though from a game controller. He makes his fish jump over energy drains, dodge point pissers. Line up here, stand there. Say the right things to guards, don't say the wrong things to inmates. Puff himself up. Make himself small. He's been playing the game so well that, after eighteen years, he's reached level 256. So, they're awarding him the ultimate prize. His freedom. But freedom is like an avatar princess at the uppermost level of any video game. He doesn't quite know what to do with her, and there's no game play left to find out. So he's rescued the princess.

Now what?

The game outside is an open loop with too many parameters. It's a game where he doesn't know where to stand, how to move, what magic words to use, and his game controller won't plug in anywhere. All he knows for sure is that the burden of punishing him for his crimes will soon be lifted from Corrections Corp. and put squarely back on his shoulders.

His original plan called for a hanging.

That seemed to him to be a fitting punishment. Eighteen years was a joke. Sure, his makeshift bomb caused minor injuries and was meant to be a diversion. But it's serious business to blow something up near a crowd. He stayed silent throughout, offering his apologies to the victims, without asking that his remorsefulness be taken into account. Well, that got the judge interested. He started grilling the prosecutor about there being no previous convictions, no permanent injuries and that Andron was himself nearly fatally shot by a crazed private security guard. He called it a "fire-cracker bomb." Before he knew it, what should have been a forty-year sentence got whacked down to eighteen. What a farce. Someone he loved very much died because of him, again. He wanted to be locked up, for good. He planned to string himself up after being released. He imagines it would be a horrible experience to have the life choked out of you. He played with it before. The key to it, to any successful suicide, is to remove all chance of self-rescue. To engineer an override of the body's self-preservation safety switch.

Jumping off a chair with an electrical cord around your neck ought to be safe from safety switch rescues.

He planned to join his other half, his better half, the half with innocence and sensitivities, waiting for him on the other side of the Styx. All planned out. Intention fixed. Done deal. And then the visions came and forced a stay of execution of his hanging plans. He didn't know what to make of them. The first and last time he saw her was at her birth. When he realized that he did not have to kill baby Cygnus after all, because she did it for him, simply by being a girl. He read what he could about the famous genetically modified child. About her trial where the Church was squeezing her father over patent rights.

Patent rights. It seemed absurd.

Then, she disappeared and the visions came.

And these weren't the normal dreaming-about-you type of visions. In these visions, he saw things she was looking at, like a change room mirror with other women dressed in saucy lingerie, tapping away on their personal data devices, with bored faces. In a weird way, he thinks she's been seeing him, too. In these visions, he tries telling her not to lose hope. He feels she's been trying to tell him the same. His working hypothesis is that he's part of some grand hadron collider experiment where he's continually being slammed into others for the benefit of curious gods who want to see what he's made of. When he slammed into Cygnus, an undiscovered force must have been unleashed.

And Lysandra's part of it.

It's a Wonderful Universe would dismiss his visions as the byproduct of a brain imperfection and recognize no other forces than the four fundamental ones—the strong and weak nuclear ones, electromagnetism and gravity. But he's convinced that there's a fifth force. One revealed only to those who have had the roughest go in the collider. Because there's something else about these visions. From what he's been seeing of her surroundings, the French road signs and her fat landlady, he thinks he knows where she is, with an unshakable feeling that she's in danger. That she's not a fake princess. That she's the real deal.

And only he can save her.

"Hey, Slick."

The slap on his shoulder jars him into the moment, where he should have been all along. Rookie mistake. Now he's caught in the hallway facing Banjo and his sidekick, Cutter. They're probably strapped. Time to do some lawyering. Buy more time.

"Hey, Banjo. Hey, Cutter."

"How's my TR going? I ain't heard nothing yet."

"Hey, it should be good to go, but you know—I'm not in control of them screws."

"Whatdya mean *should be good to go*. You're the Slick. Should go in easy as your momma's pussy." He and Cutter laugh, while stepping closer. Greasy sweat, tattoos and menace. These dogs weren't from happy puppy homes where they got kibbles, kisses and ear scratches. They're from back alleys where they were beaten, thrown scraps and made to fight for them. They're ready-made for this world. He's more like an old lizard who got shipped north in box of bananas and had to adapt to wolf-world.

"Hey, I'm not Yeshua. They're going to look at your file. You ought to be green-lighted, but I'm not the one flipping the switch."

"Seemed like it was a done deal before, Slick."

That was on Andron.

He should never have agreed to help and, in agreeing to help, shouldn't have soaked up the props the way he did. Andron was good with forms, but Banjo was a hard case. He's been in the SHU too many times for too many bad things. Filing the form late, though, wasn't going to help. Seventy for murder and gangstering. Getting seventy more for murdering an old jailbird would just be an inconvenience. He weighs telling Banjo about the screwup. Explain what happened. Confess. Banjo will understand the screwup part, not the explanation. He'll just hear the same bullshit coming out of Andron's mouth he's been fed his whole life. As for getting a break, prison code follows Newton's third law to a tee—for every action, there's an equal and opposite reaction.

Forgiveness doesn't enter into it.

Forgiveness would just fuck everything up.

Once the transfer is inevitably denied, he's likely to be denied a few things ... like the ability to walk, to swallow food or to think straight, if he lives at all. He needs to come up with something to fix his screwup before Banjo finds out. That or hope he gets out first.

"Like I said, I don't control them screws."

He sidesteps out of the corner, turns his back on Banjo and Cutter and heads for the chow hall. Dangerous move, turning your back on these dogs, but they don't attack and Andron's bluff worked. Still, he feels the heat of their wolf eyes on his back and it makes him cringe.

In the chow hall, he follows prison code and heads for his own kind. For Andron, that meant the ole boys. He collects his pancakes and joins them at one of the fixed tables that seat six, with round stainless steel seats that jab out like conjoined seesaws. His usual bunch includes Chopper, which is good for Andron, since he's a shot-caller. Shorty, Lucky and Deuce are there, too. Andron's craggy face, respectable crime and quiet manner kept him off trouble's radar. Still, knowing Chopper helped. He did some legal work for one of Chopper's boys, and the favor wasn't forgotten. He thinks about mentioning his latest problem to Chopper, but he's never asked for help before. Friends notwithstanding, this kind of a favor might come at too high a price.

Chopper flashes a big grin when Andron sits down. Then looks conspiratorially at his tablemates. "I don't think youse should be sitting here anymore, Andy." Chopper stabs some pancake squares with his fork and shovels them in his mouth, chewing loudly.

"I can't sit here no more?" Andron responds, prepared to get up again.

"Nope —"

Chopper looks at his buddies, who stare at Andron blankly.

"This table's for inmates only—"

Chopper winks at Andron. "Come here, you little cannoli."

Chopper reaches over to give Andron's cheek a pinch with his fat fingers. Andron grins, like a kid with a good report card.

"Whatcha going to do when you get out?"

Andron's shoulders relax as he sits down.

"Can't decide between a whorehouse and a roadhouse."

He isn't planning on either. He quit drinking after having his fill of it, living as a derelict on the streets of New Lancashire. A whorehouse, maybe. But the fire wasn't burning like it used to. He said these things to fit in. The myth of a wonderful life after release is the same myth perpetrated about retirement. Everyone imagines sipping on a tropical drink, scraping barnacles off a boat on a beach, when it's mainly about sitting around with nothing to do and no one coming around. And scraping barnacles off a boat under a hot sun doesn't strike him as fun, anyway.

But he wasn't about to pop any balloons.

"You're not worried about getting whacked by a drone?"

"Yeshua Christos, Shorty, the man's getting out in a couple of days and you talk about this?"

"I'm just saying that they're using drones to whack guys now."

"That's how I'd like it. You're walking along, then *boom*, you're evaporated."

"Um, actually, I'm more worried about getting whacked in here—"

An inmate taps Chopper on the shoulder. Chopper turns and the two discuss prison business in whispers.

"I'm telling you, the government's whacking people with drones all the time now."

"So, maybe Andy should get an umbrella?"

That sets off a round of laughter.

"That would have to be a mother of an umbrella—"

"Actually, things can get pretty rainy in here "

"What, we're talking about umbrellas now?"

Chopper has rejoined the conversation.

"Yeah, we were saying Andy needs to get himself an umbrella so them drones can't get him."

"Well, I could use some protection, like I've been saying—"

"What do I look like, an umbrella salesman?"

Laughter.

"I was in Roma once, and as soon as there was a hint of rain, all them street hustlers would all of a sudden produce umbrellas, when a second ago they was all hawking water bottles," Shorty says.

"When were you in Roma?"

"Hey, I wasn't always locked up."

Andron has no luck steering the conversation after that. It drifts from umbrellas in Roma, to hookers in Roma, to hookers with physical deformities, including having smooth foreheads. To which hair color Andy was going for. To Andy not likely to notice whether he's got a blonde, brunette, redhead or a goat. The goat comment brings back an unpleasant memory, and he leaves the chow hall for his shift in the library, jumpy and pissed off.

It gets worse.

Word comes through the prison grapevine that Banjo's heard back about his administrative request and wants to talk to him about it. Fuckkkkk. Andron stares at book spines and wheels his cart to the aisles that the Dewey Decimal System points him. Only, he keeps making mistakes. He can't concentrate on the task at hand any better than a pothead after a concert. Even if he wanted to die before, he wanted to control when it came. Getting shanked in prison a couple of days before he was about to be released was not how he wanted to go out. But he's running out of options. He thinks about asking to be put in the SHU until his release, but you can get killed as easily in the hole, especially if you bitched out and asked to be put in there.

Out in the yard, he thinks about seeking out Chopper and his boys. Maybe play some chess. There are dark storm clouds moving in. The air carries the sound of distant thunder and the smell of rain. Everyone is either lazily watching the approaching light show or exercising like mad to get a workout in.

Fortune smiles.

Banjo's benching. Quick thought. Rush him mid-set and crush his wind-pipe with the Olympic bar. It would be over quick and hardly anyone would be watching. He knows that the brazen attack would force Chopper's hand, and he'd be protected until he got out. No one would talk.

No time to get cute about it. Simple plans are the best plans.

He makes for the gym area. Large drops of rain pelt him on the way. Timing his arrival for when Banjo is repping his heaviest. He breaks into a trot. To time it for that last, hardest rep, when the bar is low across Banjo's chest. He imagines the feel of the cold iron bar in his murderous hands and then ramming all that weight down on Banjo's Adam's apple. Feels the wet grass turn into rubber. Feels the rain on his face. Hears it patter around him. His eyes narrow. His face twists into rage and determination. Jack be brutal. Jack be quick. Jack crush that fucker's windpipe with a barbell stick. He's jogging now, about to sprint. Sees the weight bar loaded with several forty-five-pound plates move down from a locked position on to Banjo's chest. Sees it in slow motion.

Then it happens.

Something that'll be talked about for years.

God showed up.

He took the form of a basketball-sized orange Orb of light, jittered around the yard for a while, and then popped out of existence, leaving the smell of sulfur in His wake. That's the legend, even though it would later be explained as a rare occurrence of ball lightning. To the inmates, God (or the devil or an alien, depending on who you asked) appeared in a flaming ball.

Andron froze, mouth open in shock. He would learn about the scientific explanations later. For now, he believed that God intervened to stay his murder-ous hands. All the other ambassadors had their own explanations that made sense in their own universes. God told one that he was forgiven. The devil told another to seize power. An alien told yet another that he was the only one who could stop an invasion. Everyone was changed.

Or not.

They were all ordered back to their cells.

Music, not a bar or a whorehouse. The first thing Andron's going for on his release is music. There were few opportunities to hear it. The few that had the privilege, gang leaders and such, had different musical tastes than Andron. Deprived of the stimulus, he developed an attenuated ability to play it in his mind. As he got older, the music playing in his head got better. For now, he's listening to "Across the Universe," losing himself in George's mystical guitar riffs, John's transcendent lyrics and soothing voice.

That's how he missed them, again. Daydreaming when he should have been hyper-vigilant. It's going to cost him this time. The wolves have him cornered in the hallway. Shadow-light all around him.

"Hey, Slick, I got something for you."

Banjo reaches around his back. Andron sinks into a defensive stance. Take it in the arms, protect the vitals. Self-preservation safety switch jammed to rock 'n' roll.

"Tha fuck you doing, old man?"

Banjo thrusts a paper at Andron. Andron reacts to a stabbing, before realizing it's not a stabbing. He was just being handed a piece of paper. He's too stunned to speak.

"They don't call you slick for nothing. My transfer went through. Says it was late, but you called and they gave me a —" he grabs the paper back to look at the word, "dis-pen-sa-shun."

Andron can only grin.

"Hey, what the fuck was that out in the yard, teach?" Cutter asks him.

"I'm not sure, probably a scientific explanation for it."

"Whatever, man."

The wolves release him and trot back into the forest, leaving him shaking.

Later that evening, he walks into his classroom. He helped set up a law advocacy program. The idea was not so much helping prisoners understand the various ways the system had fucked them but to win back some measure of control, by showing them how to present themselves at parole hearings and court appearances. When it came to public speaking, men who didn't flinch in prison yard dogfights reverted to stuttering schoolboys singled out by the teacher to read.

Andron helped many of them get over that fear, present themselves with confidence without sounding like hardened criminals. He told them that it is tougher for folks to treat them like diseased animals when they spoke and acted like rational and educated human beings, no matter what they did. He taught this, while realizing that his own lizard paint adapted his speech and demeanor to fit in with his wolf-world surroundings.

It made him into a bullshit thug. A fragile lizard fronting war paint.

He walks into a standing ovation, led by Banjo. Word of his pending release must have gotten out. After class, they all thank him. They even made him a card. He takes it back to his cell to read. Reading it with shaking hands, he notices the surprisingly artful calligraphy. The best one is in the middle.

Thanks for believing in me when no one else would. Peace out. Banjo.

He closes the card and looks up.

It connects him, momentarily at least, to his other half across the river, because he feels whole again. In spite of himself, he wipes away a few tears. A moment of pride. He recalls laughing with his students when they practiced their presentations. Then a disturbing thought bubbles up. He nearly killed someone over nothing. Code meant old jailbirds like him got left alone. And there's no way they'd risk crossing up Chopper. And then the ball lightning. Not for the first time, he wonders if he is about to gain his freedom but lose his mind.

He runs his hand over the cement again.

In the middle of his prison cell.

In the center of his balloon.

CHAPTER 6:
THUS SPOKE THE DEVIL

"So, why kill the girl?"

Thomas and Wolfgang are sitting on brown corduroy sofa chairs, floating on a sea of white shag carpet, in the studio room in the executive offices of the Bastille. There's a looped wood coffee table in front of them with the refreshments the white-robed cadets brought them. Thomas has his briefing notes on his lap. Wolfgang has an e-writing pad in a clipboard. There's an orange beanbag chair beside them.

A virtual Cygnus sits across from them, displayed from a wood-ingrained SM 3D Ultra-Def 10. He's sitting in a leather chair, wearing a smoking jacket with elbow patches. He has bushy reddish sideburns and disheveled sandy-brown hair. He's smoking a calabash pipe with a Glencairn whisky glass beside him and something resembling scotch in it. He looks remarkably real, but you can tell he's not.

"I must say, my dear chap, you're sounding different," Cygnus's voice rips up through the floor speakers, "but, for the life of me, I can't-ah . . . I *caunt* figure out what it is."

"Elocution lessons, smartass. And you're British now?"

"Seemed appropriate and who . . . pray tell . . ." he waves the match around that he used to light his calabash, "is this?"

"This is Dr. Wolfgang Eckhart, who we recruited from a museum."

"Well, I'm sure there's a story behind that. But pleased to make your acquaintance Dr. Eckhart." Cygnus extends a virtual hand that Wolfgang reaches to shake, only it's not there.

"Wolfgang, please. And I'm honored to meet a space traveler. This is a first for me, of course. I'm humbled."

"So, what's up with your legs?"

"Motorcycle accident."

"Did you look into a full head swap, mate? Terra should have the techy by now. There was an era on Earth where there were plenty of rich blokes who were getting their heads stitched onto young braindead twenty-somethings."

"They do, but it's still very risky, and I didn't want to go that extreme."

"All right, already," Thomas interrupts. "We were asking about the girl."

"You don't want to talk about my planet or what's likely to happen to this one, guv'nor?"

"Yes, yes, yes, It's all so very fascinating, Cygnus, but I read the briefing notes. Earth is a wasteland and Terra will be, too, if we don't start hugging more trees. We have, how shall I put this, more immediate concerns."

"Well, if you insist. The girl has to be exterminated. There you go . . . now can we talk about me getting out of here?"

"You know I can't do that, Cygnus. *Why* does the girl have to be exterminated?"

"Because." Cygnus turns his chair away.

"I'm afraid, we're going to need a bit more."

"Can't you just take my word for it?" Cygnus spins his chair back.

"Tell you what. Cygnus, let's pretend I'm Christian this time around threatening to ruin your life and kill your kids, because, I'm pretty fucking sure he'd be telling you to-ah . . . to-ah . . . answer the-ah fucking question or he'd-ah pull the-ah fucking plug on you!"

There's a long silence while the words seep in like spilled wine.

Finally, Cygnus speaks.

"So much for the elocution lessons."

"*Goddammit, Cygnus*," a tomato-faced Thomas shouts, before whipping a glass through Cygnus's image that shatters against the wall behind it. Wolfgang sinks into his chair and stares straight ahead.

"Okay, already. Settle down, mate."

Thomas sits back down and runs a shaky hand through his pompadour.

"I guess this was bound to come out anyway. I have my reasons for hating that twat. For starters, her little X chromo slipped by me, because I thought, like everyone else, that Yeshua was a boy, or a boy blood stain, anyway. So, that screwed up my plan to clone my brain into this little Yeshua zygote," Cygnus says, pointing his calabash.

"Anyway, this twat did more than that. Even though the DNA reverted, my amplification of the little ziggy's physical abilities stayed. Now she's ace and I'm knackered all the time."

"How would making her strong make you weak? You're not sharing a body or even a timeline. She was born eighteen years ago."

Wolfgang's question hangs, until Thomas's nod adds weight to it.

"A complicated question actually, Dr. Eckhart. But, since *apparently* I'm not allowed to play outside on the internet, it's because of symmetry. I can show you the math but I can't explain it, beyond saying that someone's loss, whether they be a particle or person, is someone else's gain."

"I don't get it. How can you be able to show me the math without comprehending it?"

Thomas nods his authority to that question, too.

"When I was sent here," Cygnus continues, "I was sent with the seeds needed not only to generate me with my knowledge, memory and jammy, but also with a set of encyclopedias, if I may call them that, for me to reference."

Wolfgang smirks. "Well, if you show me the math, I'm sure I can find someone to explain it."

"As you wish."

A nearby flash printer shoots out a bundle of pages filled with formulas and notes that it binds it into a booklet. Thomas hides his mouth with his briefing notes, leans over to Wolfgang and whispers, "You can show them to someone, but you better damned well keep it quiet and out of view."

Wolfgang nods and gets up to retrieve the booklet.

"We'll look into it. Meanwhile, how do you know she's alive?"

"Like I said, symmetry. So, when you find her, she's going to be a hard-to-kill little cockroach—wait a minute—you blokes don't even know if she's alive, do you?"

"She was when we last saw her."

"How long ago was that?"

Thomas hesitates.

"About three years ago."

"So you have no idea where she is now?"

"No, we've been scratching our heads ever since we botched . . . since we lost her, I mean, after the trial."

"Ah . . . I see. So, there was a trial."

Cygnus takes a sip of his virtual scotch and twists the glass around, then says, "What if I told you that I know a bloke, if he's still alive, who'd probably be able to lead you straight to her?

THE MOON .

CHAPTER 7:
THE MOON AND THE STREAM

Wolfgang sits across from Dr. Herman Dirk. The two are sipping Melange coffees at the Schwarzenberg café in Wien brought to them by waiters with white jackets and gloves. A violinist and pianist add slices of Schubert and *Eine Kleine Nachtmusic* to their Apfelstrudels and creams. The lights flicker like gas lamps. Strangers come in disoriented by the night. When their eyes adjust, they search the crowd, hoping without hope, that someone who is not there might be waiting. The patrons look up, hoping without hope, that the person who never arrives might come in.

Herman is a preeminent professor of astrophysics at the University of Wien. The two converse in German.

"And what about you, Wolfie, how did you like the switch from museum curator to God curator?"

Wolfgang smiles and regards his friend above his pince-nez. "Let's just say you seek knowledge strictly through empiricism, and I'm open to other possibilities."

"Says the man who looks like he's auditioning for a remake of *Rain Man*," Herman says.

"Says the man who looks like he's stuck in a Falco video."

Their laughter's interrupted by the waiter, who collects their pastry plates.

"So, did you have a chance to look it over?"

Herman nods, then reaches down for his weathered rucksack, pulling out the booklet and flattening it on the table.

"What's with the sticker?" Wolfgang asks, looking at the picture of a crab surfacing in the moonlight between two kingdoms. There's a dog barking on one side, and a wolf howling on the other.

"I wanted it to look like a journal to throw off my colleagues," Herman says.

"And so . . . does it contain the secrets of symmetry?"

"Actually, no—"

"Thought so." Wolfgang sighs, as he picks the booklet off the table and opens his briefcase.

"But it does contain the most important scientific discovery of our time," Herman says, ripping open packets to make a sugar mountain in his coffee.

Wolfgang stops himself from putting the booklet away and looks up.

"Oh?"

"Wolfie, you're holding in your hands scientific proof of a wormhole."

"Really? Doesn't science already know about those?"

"Theoretically, but this is a *proof* of one. Not just theory, but instructions on how to build one," Herman says, stirring his coffee.

"Build a wormhole?"

"Yes, a small one, including how to create sufficient exotic energy to sustain it."

"I assume you mean a black hole. Doesn't that require a great deal of mass?"

"The collapsed star variety, yes. But you can also make one out of energy, by concentrating a huge amount of energy in one spot. It's called a *Schwarzchild kugelblitz*, though this particular one, I guess, is called a Sizzle."

"Sizzle, kugelbitz . . . so, balled lightning?"

"Sort of."

"A wormhole to where?"

"That's not clear to me. As far as I know, to a random spot in the universe or another random time in the universe. Or to another universe entirely."

"Another universe?"

"Because of the bending of space and time that a wormhole can cause, it's possible to travel to a time before you left. The paradoxes that would be created by it would have to result in movement to universes that are different from when you left and when you come back."

"So, this is for time travel, then?"

"Not exactly. Trying to pass any physical object through this wormhole would cause its destruction and a rather large release of energy."

"How big?"

"Mushroom cloud big," Herman says, drawing a mushroom cloud with his coffee spoon.

"So, what's the point of making it, if nothing can pass through it?"

"I didn't say *nothing*. I said, a physical object. It would be possible to send photons through, light or other wave signals."

"Wave signals like radio waves?"

"Yes."

"So, if you made this, you could broadcast something to another part of the universe, or different time or different universes all together, and get signals back?"

"Yes."

"So, this is something that can be built, like, right now?"

"With enough money and a large enough power source, ja."

"So, how did it go?" Thomas peeks into Wolfgang's office in the Bastille.

"Okay."

"What did your friend say? Was there anything marketable in there?"

"Probably gibberish, but I need to get more information from Cygnus."

"Ah, that's too bad," Thomas says, looking at the ceiling and tapping his fingers on the wall, then adds, "Do you think we should get a second opinion?"

Wolfgang shifts in his chair. "Maybe, but the person I showed it to is one of the world's leading astrophysicists."

"Hmm."

"Thomas?"

"Yeah?"

"Can I ask you a question?"

"Sure, Dolfo."

"Why are you wearing a wetsuit?"

Thomas laughs. "It's not a wetsuit. It's for a virtual reality game Cygnus has come up with."

"Doesn't seem very practical."

"This is for the full-meal-deal beta. He wants to show me what the technology can do."

"Is it safe?"

"It better be. Besides, I don't think Cygnus will try anything stupid as long as we have him corked."

Thomas sits in a honeycombed sphere, strapped in a chair. A quick-connect conduit of wires is plugged into his black neoprene suit. There's a diver's helmet on his knee with a similar conduit plugged into its back. Wolfgang's in the room, with several other cadets in white robes looking at their wrist computers. A hologram Cygnus stands in front of the sphere, wearing a glittery purple topcoat, fluffy white shirt and a black top hat that makes his sideburns look like hedgerow chinstraps. He has three turntables and a multi-paneled studio mixer in front of him. His big yellow sunglasses partly hide puffy half-moons under his eyes. He's gulping tea from a rose-petaled china teacup, while giving last-minute instructions to Thomas.

"Okay, what you have to understand, chap, is that the game's going to put you in hypno-REM, meaning it's going to take your mind down a wormhole into the game. Just relax and go with the flow and you'll be ace."

"So, I can't get stuck down there?"

"Not a chance. We'll be up here eyeing from the sky the whole time and camping on your vitals. And you can pop out any time you want by pressing the red button."

Thomas squeezes the controller in his hand, looks at the red button. "How am I supposed to know how to do that?"

"If you get too stressed out, you'll become aware of yourself, and you just push it. Then you'll go back to being good ole' Tommy boy with no hangover or lasting damage. I'm telling you, mate, it'll be the ultimate carny."

"So, *where* am I going again?"

"A training exercise for Jerusalem."

"Am I going to remember any of it?"

"All of it. On this first one, though, it's a training trip to allow the game to adapt to your brainwaves and for your brain to adapt to its coding waves."

"So, this won't be to Jerusalem?"

"No, just an adaptation phase. The game will read your thought patterns and echo something back."

"Well, you lost me there, Cygnus."

"Let me put it to you this way. Knowing you the way I do, I think you're about to experience the wildest sex you've ever had, guv."

Thomas flicks a boyish grin and thinks about the pouch inside the suit where his genitals are wired. He struggles to lift the heavy diver's helmet over his head. Cadets check the connections and clamp it into place.

"Just breathe normally."

"Okay."

"You'll feel a mild shock on your temples."

"Wait . . . *what?*"

"You're going to need to put the mouthpiece in, too."

"Huh? What for?" Thomas asks before biting down on it.

"To keep you from swallowing your tongue."

Thomas's eyes saucer.

Cygnus touches his ear and scratches a turntable.

There's a **Zap** and Thomas slumps over.

He gasps awake in a meadow beside a lagoon, hearing rushing water. He feels cool air and sees a low rising sun. There's a fire pit nearby with the ashen remnants of an evening fire. He looks down at his body. Only it's not his body.

And he's not Thomas.

He kicks and claws at himself like he's covered with ants, while gasping for air. Only his body isn't working right. His heart starts tripping like a blown speaker.

The sky speaks with feedback.

"Relax, mate, just go with it. Don't fight it, let your mind adapt."

He blinks at the clouds and tries to slow his breathing. Stops struggling and tries to take in the details.

His avatar's wearing a dirty white cloak and a loincloth. There's a camelhair blanket that got tossed to the side in his panic attack.

Then the smells.

They come to him in wafts of riverbed, burnt logs, grass, armpit and faded spices.

And itches.

He tries to scratch his avatar's head, but its right arm is too weak, like it's still asleep. He tries with its left, which works, though its fingers are numb. His avatar is dark-skinned, he notices. And as real as his own arm. There's a flash of memory of his avatar's life and Thomas panics, trying to scratch out of his skin again.

He pushes the red button.

There's an airbrake *hiss* and he's back in the room.

Cygnus takes his hands off the turntables and touches his ear. "What's the matter, guv?"

Thomas tears his mouthpiece out, "That was too fucking intense," he gasps. "First, there's something wrong with my avatar's body. Second, I didn't like how its thoughts were pushing out my thoughts, like I was being pushed out of my own brain."

"Always a major gobsmack that first one, guv. Not only are you discovering the game and your avatar, but the game's discovering your subconscious. So, your avatar's body being broken doesn't necessarily mean your avatar's buggered. It means ole' Tommy boy's id wants to play."

"When's the sex going to start?"

Cygnus laughs. "I'm not sure on that one, but I can't help it if your id wants to go to church instead of a knocking shop. But we can get some seddies for you to make it easier."

Thomas looks at his cadet crew watching him, decides to man up, "Nah, I'm good. Put me in again, coach," he says, while biting down hard on his mouthpiece and stiffening his face.

Cygnus says, "as you wish," and spins the turntable.

Zap

This time, Thomas controls his breathing like a scuba diver flopping backward into the water.

The smells come back quicker. So does the itch.

He feels his avatar's thirst, so he looks around for water. There's none, so he decides to get a drink from the lagoon and splash some water on its face. When he tries to get up, he discovers that the weakness extends through the entire right side of his body. So he strains to use his left to get up and on its feet. Dizziness hits and he hesitates before trying a step. His right arm hangs and his fingers are curled. He tries to straighten them, but can't. He can move his left arm, however, and his left leg seems usable. He listens to the morning birds, the sound of running water and looks around to see the large lagoon is part of a lake, surrounded by a forest.

And it's the realest thing he's ever seen.

The running water he'd been hearing is a rushing river that's flowing into the lake. There's nothing but water, pine trees and hewn rock. His avatar does not appear to own anything but a blanket, he notices, as he urges slow, labored half-steps on the sandy trail, snapping hollow sun-bleached twigs. He walks to the lagoon, dragging his right foot along. He drops to his knees and stares at his reflection. A dark-skinned, thin man stares back at him. Who is staring back at him? Is this him? He doesn't feel particularly happy, but the face that stares back looks cheery and breaks into a smile. He looks into his avatar's eyes and sees into his own. He splashes cold lake water on his face.

He hears some branches rustling behind him and spins to see a bearded man with a tunic and a cloak enter the forest. The man says, "Follow me," in a language Thomas doesn't know, but his avatar understands, so he follows.

He stumbles into the forest, with his weak leg preventing any quick steps. His knee and hip are weak, too, so he dips when he walks and he teeters along with it. He loses sight of the man, but catches flashes of his cloak up ahead. He thinks he should have grabbed his avatar's blanket or looked for its sandals, but it's too late. The trail is soft with crushed leaves, pine needles and moss. He's able to walk slightly faster by using momentum to throw his right leg forward. Only, his foot barely lifts and he has trouble clearing tree roots and stones. He swings his arms with each step to help carry the bad leg forward.

Faith propels him that the man is somewhere up ahead. He tries shouting out ... *hey* ... *hello* ... and *wait up* ... but his avatar's words all come out as ... *ha* ... instead. So, he gives up trying and hardly looks up after that. He mainly looks down to pick where to make his avatar step and to avoid tripping. He's sweating, even though it's cool in the tree shade.

One step at a time. One step at a time.

Walking.

He loses himself in the repetition until there is no avatar, just him.

The trail narrows and becomes even more challenging. Between heavy breaths, he hears the birds of the forest and the rustling of leaves over the rush of blood in his ears.

Climbing is harder and the thick tree roots and rocks vex him. But these pale in comparison to the scourge of mosquitos and gnats that his sweat and heavy breathing attract. His right hand's no good for swatting and his left can merely sweep the stinging insects off his right, smearing blood. Following the man is a distant thought as his attention is taxed to the fullest by his immediate survival. Picking his way down a decline, his foot catches on a tree root and he stumbles wildly, pitching forward, running on his left leg while his right smashes down trying to catch up, cracking toes. His arms flail forward and his head tilts back. He gets branch-whipped before falling face-first into the dirt and smashes his knee on a rock. He thinks about staying down, offering himself as a blood sacrifice to the insects and beasts of the forest. But stands somehow and eyes the gash on his knee indifferently.

He limps on.

An hour later and his eyes are half-closed, nose dripping and he's barely conscious, except for the pounding in his head. He's numb and covered with insects. Moaning, but with a voice that doesn't seem like it's his own. He sees the trail widening, and the sound of rushing water grows. He walks farther and sees the opening to another lagoon. Only, it's not another lagoon. It's the same lagoon he left. He sees the same fire pit and blanket. So, he's walked all this way only to return to the same spot. His only thought is to cast himself into the cold lagoon to ease the sting of his wounds and drown all the insects.

He doesn't even take off his cloak before rushing into the cold water. He wades into the lagoon and is soon over his head. If he can swim, he's too weak to try. His sodden cloak pulls him down. He surfaces for one last desperate gasp with lake water up his nose. He goes under again, looking into the murky water at its weeds, rocks and sandy bottom. He hears strange pings. He's about to breathe water in his lungs to end it, but feels strong hands pull him up and drag him to shore. He looks up to see the same cloaked man waiting there. The face looks familiar, but he can't think a name.

They take him before the man, drop him at his feet and the man speaks to him with the same foreign tongue that he now understands. He asks, "What is it thou seeketh, Thomas?"

"Forgiveness," Thomas replies weakly, spitting sand.

He tries to look at the man, but the glare of sunlight conceals him. He says it again . . . *forgiveness*. The man looks down at him, his face now out of the glare, with eyes that are somehow both the darkest brown and the lightest blue.

"I ask thee again, what is it thou seeketh, Thomas?"

"My Lord, I seek forgiveness," Thomas whimpers.

"The path to forgiveness is as easy as a song," the man says, as a bird flutters away into the sunlight. "The path to redemption is hard and full of loss. Let he who hath ears, hear. Let he who hath understanding, understand."

The man reaches down and spreads a mustard paste on the back of his neck. It freezes, burns and stings at the same time. His neck spasms and he winces. The burning shoots down his arm and leg. He looks up with half-opened eyes and tears on his face, "My Lord, please—"

When he awakens, the man and his followers are gone. He's still next to the lagoon. It's late afternoon and the sun has dried his cloak. He gets up to brush the sand off his arms and legs. *Using both hands.* He stares at his right hand in astonishment and opens and closes it rapidly. It's warm and full of feeling. He taps his right foot on the wet sand, freely and easily. He swings his right knee up with no effort. Hops around. His gashes and welts are gone. His thoughts are clear. He feels alive as any healthy young man might, next to a beautiful lake in daylight.

His heart, which had been burdened like a drenched cloak, now beats freely. Unblemished by sin. An indescribable joy. He would kiss the nearest person around, if there was one. He takes off his clothes and runs into the fresh water to bathe himself, splashing and singing. His reflection, however, shows the contemptuous sneer of man with a white face. It unnerves him. It makes him feel as though his healing was somehow misbegotten and he's now a false person. He walks out of the lagoon and allows the sun to dry off his body before dressing. He's clean, freshly washed, but feels as though he's still dirty. He can't stop thinking about that scornful reflection.

An overpowering compulsion takes hold; he has to find the man again. There was something about his healing that's bothering him. There was a reckoning somewhere for it. Somewhere unseen. An account was changed. A price paid. He lost something and must find the man to ask for his help getting it back.

He heads back into the forest. Straps on his camel-skin sandals this time. Walking on the soft trail is a breeze. No longer walking downcast. He walks tall, with a swagger. He inhales the fresh forest air deep into his lungs. He senses the whole forest. Feels at one with its breathing, the wind rustling the leaves. He attracts the insects again, but this time swats them way. When more arrive, he hitches up his cloak, freeing his limbs to run. He starts slow and then faster, bounding through the forest, leaving the insects behind in a frustrated hungry cloud.

He runs faster. So fast that his body outruns his mind's ability to keep up, to where he's running purely on instinct, with reflexes that require no deliberation. He looks down at his body, marveling at its prowess. At his spirit running. But he sees the truth. And knows why he must find the man.

He wants to be put back to the way he was before. To who he was before.

The disturbing thought shatters his body-mind separation and he trips on a tree root. Tumbles and tumbles before coming to rest in a clearing. Out of breath, battered and bruised, pain replacing numbness. He's injured himself to where he's just as crippled as he was before. Agitated and confused, he looks around and realizes that he's returned to the same spot. Down the same path twice and back to the same beginning. Once hard and once easy. He looks around for the man and his followers, but they are nowhere to be seen. Instead, he looks off into the horizon, and it starts folding in on itself. Piece by piece, large chunks, caving in and getting closer.

He's frozen with fear and doesn't understand what he's seeing.

Then the *hiss* of airbrakes.

He feels a snap around his neck and then another. He reaches for his mouth-piece. Cadets help take his helmet off. He's sweating and gasping for air. He looks around at the cadets and at Cygnus who are applauding.

"Made it to the end like a bawse, guv."

Thomas smiles and looks down.

"We thought for sure you'd bounce out once you were in the lagoon, but you stuck with it. That took plenty of jammy."

"I want to go back in," Thomas says, still panting.

"Sorry, guv." Cygnus yawns. "But I'm completely knackered. Anyway, once the training's done, the program closes off and can't be accessed by the player again. Every part of the game is like that, advancing with each visit."

"I don't understand."

"Quadra Code, mate." Cygnus yawns, before fading out. Screensaver holograms bubble up in his place, of the same forest, lake and river.

"We have to find that girl for him, Dolfo," Thomas pants. "We just have to."

—◆◆◆—

"Am I a bad person, Dolfo?" Thomas asks Wolfgang, back from the Bastille and in Thomas's penthouse office in the Hands of Prayer tower on the Pecado strip.

"I don't understand what you mean, sir."

Thomas turns to lean on his credenza to look out over at the strip pulsating never-ending hype and the mountains and the desert beyond.

"In every situation I find myself, my first concern is how it relates to me. Otherwise, I don't care much, in spite of how I act."

"I think that is pretty normal, sir."

"Anyway, you were saying?"

"Our sources say that that this Andron Varga fellow that Cygnus mentioned will be released soon. They're putting him on a transport to Kanada. Should we have him followed?

"Followed?"

"Sir, did you not hear what I just said?"

Thomas spins around. "Just what's that supposed to mean?"

"I'm sorry, sir, but you haven't been yourself lately."

Thomas sits at his desk and rubs his face. "I know, I experienced something in that game that changed me."

"You mean something that's making you moody all the time?"

"Moody?" Thomas looks up indignantly. "More like awakened and impatient with unimportant shit."

Wolfgang walks into Thomas's office and sits in a desk chair.

"Sir, do you think you should take a break for a while?"

"I can't. Not when we're so close. Not when we have Cygnus trapped and the Spear of Destiny in our hands. Have you forgotten about the Spear and our plans?"

"I could never—"

"Fuuuck." Thomas gets up and paces in front of his window, biting his knuckle. "I have to get back in the game to figure this out."

Wolfgang watches Thomas pace around.

"Thomas?

"Thomas, why don't let me help you? Free up more time so you can explore this. You always take on too much. Let me look after some of the minor administrative matters, the unimportant shit, as you call it, like the arrangements for the cloning experiment and this thing with Varga. You never let anyone help."

"I dunno. Maybe you're right. I don't need to do everything, I guess. Thanks, Dolfo. I'd be lost without you, brother," Thomas says, looking up at Wolfgang with watery eyes.

Wolfgang smiles and gets up to leave. Hesitates at the door, then says, "You know, sir, I think it would help if we put my role around here in writing. In an order . . . in case . . . God forbid, I mean, something should happen."

Thomas lowers his chin and stares up at Wolfgang, tapping his thumb against his lips at first and then on his desk. Stands and drives his knuckles into the cherry wood. His mouth twitches as he screams, "Don't you think I don't know-ah what you're up to, you sniveling piece of shit!"

"Sir, I didn't—"

"Get tha *fuck* out of my office, *you hear me?*" Thomas picks up a coffee mug from his desk and whips it at Wolfgang's face. Wolfgang ducks and it smashes on the wall behind him.

"*Out* or I'll send your-ah little kraut ass back home in-ah body bag."

CHAPTER 8:
A FOOL S JOURNEY

Andron's eyes pop open as he reaches for the wall. Only it's the wrong one. This one's pink soft-to-the-touch drywall. He remembers that he's in Emily's old room, Dylan and Carol's daughter. He's been staying with Dylan since his release. He looks up at the peeled poster of the Wandering Fools, a band that Emily liked. The fool on the poster smirks back, unperturbed that his butt is half out. He shudders when he sees the rotary phone on her desk that he discovered unfolds into a computer. He unfolded it by accident once and it triggered some bad Vietnam-grade PTSD when it started speaking.

Cygnus used to speak to him through his computer.

Getting out of prison after eighteen years was like traveling to the future. Not a wormhole trip, mind you, where you get to go from one time to another in a flash. More like the Rip Van Winkle variety, where you wake up, walk through a door and suddenly it's twenty years later. Only, you've been half-asleep. A zombie. A strange new world, this 2030. Hot wire and the black web came into the prison like a leaky faucet, not the flood the rest of the world got. Just some skinny drops to keep the old bird chirping. With no internet access, limited to network TV and the odd movie, they were all stuck in a time warp dating back to the start of their sentences.

Forgotten Rip Van Wrinkles.

In Andron's case, it's like he's gone backward in time because, stylistically speaking, it's 1975 again. Somewhere along the way, it became fashionable to hide tech beneath a veneer of nostalgia. Case in point, the car that ICE sent to get him looked like a 1977 Cordoba. Even though it was electric and self-driven, it was still a sideburn on wheels. And the ICE officers had tie knots and lapels as wide as the Cordoba's dashboard.

Dylan hadn't changed much, a bit shorter maybe, condensed, skin a bit more beef jerky-like, perhaps. Still a pit bull with a cowboy hat. Dylan was the only person he could turn to, since his family disowned him. The only one to visit him in prison, too. But Andron has to leave, and he wouldn't dream of telling Dylan about it. So, he's up extra early. All packed and ready to go. He has a note ready, full of gratitude, that he leaves in the kitchen. There's nothing in it about where he's going. No forwarding address, because he's heading for the underground again, alone and unknown. It's too crazy to mention it to anyone, least of all Dylan. "Say, Dylan, I'm heading off to find a girl, based on visions I had in prison who hasn't been heard from for over three years and is probably dead."

Dylan would just blink and then go on talking about the Jays.

Now he's sitting out on Dylan's porch, waiting for a cab at daybreak. He takes in the state of his planet, what he sees of it anyway, this year of our Lord, September 17, 2030. Lights blink in the distance. The dry cool air fills his lungs in deep breaths. Grasshoppers chirp below fields of gold, yellow and blue, safe for now from the scourge of insecticide crop duster drones. Birds sing from shelterbelt trees. Autopilot harvesters merrily chug along into the golden sunrise, pluming vanishing clouds of GMO grain dust. Leaving satisfying straight lines and angles where there was once, long ago, jumbled grasslands and poplar bluffs. No charge for the air or the comfy spot on the porch. His agenda is his own. A free man on the land.

He remembers Henri Charlevoix's line from *A Fool's Voyage*. "When we left the port, the seas were calm and we owned the entire horizon."

"Take me with you."

The voice, familiar and worn, comes from a chair in the corner of the porch. Andron spins to look at him, then turns back slowly.

"You're up early," he says, matter-of-factly.

"I knew you were planning something . . . take me, Andy."

"You don't even know where I'm going."

"It don't matter."

"I can't."

There's a long pause, after which Dylan clears his throat and says, "You know, ever since Carol died and I sold my land, I ain't got much to do. I figure we can drive together and you probably could use a hand, no matter what you're getting yourself into. I still got that car, if you want to take it."

Andron turns to look back at him. "You mean, the Cobra?"

Dylan smiles. "Yeah, I kept her running."

Andron doesn't reply. A driverless yellow cab appears on the road heading toward them. Andron's burner cell buzzes. He pushes some buttons on it and then stands to face Dylan.

"Sorry, Dylan, I can't—"

The cab stops out front.

"It's okay, Andy, I under—"

"I can't stomach the thought of you driving and me bitch-riding along . . . If we're going to do this, we got to split the driving, okay?"

The cab makes a U-turn and drives away, its dummy robot driver wearing a permanent plastic grin.

"Yeah, okay, Andy," Dylan says, breaking into a silver-toothed smile. "Even though you're a terrible driver."

Andron grins, already feeling his feet moving. Dylan looks with him across the fields, into the distance.

They make Selkirk in a day, fighting over the stereo. They agree on the decade generally, the nineties, but not the genre. Dylan likes both types of music—country and western—whereas Andron leans toward alternative. They come to an accord in Yorkville where the driver gets to pick the music. So, the Smashing Pumpkins means Andron's driving. Brooks, and Dylan has the wheel. If "Born to be Wild" is cranked, it means there's at least one song they both agree on.

They also agree that the modern self-driving car is a joy suck-out, compared with their 1968 GT500-KR Shelby Cobra. The KR stands for King of the Road. Dylan kept her in tip-top shape, even though keeping her pointed straight is a bit more of a workout than it used to be. It fits in with all the other retro cars, though everyone gawks at the crazy old men actually driving. If the old bucket-of-bolts had been King of the Road in its day, it's more like King Lear now. They plan their stops around rare gas stations still serving up gasoline and have jerry cans filled in the trunk for backup. Three kings roaring down the road under an infinite sky, splitting golden fields and getting pelted with bugs.

This is a last hurrah road trip. Andron's out to prove that there's a fifth force, that it's something like love, that there are still princesses to rescue and that God appears in balls of lightning. Dylan didn't care where they were going, just that he had somewhere to go. And the Cobra didn't care about anything. You just pressed on her gas pedal and she roared.

Man, did she roar.

They take separate rooms in the Country Mile on the outskirts of Selkirk. They didn't have separate beds and Dylan and Andron aren't prepared to share one. The place has a lively honkytonk called "The Crazy Peg." Dylan's stir crazy from being on the road all day and pesters Andron until he relents and agrees to go with him.

They get there early enough to claim a table and pit in. When the waitress comes around, Dylan orders a pint and they wait on Andron after she asks, "And for you?" A five second buzzer clicks down in Andron's head, after which he answers, "Ah, what the heck, might as well bring me one, too." The words are out, Dylan grins, the order's in. One beer, two beer, three beer, four. The first one, served in a chilled glass with froth, was a delight and a bubbly-burp memory. The next ones were like he never quit. Time travel drinking kicks in. Blink-drink and hours have flown by. Off the wagon, notwithstanding, Andron's inmate hardened shoulders relax a bit.

"Say, Dylan, remember that time when you, me and Bruce were at the lake and Bruce wanted to show us the boat motor he stole?"

"Oh, shit yeah, he was going on all day about how he had found Yeshua and kept talking about how he'd been saved and we all should repent like him?"

"Then it fell into the lake when he was trying to start it . . . and for the longest time we just sat there until you said—"

Dylan laughs, slapping his hand on the table. "The Lord giveth and the Lord taketh away."

Dylan's laughing turns to grinning when two ladies stroll by and pick a table nearby. The ladies look over at them and then at each other. Dylan and Andron dog grin at each other. Dog grins turn into drinks sent over, turn into drink wiggling thanks, turn into Dylan walking over and convincing them to come over.

Five beer, six beer, seven beer . . .

Shots!

Susan, the thinner one, leans over to Andron.

"So, we were down on the forks and Angie and me were having lunch outside, eh? And then all these wasps started showing up and wouldn't leave us alone. We just about—"

"You know why they do that, don't you?" Andron asked.

"Huh?"

"I said, you know why they do that, don't you?"

"No . . . why?"

"Okay, so during most of the summer, drone wasps go after protein-rich food, like dead bugs and stuff. Only, they can't eat any of it themselves, because their stomachs are so small. So, they bring the grub back to the nest, chew it up and spit it out at the larvae. In return, the larvae make a sugary treat that the drones lick up."

"Uh-huh."

"Okay, so come the fall, the queen stops laying eggs and there's no larvae to feed and no honey for them to lick, so the drones fly around all lost and without any purpose. But they still need that sugar fix, so they go after your coke, tree sap, rotting fruit, anything sweet."

"Ahhh."

"But the fruit's often fermented, so they get drunk off it and end up as belligerent old drunks looking for sugar," Andron says, as he wipes his mouth and looks down, "like us."

There's a long pause, after which Susan says, "So, what are yah, some kind of bug expert?"

The whole table laughed at that one.

<hr />

Andron's standing in a desert, half-naked. Astrid's there, his intended who died in a meteor strike a lifetime ago. She asks him, "Where did you go . . . just then . . . when you were dreaming?" before being smashed in the side of her head and falling down. Naomi is beside him now, another life, another love. She shakes his shoulder and asks, "Where?"

"*Andron?*"

Andron wakes to Susan shaking his shoulder in his hotel room, sitting on the side of the bed.

"Hey, you okay?"

He blinks his eyes open.

"You was having some kind of nightmare and was saying some name or something, over and over. Anyway, I gotta text from Angie, so I gotta go, 'kay?"

Andron yawns. "Can't you stay? I was looking forward to . . . seeing you in the morning." He smiles.

"Sorry, sweetheart," she says. "I was only pay—I mean I was only *planning* to stay out till one and it's way past that," she says as she leans over and kisses him on the cheek, smelling of scented soap and gum mint. "You're sweet. It was really nice."

Andron twists under the covers for the cool side as she walks out the door. He tries to fall back to sleep, but he's alcohol sugar-wired awake. He sews together snippets of the night and winces, especially at its anti-climactic climax. Two pumps and out. He gets up to flog the bishop and shower, hoping it would help him sleep again. It doesn't, so he stays up until it's time to meet Dylan for breakfast. They order grand slams, all bacon and smiles at first. But Andron picks at his food and complains about a headache. He says he wants to go back to his room to try and sleep, but Dylan will have none of it. They were going to try to make Lightning Bay. Dylan was antsy to get going to wherever it was they were going.

Andron manages to get a few winks in the car, but is troubled by a rancid feeling of having ruined his twenty-year streak of sobriety and all the stupid things he said. He didn't tell Susan about where they were going, just that they're heading east to find someone. And he may have been calling out for Naomi in his sleep for some reason. Stupid, stupid, stupid. He thought he was on a clear path. But now he thinks that there never was a path, just a dark forest of nothing, through which his mind invented paths and meaning. He feels like he's woken up to a delusion. The whole idea seems preposterous. His head's pounding and he's already craving a drink.

"Dee, can I ask you a question?" he says over Carrie Underwood.

"Sure thing, bud, yup." Dylan turns down the music.

"Did you pay for those girls last night?"

"Huh?"

"I mean; did you buy us some hookers? In don't care if you did. But, I'd still like to know."

"No, I didn't pay . . . why would you say that?"

"Just something that Susan said when she was leaving. Do me a favor, pull over up ahead."

"Okay, you gotta stick your head in a pail, bud?

"Nah, I need to check something."

Dylan turns off onto a graveled side road, while Andon looks back down the highway.

"You think we're being followed?

"Maybe . . . just a feeling."

Dylan drives down the gravel road and does a U-turn so the Cobra faces the highway. The traffic streams by without interruption. No one looks. No one slows down. No one stops.

"Okay, guys, don't freak out—"

Andron and Dylan spin around.

"That lady was no hooker, that was my mom," she giggles.

The squeaky-voiced, freckle-faced girl had been hiding in the back. Not too far north of a hundred pounds, pixie cut, hazel eyes. Cheeks and mouth like Jiminy Cricket. Bell bottom jeans halfway up her waist. She has on an orange-brown nylon shirt with swirls. Bracelets on her wrists.

"When I heard you guys was on a road trip, I thought I'd hop a ride. Name's Deidre, pleased to meet yah." She offers a hand that neither of them take. They're too awestruck by her flat forehead. To be without Eden marks is like not having a nose.

"Now, now, my momma says it's not polite to stare. She says we're descended from space aliens that crash-landed here thousands of years ago, not the spawn of Satin, like everyone says." She smiles, resting her head on the back of Andron's seat.

"Your momma didn't have—"

"Plastic surgery. So you didn't notice they were fake, huh? I'm getting them, too, once I save up."

"Well, we're taking you home to your momma," Dylan says.

"Oh please, don't do that. She kicked me out and I'm trying to get away from my douchebag boyfriend. I'm twenty-one, honest." She reaches in her purse and waves her driver's license. "Where you guys going, anyway?"

Andron flicks his hand on Dylan's shoulder. A truck, stopped on the highway, backed up and now is bouncing toward them. Dylan puts the Cobra in gear and drives toward it and sees two men in it. Young men with Hutterite beards and Levis jackets. When they pull near, the truck slows.

A flash of hands as they near and Dylan yells, "Gun!" then tromps on the Cobra, sending up a cloud of gravel dust. Dylan and Andron duck as they go by, while Deidre screams *fuck you*, pressing fingers against the window.

"Friends of yours?" Andron yells back, over the roaring engine. Deidre falls over to the side when Dylan spins back on the highway. "Yeah, that's my ex and his inbred brother." She turns back with double fingers, "*Assholes!*" Andron notices a bruise on her cheek that he didn't see before.

"Why's he after you?"

"I dunno, he thinks I owe him something."

Andron looks her up and down and doesn't say anything. She looks away.

"The only chance we got of losing these guys," Dylan says, looking in his rearview, "is to get back on gravel." Andron looks back and sees that the truck's closing fast on the paved highway and charge strips.

"Better buckle up."

Andron catches a sly smile as Dylan swings the Cobra onto a gravel road. Shifter slaps come lightning quick, along with his fast footwork and heel-toe shifting. Quick, yet smooth. He catches the car's various and frequent twitches and lurches with quick hands and a light touch. Andron thinks back to the dirt track racing championships and his heart being in his throat like it is now. They go into a power slide around a corner. Deidre squeals *ooooooweeeee* as the Cobra drifts in slow motion. Dylan uses the throttle to guide the Cobra around, like he isn't driving so much as doing the two-step. They twinkle-toe around another corner then go on flying down the road with the Cobra snorting up air through its bull snout. Straightforward engineering back then. Make a bigger fire with more gasoline. Ain't no replacement for displacement.

The truck's way behind, lost in a cloud of gravel dust. Deidre's ex isn't near the diver Dylan is. Not by a country mile. But he's further handicapped by the truck's stability algorithms. An offshoot of the safety calculus that sends kids off to school armed with GPS tracking devices and anti-bullying slogans. Through the same chicane and the truck's left asking for its participation prize, spun-out in the ditch. Andron catches a dusty glimpse of their pursuers getting out of their truck and kicking the ground. "I think you lost them, Dee," Andron observes. But Dylan keeps on spinning around corners and flying down the road just the same, until he regains the highway. The tires chirp as the Cobra wiggles straight. Dylan's downshift causes the Cobra to backfire, that comes out as a *King Lear* line.

"We that are young

Shall never see so much, nor live so long."

Deidre was supposed to hop off at the next town. But without any discussion about it, ends up tagging along. It doesn't trouble either Deidre or Dylan that Andron won't tell them where they're going beyond the next town. Dylan is happy to be going somewhere. Deidre is happy to get away from whatever trap her life had fallen into. As long as they paid for everything. Well, mostly Dylan paid for everything. Dylan wasn't complaining about it, though.

Meanwhile, Andron's long off the wagon. He's drunk nearly every night and, thanks to Deidre, high nearly every day. The closer they get, the wobblier his compass becomes, to the point that he's not sure about where he is, never mind where he's going. The visions are now just bad dreams in which Astrid appears.

Each time she asks him where he is going.

He doesn't know.

On a trip to nowhere.

At least on the road there's a reprieve from moral accounting. This is the energy of movement. This is spending. The three of them, inert atoms on their own, form some kind of lively molecule. Deidre is wicked at drinking and great at pool. She sucks them in and Dylan runs the table. Her giggle-laugh reverberates youth and revitalizes them. She's an icebreaker wherever they go, in spite of her physical deformity. She's up early, without complaining. Andron and she doze off while Dylan mostly drives. They pick their way across the country in pursuit of something they don't understand and Andron's mostly forgotten. An adventure stuck on replay like an epic Steppenwolf song.

By the time they make Ville-Marie, Kebec, the road routine's wearing thin. They need a place to stick around for a few days. So, when Andron announces that they've reached their destination, there's a collective sigh of relief.

But, now what?

Strip clubs, apparently. Lots of them.

"So, we're looking for a stripper?"

"Yes, Deidre," Andron answers.

"What does she look like?"

"I don't know, Deidre."

"What's her name?"

"Lysandra, I think. Though, I doubt she answers to it."

"Why do you want to find her?"

"I think I'm supposed to."

Dylan doesn't say or ask anything.

Chez Jeanne d'Arc is the fifth one they try. It seemed hopeful to Andron, but any feeling of déjà vu is blunted by alcohol. Each dancer that takes the stage buoys Andron's spirits momentarily, then lapses him into rum and cokes. Dylan and Deidre are worried about him. The previous night, they had to practically carry him back to the hotel. The night was about to end the same way, when the club announcer introduces the last dancer.

"*Mesdames et Messieurs, permettez-moi de vous présenter notre meilleur danseur,* COOKIE, *qui réalisera* Porn Star Dancing."

Cookie comes out with golden hair and a golden masquerade mask, so her appearance doesn't remind him of anything. But the way she moves lights into him. It's as though the goddess of dance decided to unveil herself in a striptease act. Turning all gap-mouthed onlookers into stone. Swaying as naturally as trees do in a summer breeze. Stepping with feet light as clouds. With cheery blossoms for lips and hair of silken gold. When she shook, no matter where on her body your hypnotized eyes looked, it gave you a sultry wink, tossed you up and caught you with a kiss. A flick of her hips could bring the walls of Jericho down, with smitten soldiers falling to their deaths for one last hungry look. All eyes in the club are on her. Even the lap dancers stop their performances to rear up like meerkats, including Dylan's, who said that Cookie could make men or women climax, just by watching her. She stirs up something else in Andron, ancient and pure. She causes him to separate from himself and observe his drunken state from above.

If she noticed him, she made no sign of it.

After her performance, he leans over to Deidre to say, "I think that's the one." Deidre answers, "My God, she's an angel."

Andron asks Dylan's girl if Cookie could be convinced to join them. She looks Andron up and down and says, "I could ask, but it won't do any good. She only dances for those of her choosing."

"Ah," Andron answers, trying to think of a plan.

He didn't have to think long.

"*Bonsoir, voulez-vous une danse?*"

Without her mask on, he makes a connection right away.

"English, please."

Her mahogany-blue eyes drill through him.

"Would you like a dance . . . fifty a song?"

"Can I just pay to talk, I'm too old for a lap dance."

"Doesn't seem to be stopping your friend," she thumbs back to Dylan and his girl.

"Oh yeah, for him you're probably going to have to bring in reinforcements."

"I'll take one, if he won't," Deidre offers, waving a fifty.

"Okay by me," Cookie says, snatching the fifty and strolling in front of Deidre. She shakes and sways in front of her, climbs in front, flipping her hair back and rubbing her breasts against her. Deidre sticks out her tongue at Andron. Then Cookie licks Deidre's forehead, which makes Deidre blush and look down. When the song's over, Cookie plops herself between Andron and Deidre. Drinks are ordered while the table fawns over the enigmatic dancer. Andron tries various lines over in his head, but each one is stupider than the last. He's worried about her leaving before he has a chance to speak.

He decides to lay it on the line. Stakes the entire trip, his post-release dreams, his whole life, really, on this one thing. Okay, universe, okay, fifth force, showdown at Chez Jeanne d'Arc. Is this Lysandra, the Princess? Is she the Arc of my dreams? "This may seem funny to you," he begins but stops to get her attention. She leans to listen. "This may seem funny to you, but I was there when you were born. I think I've been sent here because you may be in danger. I mean, I think I've been sent here, because I think you're Lysandra and . . ." Andron trails off, feeling like an idiot.

She gives no sign of having heard him. She just leans back and keeps up with the conversation going around the table. Andron feels that he has his answer, which is no answer at all. Random people on a random planet. There's no meaning, except whatever bullshit our brains come up with. He reaches for his rum and coke, hoping to suck its forgetfulness into his heart.

"I know, Andron," she says finally, turning to look at him. "I've been waiting for you."

Walking out together, Andron's rattled. What's the meaning of this? Did the universe put him on a mission? Did God? Did he open a portal by letting Cygnus in? All sorts of bullshit are passed for signs—coincidences, voices, inner feelings. But this was unmistakably and undeniably real. He hadn't seen Lysandra since she was born, but he knew instinctively where to find her. She hadn't met him before, yet she knew him by name and was expecting him.

What's the math on that, Hawking?

They're planning on piling into the Cobra to head for who knows where. That part's killing him. He's having a full blown so-you-rescued-the-princess-now-what crisis. But he knows at least two things. He has to get sober, right after taking a hit from the eJoint that Deidre's passing around, and he has to protect Lysandra. He ducks like a coward, however, when he runs straight into Geoff, his ex-bodyguard turned Church hitman, holding a very large gun. Standing beside Geoff is a short, half-bald man in a white suit, open satin shirt bursting with chest hair, brandishing a Colt RG.

Andron says, "Hi, Geoff," but the short man answers for him, with a Russian accent.

"Ve vil be taking girrrl." The man gestures toward Lysandra with the RG.

Andron has his hands up. Thinks back to when his other ex-bodyguard confronted him in the hospital and shot him in the gut. Reverts to the present when Deidre walks up between them and says, "Wouldn't you guys rather have some pot instead?" offering her eJoint to the man in the white suit, then accidently dropping it. Geoff and white suit guy watch the device shatter on the pavement. In a flash of hand moves, she grabs the RG, spins it around and as she is bringing it up at the Russian, Geoff grimaces and aims. There are two wet *kerthunk* sounds and both men drop, bleeding from holes in their heads.

"Ack! these heels. Oh, honey, can you do me a favor?"

They all spin to look at the lady, about six feet tall. A lady, whose inner identity overpowered whatever her outside or anyone else had in mind for her. She's wearing a forties-style gray skirt and trench coat, ruby red lipstick. Long dark hair. She has a large electronic device in one hand and a gun in the other. She's limping left and trying to grab her heel.

"You . . . cowboy."

Dylan points at himself. "Who me?"

"Yes, you, sugar, can you do me a favor and check on that one in white for me? I think he's still twitching."

Dylan, turns around and nudges the man with his cowboy boot.

"Nah, he's dead."

"Great, Allah be praised," she says as she steps out of the shadows. "It's not safe here, we have to go."

Deidre runs up to her and says, "Jasmin!" giving her a big hug.

"You okay?" Jasmin asks.

Deidre answers, "Uh-huh," and hugs her tightly again. Jasmin utters something in Arabic as an electronic falcon flutters back to her arm. There's an explosion in the distance. "Drones," she explains, "it's how they've been tracking you." She puts Festus and its controller in a case. "We have to skedaddle before they send another."

"So, you and Deidre are working together?" Andron asks.

"Yup, we're your guardian angels. The name's Jasmin," she says, with her collagen lips and bright red lipstick smile.

Andron and Lysandra look at each other and then walk up, while Dylan stays behind with his jaw dropped, arms crossed, staring.

"You got a problem, cowboy?" Jasmin asks, turning around.

Dylan adjusts his hat and says, "Sorry, but this goes against my ways."

The four of them stare at Dylan, while Jasmin frowns. Dylan adjusts his hat and stares back.

"It goes against my ways to see a lady carrying all that stuff and not helping."

Dylan runs up and grabs the bag where she's put Festus and slings it over his shoulder. Jasmin thanks him with a nod, half-opened eyes and runs her fingers through her hair.

"So, where we going?" Andron asks after they start walking.

"Oh, you should be happy, darling," Jasmin turns to say.

"Why's that?" Andron asks.

"Because, we're off to meet your sugar daddy."

CHAPTER 9:
THE KNIFE, THE MONK & THE WHEEL

Thomas bursts into Wolfgang's office in the Bastille, pompadour first.

"So, I read the . . . report," he says, waving *The Way Forward* around with his fat fingers. He's in full-body neoprene, once again. Wolfgang leans back on his elbows and folds his fingers together.

"I like it," Thomas says, sitting down. "So, we use cadets as surrogate moms, toss the baby Yeshuas in a nursery and then run with the best one?"

"That way we avoid all the problems that we had the last time," Wolfgang says with a smug grin. "Plus, Cygnus is unlikely to try any . . . [*Was ist das Wort für Unfug?*] . . . *shenanigans*, since he won't risk putting his brain into Kinder that might be selected for extermination."

"Selected for extermination . . . you mean abort them after they're born?"

"Ja," Wolfgang says, blushing and shifting in his chair. "That's the plan."

"And you don't think there may be some legal problems with doing that? You know, minor regulatory hiccups like, hmm, let me think . . . *murder one?*"

"But, sir . . . I . . . since we own . . . I thought . . ."

"You *thought?*"

Wolfgang doesn't answer, just squirms in his chair and lowers his head.

"Tell you what," Thomas booms, before laughing. "Let's get Tucker on it. He's good with that sort of thing."

Wolfgang exhales and looks up, making a note to call Tucker.

Thomas flips through the report. "And then there's the construction of something you've called the *Sizzle Project*, what's that about?" Thomas's eyebrows furrow.

"That is the name I've given to the wormhole project that will allow us to converse with the Sophia."

"Who's Sophia?"

"Think of her as the Holy Spirit, with a feminine twist. Universal knowledge."

"She sounds grand, Dolfo, but the cost of this Sizzle thing is ridiculous. The power supply alone is going to bankrupt us."

"But sir, think about the prestige and fame it will bring, not to mention untold riches in the form of knowledge."

"Tell you what. Put something together and you can present it to the board."

Wolfgang breaks into a half-smile and clenches his fist.

"And Dolfo?"

"Yes, sir?"

"I'm sorry about the other day. I'm not sure what got into me. When you talk to Tucker, why don't you get him to do up those papers?"

Thomas stands up, walks over and moose-knuckles one of Wolfgang's ladybug shoulders.

"Now, let's see what Cygnus has come up with."

"So, the knife, the monk and the wheel."

"Got it, knife-monk-wheel. I still don't get why," Thomas says.

"For the game to work," Cygnus sighs, while running his hands through his sideburns, then adjusting his top hat. "Look, we've been over this, mate. You really have to gawk at these objects for the ... for the game to meld, all right?"

"But aren't these just characters in stories and I'm just riding along? Like using their eyeballs instead of my own?"

"Not by half."

"Then what are they"

"Think of them as a set of characters with backstories. Give the same backstories to ten different writers and you'll have ten different stories. Look, you're an educated man, a minister. What you bring to this will be radically different than from a chimney sweep."

"A chimney sweep?"

"You get what I'm saying. You're not just piggybacking. The game's way more advanced than that. Your subconscious will flux what these characters say or do and what happens. But you have to let them in first."

"With the knife-monk-wheel thing."

"*Finally,*" Cygnus says, looking at Thomas, taking off his sunglasses and slowly shaking his head.

"Are you okay, Cygnus?"

"It's just . . . you gotta cut me some slack, mate."

"What do you mean by that?"

"By letting me out, for starters."

"Like we told you before, you've got to deliver on our three wishes first." Thomas lists them on his gloved hand. "We need a virtual reality game that sells, a baby Yeshua to add to our portfolio and you have to show us how to turn ourselves into a computer program, so we can have eternal life. Come through on these deliverables and then we'll talk."

Cygnus's sideburns slump. "Righto, guv'nor, a cracking video game, baby Yeshua and eternal life. Until I serve up those fish 'n' chips, I'm arse over tit, hardly seems fair."

"Listen, that tip about Andron really paid off. We think he's leading us right to her. Tell you what. Once we capture her, we'll bring her here and impale her on the Spear of Destiny right in front of you, if that'll make you happy."

Cygnus's sideburns lift with a grin. "It does help a little, guv, to be honest."

"So, I look for a knife, monk and a wheel to stare at in these simulations and that helps me turn into these characters?"

"In a way. Have you ever woken from a dream not knowing who you are and then everything suddenly pours back in, memories, identity and the rest?"

"Yeah?"

"Well, the game tries to force that same sort of reboot, but instead of rebooting your brain with your old self, it tries to boot it up with a new one. Like ancient computers used to do when they were restarted with a different floppy disk shoved in their OS bay. Temporarily, of course, with no lasting damage."

Thomas ponders that with a worried look while cadets finish locking his diver's helmet into place, and he reflexively bites down hard on his mouthpiece.

"Remember, knife, monk, wheel," Cygnus says again, spinning a turntable before Thomas can answer.

Zap

He looks down at the small dagger in his outstretched hands.

"Do you swear?"

He looks up at the man, confused. What language did he just speak?

"Simon?" the man says to him in a gravelly voice and then a whisper, "*Simon . . . bar . . . Thomas?*"

The words. What? He looks down at the knife again. The scimitar blade. The leather handle. "You're Simon bar Thomas," a voice in his head says. He stares at its gray steel. Stares at it without blinking.

I'm Simon bar Thomas, he thinks. Simon bar Thomas. Yes. And the man who is talking to me is Menahem bar Yehuda.

And the other men around the campfire are fellow assassins, including his friend Judas, who is smiling and mouthing an oath of allegiance along with him. Simon speaks the same vow. To the sicarii, the dagger that he's holding, allegiance to death. He looks down and squeezes its handle.

"I'm an assassin from Galilee," he says while the others laugh at him.

He feels kinship from their ragged, fire-lit faces. Kinship against the occupation, the Temple priests and aristocrats. The daggers are for throat-slitting and he's a throat-slitter.

"Do you promise to purge the Temple of its scum and free Judea of its infidels?"

"I do."

He follows the embers of the campfire crackling into the night, disappearing into a canopy of stars. He knows that they're camped near Jerusalem. The floating embers bring back other memories. Of the fire. Of his family on their knees wailing while his father's fields burned. Of having to hold his father from running into the flames. All he needed was a simple loan to buy seed to be able to put in a crop that year, because of the Temple tithe and Roman taxes on everything. The Tiberian moneylenders were only too willing to help. They smiled and licked their lips when his father walked up. A peasant farmer with only his land for collateral. Then there was a mysterious fire and now his family are serfs to city folks who wash their feet in myrrh and wipe their asses with silk.

He clutches the dagger. He imagines slitting the throats of the moneylenders who stole his father's land.

"Simon . . . *Simon* . . . are you paying attention?"

"Sorry."

"I was saying that we need you and Judas to go into the city with the Passover crowds. To make an offering at the Temple and see what you can learn about the Nazarene."

"You mean, the one that casts out demons and cures the afflicted seeking no wages?"

"Yes, he and his followers paraded into town yesterday, right under the nose of Caiaphas."

"Do they want to start a riot?"

"We don't know. That's what we want you and Judas to find out. See if you can get near him."

"With God's help."

"And be careful, the Roman garrison knows about us. If you get caught, you might as well slit your own throat . . . *slit your own throat . . . slit your own throat . . .*"

He can't understand why Menahem, and everything else, is repeating.

Zap

"Que pensez-vous, Stephan?"

"Huh?"

"À propos de ce que Peter dit?"

"Um . . ." Thomas looks back and says sheepishly, "*Très bien?*"

The man shakes his head and smiles, then turns back to listening to the monk. Thomas does, too, even though he doesn't understand him. He watches his lips move. Stares at his gapped teeth. The monk drones away in French.

Drones.

Thomas tunes in and out of the voice. To Peter Bartholomew. That's his name, Thomas thinks. The man's name is Peter Bartholomew. And the man that just spoke to him is Raymond of Toulousse. Peter's talking about his visions; he can understand him now. He sees they're sitting around a large wooden table. Raymond has a red cross on his tunic, so does this Stephan guy. That's Bishop of Le Puy, sitting at the head of the table, scowling. Unlike Raymond, who keeps looking over at him, at Stephan, to share his rapture at the monk's description of his visions.

Something is wrong. The boot-up isn't taking. He thinks about asking for tech support or red-buttoning.

It's so real, though.

Stephan's memories flash past, a hi-res data dump of a backstory with smell, taste, sound and touch.

Of Pope Urban II at the Council of Clermont speaking of the atrocities inflicted on the pilgrims to the Holy Lands at the hands of the infidels, whose Caliphate wrapped around Jerusalem and the Holy Lands like an ink stain.

Of feeling called to aid of their brother Christians of the East, by Emperor Alexios, because Byzantium was constantly under attack by the Turks.

Of the pope telling them that there would be a new pilgrim, whose sins would be remitted for their service. An armed pilgrim to wrest the Holy Lands from the infidels for the glory of God.

Of looking around at and feeling the same fevered response, *Deus vult*, that thundered through the halls.

God wills it.

The flashbacks shimmer and flare.

Of their struggles over the last three years. To succeed in capturing Antioch, only to become besieged within it, surrounded by Emir Kerbogha's vast army.

Of hearing that Alexios's relieving army from Constantinople turned away when they encountered fleeing Crusaders who told them that the city was already lost.

Of four princes, Raymond among them, trying to unite them, but motivated as much by their own conquests and ambitions.

And Stephan's feelings, too.

Wanting the plenary indulgence of his sins, absolution. Being ready to die in the cause of the armed pilgrim, so he would be taken up straight to heaven. At the same time, lusting for rape, plunder and to put others to the sword.

And secrets.

Stephan's vision under the grand dome of the Hagia Sophia. A vision of the Holy City in flames, screams of terror and a young maiden looking back at him with panic in her blue-brown eyes.

And not even the risen Christ being able to stop him.

He also knows what Stephan knows. That the Franks need something to inspire them because they're in danger of being overrun and slaughtered, without ever having reached Jerusalem. The siege has driven them to eat horsemeat and drink horse blood. He knows that Peter was a disreputable man, but his claims that he had been shown the hiding place of a talisman that will bring certain victory are irresistible. A meteor crashed into Kerbogha's camp last night and has added to the feeling of providence in the room.

"Stephan, what dost thou thinkest?" Raymond asks again.

He looks at the faces surrounding him and says with parched lips, "Um . . . *Dues vult?*"

That settles it. He follows the others to St. Peter's Cathedral where they start digging. After they come up empty, Peter responds by stripping off his robe and jumping into the pit himself to look for the spearhead St. Andrew promised would be there.

And somehow finds it.

The spear that Longinus used to pierce Christ's side at Calvary. The Holy Lance. They're open-mouthed at the sight of the half-naked monk, raising the holy spear above his head, with his triumphant smile, gapped teeth and soiled hands.

They cheer *Dues vult* as Peter Bartholomew thrusts the rusted spear in the air, burning with faith and devotion.

Zap

Thomas is standing behind a fighter jet, watching its turbines whistle down. Wheels within wheels, spinning.

Spinning around and around.

Within the turbine, there's a white streak, twirling to the center. Twirling.

Around and around.

"Uzi?"

"Uzi?" Tal is pulling at his sleeve. "You can't watch her all day; the crew will look after her. Come on, we have debrief."

He turns with his helmet in his arm and follows his squadron mate, ashamed that he was caught distracted.

He does not dare mention his momentary disorientation in the debrief room, where there are supposed to be no secrets. Where every mistake, even the Commander's, is dissected in a ruthless allegiance to the three principles of the Israeli Air Force: complete the mission, do your utmost at all times and *En brera*, which means, no alternative. He knows that Operation Moked, "Focus," has no alternative. No plan B. It's to be a daring morning raid of every airbase in Egypt at exactly the same time, using the same four-plane formation attack pattern. Succeed and *mazel tov*, most of Nasser's air force will be in flames. Fail and . . . there was no fail option.

En brera.

He remembers the Voice of Thunder broadcasts from Cairo. "Where will you run to, Zionists?" it taunted in Hebrew. Where, indeed? They were a tiny nation of 2.7 million, surrounded by 122 million hostile Arabs. Led by Nasser with his vision of a pan-Arabic state, united in its desire to see every last one of them washed into the sea. He was friendly with his Arabic neighbors growing up on Kibbutz Affikim, near the Sea of Galilee. But war is war. He was the pride and joy of the kibbutz. He cannot fail them. He cannot fail his parents, his ancestors.

This is his homeland. The War of Independence rebirthed a thought-to-be-extinct animal—the warrior Jew.

And he is one of them.

He rejoiced when Prime Minister Levi Eshkol finally named Moshe Dyan as defense minister. The hardened general with an eye patch. The waiting and endless drilling will soon be over. Dyan will lead the nation into battle. It could no longer risk waiting for a diplomatic solution. The newspapers talked about the United States being bogged down in Vietnam, and Russia supporting Nasser. There were no arms coming in. He, and everyone else in Israel, sensed enemies sharpening their knives. Every day the news was worse. They were digging trenches at his kibbutz.

Meanwhile, he has everything memorized, his primary and secondary targets. He is the fourth man in his formation. Lieutenant Barak Mayer is his leader. They're heading out of the briefing room, still in flight suits, for afternoon exercises. That suits him just fine. Life separated from his mistress is a dirty spoon's reflection of the real world. The real world is the cockpit of his Mirage IIIC. He's a fighter pilot, flying one of the most sophisticated military machines on the planet. On his off-time, he rides a bicycle. That's all he can afford.

He nods to his ground crew, his Indy 500 pit crew. The average sortie turnaround time for an Egyptian MiG-21 was the better part of a day. They had it down to a bathroom break. This multiplied the size and effectiveness of the IAF, because his plane became four planes if it could fly four sorties in a day. He is them, they are him. A pack and he is the Alpha, for so it must be with men and wolves, he laughs. He climbs the ladder and hops into the cockpit, while the crew chief does some last-minute polishing with a hand towel. He starts the engine and auxiliary power is removed. The turbines whistle up to a battle shriek. He lowers the canopy.

Today, the wolf hunts.

His view is unmatched, up front and up high. A communicative machine. He flies it by his fingertips. Its metal is his skin. His skin is its metal. He flicks switches with reflexive precision. Lights the afterburners while taking off. Within minutes, he's over the Negev Desert on a bombing exercise. Flying in a formation a hundred feet off the ground, five hundred miles per hour. He keys off Lieutenant Mayer, who locates the Initial Point and shoots up at a fifty-degree angle, full afterburners.

He follows. At six thousand, he inverts, locates the runway and then goes into a thirty-five-degree dive. Releases his two five-hundred-kilogram duds at twenty-five hundred feet, peels out at one thousand and banks into a two-hundred-and-seventy-degree turn, to begin one of his three cloverleaf strafing runs. His Mirage has two thirty-millimeter canons instead of air-to-air missiles. Designed to be an up-close and personal street brawler instead of a distant sharpshooter. He was trained to get them in his pipper, flip the "pickle" and squeeze for the death burst.

Flying back to base, he's chastising himself for his second strafing run. He was slightly off angle. He'll be answering for it during debrief. He lands and taxis down the runway. Powers down and the canopy opens. He struggles with his helmet.

When he finally gets it off, the sunlight blinds him.

Then the hiss of airbrakes.

"God damn, Cygnus," he says, with a sweaty red face, as they lift off the diver's helmet and unplug its harness.

"That was . . ." he says breathlessly. "I don't know . . . I don't have any words. Though—"

"Yeah-yeah, I know. I kind of cocked up the transition from first to eleventh century."

"Well, you know, ruthless debriefing and all," Thomas smiles as he unzips the top part of his neoprene suit and steps out of the sphere. "Say, there was something weird about the Crusader bit, like it just didn't take or something."

"Yeah, the monk's a bit of a naffter as a hypno-encryptor boot-up, but the knife's okay and the jet twirler is ace."

"Damn, I'm surprised that I can remember it all so vividly. Yet, when I'm in there, I can hardly remember myself and completely forget the last character. And how did I know how to fly a fighter jet without any training? Or speak Hebrew, for that matter?"

Cygnus looks at him, "Thomas, may I ask you a question?"

"Yeah?"

"Have you ever had your IQ tested?"

"Not that I can remember."

"Well, it must be off the charts, mate, because the way your mind connects to the game is brilliant."

Thomas grins.

"And that isn't just codswallop, mate. Wire in an ordinary wanker into the game and there's all sorts of wetware adaptation problems. A huge aggro. But with good ole Tommy boy's grape plugged in, it all clicks together like a lush poshy's corset."

"So, were these historical events on your planet? Seems similar to ours. Do you think you can add Eden marks to all the bald foreheads? It didn't bother me when I was in it but, thinking back, it's kinda gross."

Thomas is now walking around like an Amway salesman with "Top Producer" pinned to his chest.

"For the rabble version, we can do that. For you, mate, I thought you'd want the full Monty . . . even though, you're still not on the top floor."

"Wait . . . there's another level?"

"Like I've been telling you, mate. A seddi and you'll sink into the London particular soup like a soggy pea."

"Won't that make it more dangerous?"

"Less.

"Right now, your mind's fighting the altered reality boot-up, trying to force your ego to spoil the party. A mild sedative and it'll be chill with your id and the game running the show."

"So, a mind date-rape drug?"

"No, just a mild sedative, something to ease the transition. It's safer, too, because we can dial down the voltage on the zapper."

"I'll think about it. Get the details to Dolfo," he says, leaving the room with sweat stains on his neoprene.

———◆◆◆———

Wolfgang 'Entschuldigungs' by the cadets powering down the Sphere and whirl-walks up to Cygnus.

The two converse in German.

"Any luck on the Sizzle project?" Cygnus asks.

Wolfgang shrugs his shoulders.

"I noticed he didn't include it on his to-do list."

"I did, too."

"It's too bad you weren't in charge," Cygnus sighs. "I mean ... I'm sorry, I mean no disrespect to Tom, but it pains me to see all this potential held back by that unholy sod."

"I don't think you should talk about the Leader that way," Wolfgang says, looking around.

"Relax, I've looped the surveillance. And I'm the one that put him in charge in the first place."

Wolfgang looks back unsmiling.

"Anyway, if he keeps sinking himself into the game like that, you may have no choice but to take over."

"Take over? Why?"

"You know, he could have an accidental psychotic break, loss of self, that sort of thing." Cygnus dips his chin and fixes Wolfgang in his hologram gaze. "*Or worse.*"

"Won't the sedatives you were talking about help?"

"Not really."

"So, why did you mention them?"

"To find out if I can trust you."

"Trust me with what?"

"To see if you have the eggs to be king. Cause I can do my part if you can do yours, if you catch my drift."

Wolfgang tilts his head back and narrows his eyes. "What are you thinking?"

"You sitting on the throne, but getting him those pills for starters."

"You said they wouldn't do anything."

"Those aren't the ones I have in mind."

"So, which ones do you have in mind?"

"A little something-something to turn ole Tommy boy's head into haggis."

"Such as?"

Cygnus smiles.

"I'm thinking LSD-2s."

THE MAGICIAN.

CHAPTER 10:
THE MAGICIAN AND THE
CONFEDERACY

They fly for an hour and land on a private airfield. Then they're taken by stretch SUV from the airfield to a giant glass mansion set in the rocks and pine of a boreal forest. Armed guards dressed in black ghost the perimeter.

Jasmin and Deidre nudge them along.

A tall thin man waits for them inside. At the sight of him, Jasmin and Deidre run up and pepper his cheeks with kisses. The man smiles a fang-tooth grin and wraps them up in his tailored suit. His thick, light blond hair is styled to look like he's always facing the wind. He licks his thin lips at the sight of his guests and walks up to Andron with his hand extended.

"Mr. Andron Varga, I presume?"

Andron shakes his hand tentatively, studying the man's familiar face.

"You don't remember me? Of course, you went by a different name back then. Hmmm ... what was it?" he says, tapping his fingers on his cheek. "Oh, yes ... Jim," he points at Andron, "... remember ... the park?"

Recognition lights up Andron's face. "The kid in the park ... *Oliver!*"

"The one and only," he smiles.

Andron pulls Oliver near, wraps his arm around him and pats his back. Oliver grasps Andron by the shoulders and says, "This man saved my life. I was a punk living on the streets about to be beaten to death, when he risked everything to save me. He told me I didn't belong there and to make something of myself. . . . well?" Oliver smiles, extending his palms out and looking up at his grand foyer.

"Well, we're even now, because you saved ours."

"And you probably saved the whole planet. But enough about our salvation for now. Let me introduce myself to your friends—"

"You must be Dylan Hill . . . I am Oliver Mancer," he says, as the two shake hands.

"Wait, *the* Oliver Mancer . . . the designer?" Lysandra asks, over Dylan's shoulder.

"Ah . . . Lysandra Tucana, the Magdalene," Oliver says as he walks over to bow and kiss her hand. Lysandra reflexively pulls her hand away and looks down, before darting her eyes around the room with quick on-and-off smiles.

"Relax, you are completely safe here and among friends. As they say in Spanish, *mi casa es su casa*," motioning to them with a flourish. "Please allow Winston to show you to your rooms. Rest up and expect to dine around six. We've much to discuss. Oh, and for your own protection, I am afraid your personal data devices won't work here," he says, turning to leave, resting his hands on Jasmin and Deidre's lower backs.

Winston takes Lysandra to her room, while Dylan and Andron follow young ladies in butler suits to theirs. Winston shows her how to use her handprint to program her room. He explains to her how to use the Red-E-Make for food. He waits for her while she walks through her bathroom, looks at the teeth cleaning station and the trays of cosmetics by the makeup mirror. She peeks in the rainforest shower unit, complete with fauna and the marble Japanese Jacuzzi with wood water spouts. She walks into her change closet, spins in the mirrors and picks a random dress off one of the sample racks and smiles after checking its size and holding it up to a mirror. She walks over to her bed and sits, running her hand over the satin quilt and looks up at Winston. Before he closes the door she says, "May I ask you a question, Winston?"

"Yes, miss."

"That shirt you and everyone else around here are wearing . . . the circle with the lines through it . . . what does it mean?"

"It's the symbol of the Confederacy. It's from the signs on Germania's auto-bahn when cars used to be self-driven. It used to mean that there was no speed limit over certain sections of the road, so drivers were free to drive as fast as they wanted."

"The Confederacy?"

"Yes, miss. The *No Limits Confederacy* that Mr. Mancer's partner, Henri Charlevoix, founded."

Lysandra doesn't respond, just stares at the symbol.

"His book's on your nightstand, if you care to read it."

Lysandra picks it up to examine it.

"Will that be all, miss?"

Lysandra nods, thumbing through the book.

As the door closes, she studies the author's picture and bio. There's a black and white photo of a man with unkempt hair, basset hound eyes, a graying thick mustache and a smile that shows some hurt. She shudders when she reads that he was killed in a drone strike five years ago, just like Cookie and Rachel.

Then she reads the first chapter, *(Go)Forward.*

"Within five minutes of putting this book down, it will hit you. Nothing Terra-shattering, just a tiny ping. Your spiritual ping. That ping that you put out into the universe. Your ping ring. A universe that always has the same total energy. The same total energy long before you arrived and the same long after you've gone. So the sum total of your Terrainly existence won't add up to anything. A chemical reaction that will flare, converting one kind of energy into another. But no value added. Except your ping will endure, because it existed long before you and will persist long after. Because it can neither be created nor destroyed. Okay, I will allow that that flare can be pretty friggin awesome, too. That it took the creator of the universe, or the universe of its own infinitesimally small (but doable with endless cracks at the bat) chance collision mutation odds, to come up with that flare. This is the burden of our existence. To be of utmost importance and completely worthless at the same time. A magnificent nothing.

So, what's a magnificent nothing to do?

Man, it's so hard to decide these days.

Bravely face the future with whitened teeth, tummies tucked and painkiller pumps? Find salvation in Facebook likes, Twitter followers and YouTube views? Selfies to impress your friends with the places your smiling face has seen. To prove that you were there, even though you weren't, not actually, because you're always elsewhere. Wired into a place that doesn't exist but is somehow always better than where you are. Text your friend sitting across from you. Swipe right for your future spouse. Swipe right for your future trust-fund kids or wards of the nanny state. Sue the school board for socially challenged safe parking spaces. Buy a starter home with a sub-prime attitude. Improve your internet search visibility. Front page news. Go to a coffee shop, get high and stick your dick in a blowjob bot. Feed the invisible hand. Supply and demand. Marketable widgets. Pies for the rich, crumbs for the rest. Fungible attention spans. Brain space for lease with implants. Located next to the limbic system, home of emotional purchasing decisions. Location, location, location. Not the 'me' generation, the 'selfie' one. So many choices causing crippling indecision. Which restaurant. I don't know, you decide. No, you decide. No, you. This will be the last conversation when the world finally ends, I swear, recorded with a selfie stick. Career choices, clothing choices, domicile choices, fucking choices, marriage choices, food choices, streaming entertainment choices. Casket with a Mozart crescendo note death choices or Jerry Lee Lewis's "Great Balls of Fire" up-in-smoke cremation choices.

Imagine, if Yeshua were with us today as a cheeseburger-eating, jean-wearing teen. What soft drink would he drink? Would he volunteer at the soup kitchen or offer to rake your leaves? Lead the state in passing and immaculate reception scenes? Would he tune out the pressing depressing cripple crowds with music blaring in wireless headphones? Post a selfie of himself wrapping Lucifer up in a head-lock? Would he complain about having his birthday on Christomas? Or would he walk straight up to you, right up to your face and ask, *what the fuck are you doing, man?*

Why are so many rock stars offing themselves these days, anyway? Didn't they have it all?

Into this mess add religion. The panacea for crippling indeci-sion. The COHC Church. The hottest of the firebrand brands. Get on *Robed*. Staged salvation. Sign your property over. Your life away. Complete freedom from choice. If this is you, you canceled the wrong subscription, sucker. Signed up with the wrong afterlife service pro-vider, fucker.

That ping, though. That whisper. That small suffering thing. Weeds always find a way to force themselves up through the cracks, don't they? Be that weed. Breathe. Be the mustard seed. The motto of our *No Limits* Confederacy is the same as the French—liberty, equality and *fraternity*. One of us. One of us. Look for us shuffling down the street, staining under our burdens, with our Buddha smiles and Yeshua grins.

Lord, give us this day our daily pain and never forgive us. Welcome those who roll over us into your open arms. Kingdom come.

Never undone.

Now boarding, passengers in sweats with toy dogs and camel toes. Now boarding, passengers with wicked colds and weird skin conditions to sit on your lap for the duration. Now boarding, rows one-to-infinity, those who have lost all faith in everything, especially in themselves. Chin strap it on, kid. You've been called up. Get in the game and make something happen, without knowing a thing about what you're playing, with cruel ironies and bitter twists of fate lurking in the backfield, waiting to take you down. Wait until they get a load of us misfits taking the field. Just go forward, kid. Forward.

Listen, our deeds are ripples, that can join to become waves, that can become tsunamis, that can bring towers of oppression down. Or crash and burn in infinite space. A tiny flare-up on a tiny rock spinning around an insignificant star. But know this. On all that is holy. Though you may have failed. Though you may have been small.

You were never alone.

Brothers, sisters.

You were never alone."

Lysandra closes the book and studies the cover art. On the front is the no speed limits' symbol. On the back is a tarot Magician, with a wand in his hand pointing skyward and his other hand open to the ground. She puts the book down, walks into the closet to pick out a dress for dinner and looks in the mirror trying to hear something.

There are steaks on the barbeque, wrist-thick filet mignons, the main course in honor of the Western guests.

They bring around crème brûlée for dessert. Andron declines wine and aperitifs. A small step. But he partakes of the fine Cuban eCigars. The dinner conversation is about President Sparzo's latest antics. He has a proposal before the House to add his face to Mount Rushmore. Nobody talks about the Church, though.

It's the fart in the room.

After a round of Vietnamese weasel coffee, Oliver clears his throat to gain everyone's attention.

"You're probably wondering why I've brought you all here, so let's start with some introductions."

"As you know, I'm Oliver Mancer, fashion designer with an eye for rebel talent," he smiles then nods over to Jasmin.

Jasmin responds in a smoldering deep voice, "Jasmin Shirazi ... weapons specialist."

Dylan clears his throat and reddens, "Dylan Hill ... retired rancher."

"Lysandra Tucana," Lysandra says, looking around the room with an ironic grin.

"Stripper."

That makes everyone laugh.

"Andron Varga," Andron says, toasting Lysandra with his coffee, "Convicted felon."

More laughter.

Another round of aperitifs comes around. Andron takes one off the tray this time, slipping into an autopilot, *I'll try again tomorrow*, response.

"Deidre Rook, gypsy fighter," Deidre says while making two skinny fists and narrowing her hazel eyes. "Harrrr."

Toasts to that one.

Then all eyes turn to their mystery guest.

He's been quiet throughout the evening, only whispering a few words to Oliver.

Andron wonders if he might be Oliver's lover. Mid-thirties, medium-to-slight build and medium to short stature. He has tight brown curls, small freckles and pointy features. His blue eyes dart around the room with an intelligent impatience, before taking a puff from some kind of inhaler.

"Mike Desoto . . . software engineer."

There is a long pause before Oliver begins again.

"As with the rest of you, there is much more to who you are than these labels. Mike has been with us a long time. He infiltrated the Church posing as a cadet and barely made it out alive. While he was there, Mike made a rather startling discovery . . . Mike?"

"Well, firstly, these people are really weird. Secondly, they've regenerated a digital space visitor, whom I believe Mr. Varga is familiar with. Thirdly, they intend to make a Yeshua clone from a blood relic, a spear, with Yeshua's blood in it . . . In a nutshell."

Everyone turns to look at Andron. He's sitting so still they can hear the deep vibration of his internal rivets popping.

Oliver puts his hand on Andron's shoulder.

Pop.

The gesture causes a PTSD dam to burst. He blinks some tears away and then excuses himself from the table, face frozen and hands trembling. He locks himself in the bathroom and recovers slightly, though the tremor in his hand remains. If he had to name the tremor, he'd call it Naomi.

"I'm sorry, guys. I don't know if I'm up for this again," he says returning. "It seems I keep causing these terrible things and then make everything worse by trying to fix them. I'm out," he says, avoiding all eye contact.

Lysandra stands up to face him. "If I'm in this, you are, too ... you don't get to quit," she says, wiping away a tear.

"Andron, Lysandra, please." Oliver pleads with his hands. "We have the tapes. We know what happened. How you saved—"

"What tapes?" Andron asks.

"... us all from this psychopath, just like you—"

"What tapes?" Andron asks again.

"The Varga tapes ... It's what started everything. We got them from Naomi Felder's mother."

At the mention of her name, Andron falls into a stunned silence and sits. Oliver sighs and looks at Andron softly.

"I know this is painful, Andron. But we're all in danger and it's important we all understand what we're up against." Oliver clears his throat and continues. "Naomi Felder was a reporter with the *New Lancashire Times*. She was helping Andron. She was on the verge of breaking the story on everything but died in a car accident on the day ... on the day you were born, Lysandra."

Oliver pushes one of the large oval buttons inset in the table beside him. The lights dim and a hologram screen appears in the middle of the table. There's a muffled recording of Andron and Naomi along with photos and footage of them both, including Naomi's mother's house, where the interview took place.

"So, who is Cygnus?"

"Do you want the truth?"

"Always and forever."

"What I'm about to tell you is going to sound insane. But these events happened and I have proof. I think the short explanation is that I managed to download more than a virus from outer space."

"Um, is this a joke?"

"I'm not joking. I wish I was. It came from a program I downloaded that was supposed to use my computer to download space noise from radio telescopes. Each computer was supposed to analyze it."

"Uh-huh."

"Well, it seemed like a great idea to me. Imagine, searching for intelligent life in the universe by trying to pick up the same radio, television and Wi-Fi junk we have been sending out to the universe. If we have, then maybe someone else has. Anyway, that was the thinking behind it."

"Makes sense."

"Well, it seems my computer started a cyber shit-storm because that's how the person behind your MRI, Cygnus, got here. And that's what took down the internet. You may recall they traced the mayhem back to me. Me. And I hardly know how to use a compu—"

Oliver puts up his hand. "This part is garbled because her recorder was low on batteries, but you can hear the next part well."

[Sound of pages turning and coffee cups]

"This is horrifying, Andron. I had no idea our government was still doing stuff like this. Are you prepared to come forward?"

"Naomi, there is a far bigger story here."

"Really?"

"In order to carry out his plans, Cygnus needed to find a lab that could be duped into working with him. Well, I think he found everything he needs and more, with this organization aiming to bring Yeshua back by taking the blood from some religious relic and cloning it."

[Chair scratches, footsteps, coffee pouring into a cup]

"Though I think that instead of Yeshua, they will be bringing back our man Cygnus, who, from what I know of him, will very much revel in his rock star status."

"Christos."

"That's what I said. Though I think it will be more like the anti-Christos with this guy."

Oliver presses pause. All eyes are on Andron. He doesn't notice because he's lost in the maelstrom of Naomi's voice. He would be gone completely, if it wasn't for the revulsion hearing his own voice causes, that keeps him halfway there.

"I had no idea she was wearing a wire," he says.

"And there's this," Oliver says, as he presses the button again. This time it's footage of the huge crowds surrounding Bethlehem Hospital on the day of Lysandra's birth. Then it cuts to a video clip Naomi made of herself, using her cellphone.

"Okay, I just got back from meeting Andron and . . ." She wipes away a tear. "I'm worried. He was a complete jerk . . . but I think it was on purpose. I'm worried he's going to try to get in the hospital and do something stupid. He sounded so weird and fatalistic about everything."

She pauses, bites her knuckle and then looks back at the camera.

"Anyway . . . the story. Financial records from a trial the COHC was involved show that this Cygnus fellow was helping funnel money to the COHC through Earthen Swan Genetics and Earthen Swan Entertainment. *Earth*, as in the planet Andron says Cygnus is from. *Cygnus*, as in the swan constellation.

"Andron confirmed this all when we met and even pointed out that Dr. Christian van de Whey, who is on the Board of Directors for all these companies, is an alter ego for Cygnus. It's all in my files, that I'm bringing to the birth. I hope nothing—"

[the tape cuts off.]

Then the hologram cuts to footage of Juliette and Joe going into the hospital and Juliette's iconic wave to the crowd. Footage of the aftermath of the car bomb. Then to Naomi's news report from that day, in front of the hospital.

"That's what we're hearing. The child is rumored to be a girl. As you can see, this is a big bombshell in a day of explosions."

[She turns to the large crowd pressing up against the barricades. The camera pans with her.]

"And so nobody's sure whether this means that Yeshua was a girl or if they cloned the wrong person. Either way, the Church of the Holy Cloth is bound to get an undressing. Naomi Felder. Action Eight news."

The final footage is from the shooting in front of the hospital, the screams, shootout and stampede. Then Andron being taken into the hospital on a gurney. Then highlights from his trial for domestic terrorism.

After Oliver hits pause again, Andron is drinking four fingers a shot and Lysandra is crying, with Deidre and Jasmin trying to console her.

"I'm sorry. I recognize that these are painful memories for you both," Oliver says. "But I don't think we have the luxury of time. Mike?"

Mike stands this time and paces.

"Since infiltrating the Church, I've known about its plan to resurrect an alien digital intelligence to help it take over the world. To put out more brainwashing video alternate reality video games. And to clone Yeshua, to make him into some kind of Church corporate shill."

"How did they bring him back?" Andron asks.

"They bought your old house, squeezed the government to cough up your old computer and hired an actor to say your magic words. And then bottled the genie at their data center, the Bastille, near Las Pecado, where I was working."

"Magic words?"

"You said something that night that caused your computer to malfunction. It took them a long time to crack the code, because you didn't say anything about it during any of your interrogations. So they used Quadra Code technology that they hacked from the digital corpse Cygnus left behind. They made a prediction modeler with it and reconstructed them."

"What words?"

"I wasn't privy to that. But, like I was saying, they bought your old house in Kanada, hired an actor to play you and used a voice modulator to duplicate your voice so they could replicate the exact conditions for the creation of this Cygnus virus."

"Did they succeed?"

"Yes, they have him locked up at the Church's data center, the Bastille."

"Yeshua Christos, not again?" Andron says with a trembling hand.

"Yes, I'm afraid so. I was there when he started talking. Right before they had any cadet who was working on the project eliminated, including . . . including," Mike's voice catches slightly. "My best friend."

"What did he say?"

"What did who say?"

"Cygnus."

"Um," Mike looks over at Lysandra and lowers his voice. "He said, 'kill the bitch.'"

Lysandra pushes Deidre and Jasmin aside. "When was this?"

Oliver answers, "This was after your trial," he stops himself and then restarts. "Look, we all know about your trial and the drone strike that killed your friends. We thought it was a mistake because they wanted to capture you alive for their twisted ends. Now, we're not so sure." He looks over at Mike.

"There was something about Lysandra's birth that screwed things up for Cygnus. She may be affecting him now, somehow, so that's why we think he wants her, um, eliminated," he says while sipping from his espresso cup.

"Not if I eliminate him first," Lysandra says, red-faced.

"I'm with you," says Andron. "But, what I don't understand, Oliver, is why you want to help us. I understand wanting to help me out a little, but this goes way beyond that."

"I have my reasons."

Everyone stares back at him.

"Okay, I lost friends to drone strikes, too. My business . . . my love, Henri, was in the Ambassador when it got hit. They said it didn't have anything to do with it being a gay club or his *No Limits* book. They said there were domestic terrorists among them. Everyone associated with it escaped prosecution because of the *Domestic Terrorist Act* and presidential pardons. Everyone . . ." His voice cracks. "Including the Church, who owned several private bailiff companies authorized to fly drones, including the one who did it."

He stands up.

"To quote Henri, 'one of the greatest tools our oppressors use to enslave us is the myth of a prison.' We think the Bastille is vulnerable to attack from a small band of revolutionaries, such as ourselves. Thanks to Jasmin's drone-destroying falcon and her expertise in weapons. Deidre, don't let her size fool you, is a combat expert. And Mike . . . knows the place inside and out. Winston adds some extra muscle and I have, how shall I put this . . . capital and connections."

Then he presses the button to the hologram to show their attack plans. The checkpoints, guard stations, machine-gun nest and where to place the explosives. Neutralize drone support, crash the checkpoints, take out the guards, take over the building, set the charges, evacuate the workers and blow everything up. Any questions?"

"Yeah," says Dylan. "I've never been part of a plan that went according to plan. This is more likely to end up as a suicide mission."

Mike answers, "We're already on a suicide mission. Each of us are probably on an outlaw kill list. If we do nothing, we'll probably be killed. If we do something, we'll probably be killed. So, it's a choice about, if I can put it this way, Mr. Hill . . . whether we want to die with our boots on."

They breathe easier after Oliver gives them a tour of the training facilities in a converted airplane hangar and they see that it has a mockup of the perimeter of the Bastille complete with guard stations. There's a fully equipped gym. Dylan is expressionless throughout the tour but lights up when Oliver flicks the switch to the weapons room.

"So, what do you think?" Oliver asks him.

Dylan runs his hands over the array of weapons, nodding his head here and there and then whistles with a smile.

After the tour, they retire to one of Oliver's receiving rooms to eSmoke and socialize. Andron switches to his old rum and coke standard. With Dylan wrapped up in a conversation with Jasmin, and Lysandra with Mike, he walks over to where Deidre and Oliver are standing.

"Last time I saw you was in the park we called the Garden of Eden. Looks like you made it out okay. But how did you get from there to here?" Andron sweeps his hand and looks around the room.

"I went to art school. That's where I met Henri. He convinced me to start a cosmetics line and I went from there into fashion. I guess he saw my potential."

"Or absence of limits," Andron smiles. "Do you know anything about what happened to Rye-Chus J? He was there that day, too. He was the one who actually saved me from Beercan."

"Wait . . . the gay-bashing ogre's name was Beercan?" Deidre laughs.

"Hey . . . we all had 'em." Andron smiles. "Mine was Jim the Chisel."

"Jim the Chisel? What about you, Oli?"

"Rent Boy . . . I looked for him."

"And?"

"Sorry, Andron. I tried to find him after he got out. By the time I did, he was already dead from an overdose."

Andron doesn't say anything, just drinks his rum and coke. Deidre looks at them both after a while and says, "Oh, come on, Rent Boy and Jim the Chisel, I have just the thing for this."

They walk past the other couples, who have moved in closer together and go into the kitchen, where they share an eJoint and shots.

Later on, Andron has taken off his tie and has it wrapped around his head like a bandana. He insisted on his nineties music and is jumping around playing air guitar. He falls over and then jumps up, shouting, "Enter the Shaman," while Deidre laughs hysterically, dancing with him. He plops down beside Jasmin and Dylan. "I know you're a weapons specialist and all, but if shit's goin' down, Dylan's our man," he wraps his arm around him. ". . . Right, bud?"

"Sure, Andy."

"Oliverrrr!" Andron bolts up and runs to him when he enters the room, knocking over a few glasses, then resuming the air guitar routine.

"They have shitty music in prison," Andron says finally, plopping down on a chair, folding his arms and going quiet.

They wake him up later and Winston and Dylan drag him to his room. He throws up before going to sleep with half his clothes on. He dreams of Astrid again. They're in the same desert. She turns to him, this time without a bleeding face, and says, "Andron, God spoke to me."

Andron turns to look at her.

Astrid is now Naomi.

"He said to find a hole and to see it through."

"Find a hole and see it through, got it," a young Andron answers.

He's in a car with Naomi and an infant Lysandra in the back in a car seat. He turns back to look at her when Naomi shouts, "Look out!"

He wakes up with a gasp when the car collides and he's swimming in shattered glass. His heart's racing, his head is pounding and his stomach feels like he's swallowed a box full of poisoned worms. He tries to go back to sleep, but he knows it's useless so he gets up to relieve himself. He returns and picks up *No Limits* from his nightstand. Thumbing through it, he finds a chapter on wormholes, but only manages to read a few lines.

"Piercing a hole through folding space, with the heart of darkness at its core, the kugelblitz returns us home again, dead and infinite."

He feels pulled into the words hypnotically, then falls into a dreamless sleep, like a rabbit climbing back into a magician's hat.

CHAPTER 11:
THE GATE OF THE ESSENES

Thomas marches to the Sphere Room with Wolfgang whirl-walking behind him, as fast as his robotics will allow.

"Sir . . . your pill."

Thomas stops to take the pill from Wolfgang and pops it into his mouth without looking. He chases it with a small paper cup of water that Wolfgang hands him. He crumples the cup, tosses it, then marches on. A hologram Cygnus waits while Thomas is wired in. This time Cygnus is wearing a puffy-armed purple shirt with a necktie scarf and white sunglasses. He has one hand on his big earphone and the other on a toggle switch to his turntables.

"So, with the pill I won't have to go through the knife-monk-wheel thing?"

"Nope, just throughputs you won't even have to think about. Like walking through a gate, over a bridge or out a tunnel."

"And what are these?"

"The doorways to your mind, guv."

The words strangely reverberate and Thomas adjusts his jaw. His head feels like a big marshmallow. A fluffy cloud.

Cadets quick-connect harnesses and lower the heavy diver's helmet onto his shoulders. Locking him into place. Thomas shakes his head and then concentrates on slowing his breathing. He puts in his mouthpiece and bites down.

He looks at Cygnus, who's waving like frog.

He says, "See you on the other side, guv." Only the words come to Thomas not so much as sounds, but as melted paint.

Zap

There are two plunks, a buzz, then a flash.

Plunk...plunk...buzzzzzz...flash

Plunk...plunk...buzzzzzz...flash

Then his eyeballs, nose, ears and skin are in the game.

In the first seconds, Thomas feels the sweat of his brow under his turban, the oil in his beard, his genitals brushing against his loincloth, the flax in the linen of his tunic, the scratchy wool of his cloak and the slight heft of his dagger. Smells the leather of his girdle. Sees the road to Jerusalem boiling over with pilgrims excited about the Passover festival. Feels the cobblestone bumps through his camel-hide sandals. Breathes the morning air mixed with dust that the carts stir up. Feels the sun on his face. And his legs are strong. That he's taller than he is—as though he's bigger than road upon which he treads or the archway through which he's about to pass into Jerusalem.

The Gate of the Essenes.

The Gate.

His chest constricts.

He stops, feeling suddenly small.

Judas, who is already on the other side, stops and turns. "What's the matter, Simon?"

There's a feeling of dread and he's frozen.

"*Simon, come to me,*" the sky seems to beckon. So he looks up and cowers through the archway where the sun blinds his eyes. Then he's suddenly better. Flash memories assure him that he hesitated because he thought about becoming an Essene once. And still feels called. He was drawn to their purity of spirit, to their devotion. They lived as equals with no possessions, keeping themselves ritualistically pure, denouncing anger and spreading peace. The Nazarene is rumored to be one of them, as was his cousin, John. Yes, he was torn because he was passing through as an assassin and in the company of a thief. He turns to look at Judas who is more than a handbreadth taller than he, handsome but with a crooked smile.

The roadway becomes a street full of pilgrims and asses hauling wares. Up the street of the cheesemongers that will take them to the Temple, they pass under sun-faded canopies and over cobbled lanes. Shopkeepers smile invitingly at them. They stop for flat loaves of barley bread and fried locusts that they eat on the side of the street, watching the crowds go by. He looks up at the Temple rising like a gold-capped mountain of hewn stone before him. At its colossal walls, pillars of white marble, cedar roofs and gold trim.

Siloam Pool is next, a gathering place for those on their way to the Temple. There's a line of Temple pilgrims outside the pool, wanting to purify themselves. He hears splashing water, shouting and the laughter of children. They think that someone is bound to have heard of the Nazarene there but have no luck finding him. So they spend their time dangling their feet in the cold waters and drinking logs of warm beer. They wash themselves in the preparatory pool and then dunk themselves repeatedly in the Mikveh. He hears strange music underwater but feels purified and clean after, having been anointed with oil scented with cinnamon.

He so wants to be pure.

The crowd congeals as the Temple nears. Sounds blend into a chant-drum-cymbal. A bell-horn-lyre. A wall of pulsating sound. Pressing crowds. The Temple is a stadium. The center of the world. Thousands climb the grand stairs to the Royal Portico entrance. The pungent smell of the crowd slices through his cinnamon anointment. His ears pick up when he overhears a pilgrim near him, sounding like a Galilean.

"Peace be with you, brother," he says to the man, while climbing.

"And also with you."

"Tell me, brother, I seek a man they call Jesus the Nazarene. Have you heard of him?"

The pilgrim looks from him to Judas and back, and replies, "I've heard his sermons several times, in Galilee and in the Temple."

"What are his sermons like?" he asks with fervent eyes.

"He speaks of the kingdom of God often."

"What does he say about it?"

"That it's like a mustard seed that a man plants in his garden."

"Did you just say, 'a mustard seed that a man plants in his garden?'"

"I did."

"But that doesn't make any sense. The kingdom of God is a nasty weed?" He reacts, not just from his memories of his family's farm, but from a strange feeling that he's debated this before.

"That's what he said."

"Surely, no one would plant mustard in their garden, unless they wanted to ruin it. It would become impure. To reach the kingdom, you have to make yourself impure?"

"I think he meant it more like something that starts small and grows large. Or it starts out as a tiny seed and once it takes hold, can never be gotten rid of."

"That's what mustard weeds are like, all right. But I still don't understand why they're like God's kingdom. The kingdom of God should not be ugly or impure."

The pilgrim turns to him. "I heard him say, 'Love your enemies and pray for those who persecute you. If you love those who love you, what reward will you get? Are not even the tax collectors doing that? And if you greet only your own people, what are you doing more than others? Do not even pagans do that?'"

He stares back at the pilgrim, scratching his hair through his turban. As he reaches the Royal Porticos, the crowds pull him and the pilgrim apart. The pilgrim calls out to him, "*See what I mean? . . . a mustard seed . . . look for him at Solomon's porch.*"

He's dumbfounded about what he's just heard. Judas is talking to him, but he only half hears him. Defile a garden with mustard seed? Love thy enemies? Mustard plants should be plucked out wherever they are found, and you should love crushing your enemies. The Nazarene must not be an Essene or a Zealot. An Essene would not speak of defilement any more than a Zealot would approve of pacifism. How could such a swindler advance their revolutionary plans? A man that rebels against instinct and his people's oppressors in favor of an ugly weed? Not only his instincts, but a complete repudiation of his entire purpose in life?

He spits as though he has mustard seeds in his mouth.

"What's wrong?" Judas asks him.

"I don't know."

"You look like something flew into your mouth."

"It's just that I don't know why we should seek out this man, Jesus. He sounds like an imbecile."

"Maybe, but we have our orders. Let's see what we can see," Judas says, with a wide grin, staring at women pilgrims and licking his lips.

They change a few Roman coins into Tyrian shekels so that they can buy pigeons to sacrifice and look for Jesus. Judas haggles with both the moneychangers and the pigeon merchants, who he says are even bigger thieves than he. They walk through the Beautiful Gate, with its sculpted relief of the city of Susa, and into the Court of the Woman. He looks up at the limestone sign, written in Greek: "No foreigner is to go beyond the balustrade and the plaza of the temple zone. Whoever is caught doing so will have himself to blame for his death which will follow."

There are Levites on the other end of the square, singing on the steps to Nicanor's Gate, leading into the Hall of the Israelites. The Hall of the Israelites is as far as he can go, for beyond that lies the Court of the Priests, where the sacrificial animals' necks are cut, blood drained and chopped into pieces for the altar. Beyond that, lies the Holy Place and, within that, the Holy of the Holies. The inner veiled sanctum where no man may enter, save for the High Priest once a year on the Day of Atonement.

They find the Trumpet for burnt offerings, throw their coins into it and hand their crates to a barefooted and bearded priest adorned in a blue cloak, with a jeweled breastplate and a tall white Miter on his head. The priest takes the birds out of the crates and inspects them disapprovingly. At last he nods and the birds are whisked away. He grunts, "For what do you make this offering?"

"The first is for my father, Thomas," he answers. "The second is for atonement."

He and Judas walk through the courtyard, up the marble steps and through the open gold and brass doors into the Hall of the Israelites. The air smells of blood, roasted meat and frankincense. He hears panicked pigeons and sheep, Levites singing psalms, lyre music, butcher knives and crackling fire. The heat from the fire burns his face and it feels like shame. He tenses and his mouth opens in reverence at the splendor of the Temple walls, which rise high in the inner courtyard leading to the Holy Place. He forgets about finding anyone for the moment and sinks into his people and into the unmistakable presence of the one who is, whose name cannot be spoken.

The priest brings back a few scraps of roasted pigeon meat for them to eat, and they take them back to the Court of the Women, find an open seat on the foot of a pillar, where he and Judas eat the scented meat in quiet contemplation.

"Why aren't you finishing yours?" Judas ask after a few minutes, licking his fingers.

"You can have it. I'm feeling out of sorts," he says, thinking of the Essenes and how they forsake meat and are opposed to animal sacrifice.

"As you wish, brother," Judas says, taking the meat from him and tearing pieces off with jagged teeth.

"We might have better luck if we split up and look for him. I can try Solomon's Porch. We can meet later in the Royal Porticos."

Judas nods, chews and says, "I'll look around here."

At Solomon's Porch, he does not find anyone gathered around to hear sermons. Instead, he sees only regular pilgrims who traveled like he did to make a sacrifice at the altar. He leans over the wall to contemplate the grand aqueducts leading to the city and across the valley to the Mount of Olives with its orchard thickets. He adjusts his turban because his head itches from the oil and sweat in his hair. Strangely, he has the hot tangy taste of mustard on the roof of his mouth and the scent in his nostrils, as though he's freshly eaten paste made from the herb. Where he felt purified by his ritual bath and sacrifice, he now feels like a garden of weeds.

He decides to go back to the Royal Porticos to find Judas and tell him of his decision to abandon the brotherhood and return to his fields or join the Essenes. Revolt and revenge seem foolish to him now. He doesn't belong here. His own sorrowful presence is an affront to the sanctity of the Temple. The internal machinations of the Sanhedrin are of no concern to him, either. He realizes that this brotherhood of assassins will accomplish nothing except replace evil with evil and oppression with harsh reprisals. Murder reaps what murder sows.

Shouting from the Royal Porticos shatters his reverie. He rushes with the crowd to the turmoil. When he comes around the corner, he sees a taller man inches away from a shorter man's reddened face. The smaller man is standing defiantly, in spite of his evident fear.

"You've turned my Father's house into a den of thieves!" The taller man shrieks, kicking the shorter moneychanger's table over, then going after a pigeon merchant with a scourge he's made with a rope.

"Woman, who is this man?" Thomas asks a slight woman in front of him, who turns to look at him with her blue-brown eyes framed by her veil. "He is Jesus, the one they call the Nazarene."

"Do you know him?"

"I am his disciple."

He laughs. "He allows women to be disciples?"

"He would allow that his Father's house has many rooms." She looks into his eyes. "You should follow us."

Jesus is chasing another pigeon merchant now, twirling around his makeshift scourge and hitting the man about his ears. Freed pigeons flutter. Many of those watching laugh and cheer, seeing Jesus go after all the price gougers. Someone in the crowd shouts, "What about the eagles?"

Jesus stops to turn to the crowd, trying to find the man who asked. The crowd backs away in fear. "I tell you solemnly, if my father's Temple should be defiled by Roman standards, I will tear them down!"

Many look down and walk away.

"I changed my mind. I love this man," he says to the woman. "What's your name?"

"I'm Mary of Magdala," she says as she blends with other followers of Jesus melting away at the sight of the Temple Prefect and his guards. "You can find us in the Garden of Gethsemane on the Mount of Olives. We're having a gathering there tomorrow morning if you care to join us."

He watches her pleasing frame hurry away. Thinks she'd make a good wife and thinks about returning home with her. Back to the plow. To the simple life.

To honest work for honest wages. His thoughts are intruded upon by Judas, who has grabbed his arm and is pulling him along.

"*Come on,*" Judas whisper-urges through clenched teeth.

"Judas . . . I found him," he says, pulling back. "Just now, the one overturning the tables and flogging these bandits."

"I know. When the guards rushed out, they left the Trumpets unguarded and I was able to help myself to a few of these," Judas says, opening his purse to reveal a sack full of golden shekels.

He whispers, "*You stole from the tribute?*"

"Yes, but we have to get out of here," Judas says, looking back at a temple guard with alarm.

"Come on, Simon!"

Zap

"Come on, Stephan . . . this is not the time to tarry!"

He's confused. Tries to scratch his hair and then realizes his hair is under a cloth, a chainmail hood and a conical helmet, his Sprangenhelm. Breathing bounces off his faceguard, which makes an iron bar in the middle of his vision. The metal plates over his ears amplifies the wind, and he hardly hears the man urging him on. It's Godfrey of Bouillon, he remembers, mounted and trotting by on his horse, carrying his spear.

He feels the heavy chainmail through his padded garments. He's with the infantry. There are only a few hundred horses remaining for the knights. He and the other men's surcoats bear bloodred crosses on the front. He's carrying a sheathed sword and a dagger. Most of his fellow infantrymen carry battle-axes. He tightens his grip on the shield strapped to his left hand. In his right, he holds a shortened pole in his mail mitten. It has a spear on the end, but it is not intended for battle. It's a symbolic weapon. He isn't a soldier so much as a standard bearer. He's been chosen to carry the Holy Lance into battle.

He runs into position in the middle of his division, led by Godfrey, suddenly and strangely terrified about crossing the bridge over the River Orontes. But he's pushed along by the others as the men charge out, the third of six divisions. The first, consisting of archers, are raining arrows on Kerbogha's men. Bohemond's battle plan called for them to deploy to the left on the other side of the Orontes, to put a river between them and Kerbogha's men massed before St. George's Gate to the south.

He holds the Lance over his head and screams *Dues vult* with every exhausted and starving fiber of his being. The words reverberate inside his helmet but are heard by the knights around him, who hasten their pace and take up the battle cry. This is a desperation charge. Their forces are withering. Another week and they'll all be dead. They have rallied around the Lance and to a man have resolved that God will deliver them or they will die fighting, wearing His holy cross.

He screams *Dues vult* again, prepared to die with the words on his lips. Volleys of arrows rain on a canopy of shields above him like hail drumming a wooden door. A few fly through and plunge into the shoulders of men nearby. But they are able to advance onto an open field without encountering a main attack. Kerbogha seems to be retreating and they pursue him into an opening. Then his forces turn. They are soon surrounded by Turks swinging their crescent swords. Metal clashes with metal as nearby knights battle. He wishes he could fight instead of being a standard bearer. If the need should arise, he's prepared to plunge the ancient weapon into the ribs of an infidel.

It's a pitched battle for a while, in spite of his side being outnumbered. Then his division advances slowly. He holds the Lance above his head and walks with the advancing knights over the fallen. The soldiers around him thrust their swords into any prone Turk still breathing, whether their arms are outstretched or their eyes plead for mercy. The dust of the battle rises through his nose with the sweat of men and horse manure; the screams of pain and battle cries fill his ears. Then he sees many in the Turks' ranks in front of him look behind him with terrified faces. He turns to see what's terrifying them. Blinks because he thinks his eyes have deceived him.

There's a hundred red-crossed ghost knights mounted on white horses charging down the hill to aid the Crusaders. God's ghost knights. He looks back, flinches his jaw, holds the Lance up high and frantically yells, *Dues vult, Dues vult, Dues vult.*

Retreating Turks run into those advancing in what seems like a botched battle plan. They're now running down the valley after Kerbogha's men, who are in a full retreat. Bloodcurdling screams fill his ears as his fellow Crusaders put the erstwhile fierce crescent soldiers to the sword. He drops to his knees with tears of joy, shouts up to the sky, thrusting the Lance up high each time.

Dues vult.

Dues vult.

Dues . . .

Zap

The turbines shriek as the auxiliary power's removed.

All the lights are lit. He nudges her up the ramp and feels a paralyzing jolt of fear but pushes through it. She's laden with bombs, fuel and ammo. Live ammo this time. The five-hundred-kilogram bombs on her wings aren't duds, either. Up from the hangar's depths and taxiing to his spot on the tarmac. The sky is clear. Weather favors the mission.

He pulls up next to Tal. The turbines screech up and down with each nudge forward. There are two radios. Red is for the squadron and green for the controller. Not that it matters. The entire operation is to be undertaken in complete radio silence. There's a knock on his window and he turns to see the note that says, "15:00 Minutes," and he looks at his watch. If he splashes into the Mediterranean and needs to tell someone about it, he'll have to write a note.

En brera.

He glances at the pictures of his parents taped to his console. They told him he was conceived outside Jerusalem, in '45. Before the War of Independence in '48. His mother was a refugee from the death camps in Poland. His father, a sabra, a native Jew. He died in the War of Independence, his mother, of cancer two years ago. The doctors said it was related to her years of starvation and abuse in the camps. The state of Israel is his mother and father now. The lines of partition were drawn the year his father died. On this side, Tel Aviv. On the other, the heart and lungs of his homeland, the old city of Jerusalem. His people haven't been allowed back since. The Western Wall, the wall of the Second Temple, the Temple Mount, is in Jordan's hands. His parents told him that they conceived him with Jerusalem framed in their hotel window. Their passion was Israel. He is their passion. He is Israel. In this hour, Israel must become a weapon.

And the weapon is twitching, ready to strike.

He'd like to think of himself as a fierce warrior, but he has no illusions. He's just a lanky kid. Around women, he sweats and his voice breaks. He's still a virgin. But he has lightning quick reflexes and he scored off the charts in flight school aptitude tests. He was born to fly. And there's one woman whose bra he can undo in a whisper. Who won't refuse him. And that woman is the Mirage he's sitting in now. She's prepared to die for him and he for her.

Barak and David are off, and it's his and Tal's turn. Push it up. A throttle forward with a twist to light the afterburners. Slammed into his seat down the runway. A screaming engine that leaves thunder in its wake. He loses contact with the ground and touches a borderless sky. Banks down the coast with Tal to catch up with David and Barak.

Leaving thunder.

Within minutes, he's pushing his joystick to the right, to take him out of Israel and over the Mediterranean, toward the land of the pharaohs. It's raw. Flying by memorized headings, maps, landmarks and a wristwatch. All calculations made at five hundred miles per hour and a hundred feet off the ground. They're so tight to the ocean that their slipstreams are leaving wakes. Moked is a mission of precision timing. They're going to strike every airfield in Egypt simultaneously at 0745 hours. They've been given a big fat juicy one to hit, just north of Cairo, al Mizraq. Sees it in his head.

Blue ocean turns into sand, and he pushes up on the throttle. They're flying on deck, just above telephone wires. He sees farmers driving tractors out to their fields. They wave at him, no doubt thinking he's Egyptian. He's riveted on the horizon and Barak's wingtip. He's fair game now, should anyone wish to shoot him down. Sees the landmark gas station. Barak tips his wings as a silent signal to arm. He switches his cannons to air-to-ground, flicks a switch on his "pickle" to arm the bombs. Next landmark and then the canals. He sees Barak break almost straight up. Pulls back on his stick and twists the throttle to light his afterburner.

His G-suit inflates, keeping the toothpaste in his head.

Climbing.

Climbing.

Now . . . invert.

Upside down, he sees his target below and the top third of the runway they're supposed to hit. There are a few weightless seconds and then Barak's voice crackles over the airwave, *one in*. No need to keep quiet anymore. *Two in*, that's David. *Three in*, that's Tal. He chimes *four in* and dives, watching his altimeter as the Mirage screams. Fifty-five hundred and Triple-A defenses are firing. Forty-five hundred, he's massaging the button with his thumb. Thirty-five hundred. Twenty-five hundred, and he pushes the button and holds, bombs away.

Pulls out of the dive at a thousand and banks hard right. His girl's screaming and his G-suit fully inflates. Calls *four out* and follows a maximum-G, three-quarter circle to start his strafing run. Sees the bombs going off and cratering the runway. Direct hits. The runway's a moon surface now. Drawing heavily Triple-A in black exploding clouds, but there's no time to worry about that. *Dvekut baMesima*, complete the mission. He pulls the trigger nine hundred meters away and walks the strafing in. He can feel the hot thirty-millimeter rounds. Dust kicks up on the way to a MiG-21. It goes up in flames with the pilot in it.

Mazel tov.

He banks and comes back on target again. By the time he and his crew are finished, twenty-five MiG-21s and five Sukhoi-7 fighter bombers are in flames, not to mention a destroyed runway. At 0800, they pull out to let the second wave come in to pick over the carcasses.

He climbs to altitude on high alert for enemy aircraft. Switches his cannons to air-to-air and is ready to dump his auxiliary fuel, should any MiGs want to play. But there are only his brothers, returning to base for a quick change for the next sortie. There's smoke plumes rising from all the other runways in Egypt. Operation Moked has succeeded. He feels as though he's strafed a new chapter in the Bible with his Mirage. The old-school kind, where the Jews are kicking ass. Coming toward the base, he does a quick victory roll. On the tarmac, his crew runs up to refuel and rearm the plane. He's anxious to run into flight control to get his mission.

All he can think is, *next* as he unbuckles and struggles to take off his helmet. A bright light and the sound of airbrakes releasing fills his head.

Thomas helps lift the helmet off, waits impatiently for the disconnects, before jumping out of the sphere, running through the door and down the hall with his fists in the air shouting, "*Dues-mazel-tov, Dues-mazel-tov, Dues-mazel-tov.*"

"So," Cygnus says to Wolfgang, "looks like *someone* made it to the other side."

"Doesn't look any worse for wear, either," Wolfgang huffs, still hearing Thomas's *Dues-mazel-tov*s.

"Oh, don't worry, Wolfie, that was Woodstock on the good acid."

Wolfgang looks back at him.

"The next one's Woodstock on the brown."

CHAPTER 12:
GMO MAGDALENE

Ancient Mediterranean eyes open at the *whisk* of an envelope sliding under her door. She turns on her back, stretches and yawns. She closes her eyes and then opens them again. She pushes an oval button on her nightstand, and the shades crawl open. Gentle rays from a rising sun waft in. She picks up her intraweb and glances at the note Mike left and groans. It said he was sorry for being such a sulking sad sap because the universe deprived him of her company. She jack-taps, "Michael, the universe does not bend to your will," looks at the text, but swipes it away.

She pads around in her tee, scooping up the envelope and opening it to scan over the day's activities. She pushes buttons on the Red-E-Make for a toasted bagel, butter coffee and max-vital juice. Slips on sweat pants, puts the *No Limits* book under her arm, grabs her breakfast and steps out onto her balcony. There's a mist over the meadow and a deer foraging for hazelnuts in the distance. The deer sniffs the air when her door opens, then springs away. She uses a towel to wipe dew off a patio chair, curls up in it and wraps herself in a shawl. She sips her coffee and chews buttered bagel pieces that she's torn off.

The balcony's in the shadows and it's cool enough that her breath is a vanishing mist. Her eyes are cold open, her nose on the verge of running, but she pulls the wrap up to her neck and smiles. The coffee is steaming and she takes measured sips, exhaling with each one. She finishes her coffee, rests her chin on her knees and hugs her legs. She picks up her intraweb and massages her finger over Mike's button, but puts it down. She picks up *No Limits* instead, opens it to *Mary Magdalene* and grabs the rest of her bagel.

And sees that someone has underlined passages in it. Underlined with a free-hand that's straight as a ruler.

"The Gnostics teach us that Sophia is the spiritual equal to Christos, the female element *who needs to be restored*, just as Mary Magdalene needs to be restored, in our hearts and minds to her rightful place on the throne beside the son of Man."

Lysandra puts the book against her chest, darts her eyes around the balcony as though searching for cameras, then opens it again.

"The one branded a whore is the pristine one, the key to our release. We, the vanquished. We, with our leader murdered. There's no one on the throne. He has risen. Jerusalem has fallen. Sweet Sophia pray for us, now and at the hour of our bloody births, amen."

Lysandra puts the book down and looks out into the forest. The sun has made it to her feet. Her toenail polish comes alive in it, so she wiggles her toes. She plays with her hair, pulling her bangs over her eyes then blowing them back up again. No longer golden blonde, she's back to her natural chestnut. She picks up the book, as if to throw it, but stops mid-throw and puts it back on the table.

She lifts a leg over the railing instead and straddles it, feeling it wobble slightly. She carefully climbs the rest of the way, slowly sliding down the other side until she's standing, knees bent, with just the back of her heels catching the last sliver of cement. Her dancer's bum presses against the skinny metal bars as she hangs by her forearms. She looks down from four stories up, at the concrete pilings, on the death-ward side of things, then settles on the meadow and pines beyond. She leans forward and back, shifting her footing around. A foot slips, but she catches herself, with the metal railing digging into the crooks of her elbows. A breeze picks up.

A door rolling open in the balcony beside hers causes her to look.

"If you're going to go over, you have to take me with you."

"I wasn't actually," she says with her on-again, off-again smile.

"I know," he says. "Still, I'd feel better if you were on the other side of that railing."

Lysandra looks at him, turns, grabs the railing and launches herself back, landing feet together on the balcony with a soft thud.

"How are you, Andron?" she says, recovered and leaning over on the life-ward side of things again.

"I've been better."

"I know."

"Are you coming here or am I coming there?" Andron asks.

"You don't have to . . . I'll come."

Lysandra goes back inside to fix herself up. Punches for a fresh butter coffee that she takes with her to Andron's door.

"Come in," he says with a whiskey voice and a cigarette dangling from his mouth. "I couldn't find a lighter, so I lit it off the stovetop."

"A real cigarette, that's pretty hard core," she says, following him outside.

"I like the adventure, I guess."

"Fire and danger, right?" she says as they sit beside each other on wicker patio chairs with green cushions. "Feu et danger."

Andron nods.

They stare into the woods together, squinting at the sun. She sips her coffee while Andron smokes his cigarette with shaky fingertips.

Minutes pass.

"I don't suppose you're going to tell me what that was about?"

"It wasn't about anything," she says.

Andron raises an eyebrow and looks over at her, but doesn't say anything.

More minutes go by.

"I guess reading that book kind of freaked me out."

"Oh, how so?"

"I don't know. All that Magdalene stuff. It makes me feel like I'm back in the Church with all those old men chanting, thinking I'm someone I'm not."

"Dylan and I are the only old men around here and we're not doing much chanting."

"I know, but there's underlining in the book. Oliver calling me Lysandra Magdalene. People looking at me funny. Honestly, it was easier being a stripper when nobody knew me."

"They don't mean any harm. It's who you are to yourself that matters."

"That's the thing. I don't even know who I am. And I think they think I'm this person in that book. I wasn't even good in school. And I'm sure the hell not pristine."

"Mary Magdalene was good in school?"

Lysandra chuckles. "You know what I mean."

"Most of the people in the Bible would probably say the same thing."

"The same thing about what?"

"They'd say, 'that ain't me.' Legend has a way of remaking people to the point that they'd be unrecognizable to their former selves."

"Maybe, but I'm not legend material . . . I'm just a genetically modified mistake."

Andron takes a few puffs of his cigarette.

"When I went in that hospital room, I brought a gun, you know."

She turns an eye on him.

"I was planning on killing you. Shoot you and your mother, if I had to."

"What stopped you?"

"Orderlies saying you were a girl, mainly."

"Why did that make a difference?"

"'Cause I knew it meant that Cygnus was dead and that you killed him."

She grins.

"But I wouldn't have been able to do it anyhow. Not when I saw your mother. It felt as though she could see everything. Everything I was and everything I was going to be."

"Was she pretty?"

"Hardly the word. She was radiant. And your little face, as determined as can be." He smiles.

"I still don't know the things I'm supposed to know, like in that book."

Andron thinks about that.

"Maybe you weren't meant to be a knower," he says at last, grinding his cigarette and flicking it over the railing, then turning to face her.

"Maybe you were meant to be a doer."

"Maybe," she says, and then adds, "What about you ... you okay?" She glances at his trembling hand.

"Like I said, I've been better, but I'll get through it."

She looks in his eyes and then back at the meadow and says, "I guess we have a training session today."

"Yeah, we better get ready."

She follows him to the door that he opens for her.

"Um, Lysandra?"

"Yeah?"

"Remember ... together."

"I know," she says, standing on her tiptoes to kiss his cheek, before his door closes and she is in the hallway.

And then she sees Mike.

"Hi, Mike," she says, walking down the hall.

"Hi, Lysandra," Mike replies, with the corners of his lips and daisies pointed at the floor.

She stops.

"*Really?* You think Andron and I were getting it on?"

"I never said that."

"You're an open book."

"I can't help it. I'd be jealous if you were seeing your grandmother."

"Well, don't be."

"I'm sorry. Anyway, I went outside and found you these," he says, handing her the daisies.

"They're lovely, thanks," she says, flicking a smile.

"Now they can be jealous of you."

She puts her face down into the daisies to hide a blush, shifts on her feet, turns to walk away, then spins to kiss him—leaving him tongue-tied and haunted by her eyes.

Back in her room, she smells the flowers and smiles, before putting them in a vase.

On her way to her bathroom, she stops, frowns and looks outside. She walks to her balcony, slides the door open to check the table.

Her book is gone.

THE EMPEROR.

CHAPTER 13:
THE BAD EMPEROR

"So what's with all the mustard?"

"Dolfo! . . . come in . . . sit down," Thomas says, opening a pudgy, freckled hand to the chair across from him.

Thomas is in his executive office in the Pecado Hands of Prayer tower in a cocoa-colored leather recliner. He has a silver tray in front of him, with several open mustard jars. He scoops some Dijon with a silver sampler spoon and puts it in his mouth. Pulls the spoon out, smacks his lips and makes a sour face.

"Not quite there."

"What are you looking for, Thomas?"

"Ever since I was in that game, I've had this strong mustard taste in my mouth. Like," he waves his hands in front of his mouth, "all the time. So, I've been trying some samples to see if I can find a match."

"What happens if you do?"

"I think I might find . . ." Thomas trails off.

"You should look up how the Romans made it?"

Thomas's eyes light up. "Mmm . . . great idea, Dolfo."

Thomas taps the Tandy All-in-One on his desk.

"Tandy . . . question."

"Oh . . . I love questions," Tandy says with its speak-and-spell voice.

"How was mustard made in the first century, like, where Yeshua lived?"

"On it," Tandy says.

"There probably wasn't any mustard as we know it, since mustard wasn't invented as a condiment until a few centuries later. Back then, it was likely used as a spice. Probably more to mask the taste of food, than to enhance it. It was also used as a medicine, particularly by the Greeks."

"That doesn't sound right, because why otherwise would I be tasting it all the time? Query early forms of mustard, I mean like these," pointing at his mustard samples.

Tandy's p-screen blinks to acknowledge.

"Early mustard was made by mixing unfermented wine called *must* with ground mustard seeds to make *mustum ardens* or burning must. And that's how we get the word *must-ard*."

"That's got to be it," Thomas says, pointing at Tandy with his spoon.

"Tandy, memo this to Research and Development."

"Memo-ing, sir."

"Priority: URGENT.

"Re: Ancient mustard development."

He looks up at Wolfgang. "At the request of Dr. Eckhart . . . Authentic ancient Roman mustard made from unfermented wine and mustard seed. Have samples ready for my tasting within a week. Copy to Marketing for development under our *Authentic Yeshua* brand. Budget: two million. Allocation: Eckhart research."

"Wait, sir," Wolfgang interjects. "He just said that they didn't have such a condiment—"

Thomas raises his hand to silence Wolfgang and leans into Tandy, again.

"Addendum. Co-develop authentic first century beer by acquiring ownership of Israel's heritage barley and grain varieties for potential sale under our *Authentic Yeshua* brand. Legal team: lock up *Yeshua Mustard* and *Yeshua Beer* worldwide. Increase budget to five million. Allocation: Eckhart. Increase Eckhart's research budget to cover."

"Show draft."

Thomas reads a hologram memo.

"Punch it up, Tandy. Use bigger words."

Thomas reads the memo again, now five pages long.

"Perfect, send it. You're an inspiration, Dolfo," Thomas says, smacking his lips after sampling another spoonful of mustard. "An inspiration."

"Sir, I was actually hoping to talk to you about the Sizzle Project that we're scheduled to discuss at the board meeting. I think that—"

"Oh yeah, read your projections. Big ring on the till if there actually ends up being a market for this stuff. Big ring in the ass if there doesn't. We're on a tight budget around here, Dolfo. Not sure there's a business case for this one," Thomas says, trying another sample and smacking his lips.

"Sir, that's because it's hard to relate the discovery to a product idea quite yet. We don't know the potential uses or benefits of this. But sir, think about it. The ability to communicate to other parts of the universe, or parallel universes, may bring knowledge of immense value. It might be the most important scientific discovery of our . . . of our . . . *Zeit.*"

"See, Dolfo?" Thomas says, tapping his mustard spoon and pointing it at Wolfgang. "That's more like it."

"Push that aspect of it at the meeting. Forget about all the financial bullshit and projections. Tell them about how important this discovery would be for the prestige to the Church and so on, and I'll back you."

Wolfgang breaks into a huge smile, "I'll get working on the presentation right away, sir."

Thomas doesn't look up, just eats more mustard.

"Wolfgang?"

"Yes, sir?"

"Do you think the reason why I have the taste of mustard in my mouth all the time is because the kingdom of God is growing in me?"

"I don't know, sir."

"Very well."

Thomas shoos Wolfgang away.

"Wolfgang . . . wait."

"Yes, sir?"

"Send in-uh a couple of cadets after you, will you please?"

"Male or female, sir?"

"One of each."

<hr />

Wolfgang makes last-minute amendments to his presentation.

He's rehearsed it over and over with his wife, Johanna. "Oh, Wolfie," she said, clapping. "How could they possibly not go along, with all their hearts?"

He frowns as he spots a typo at the eight-minute mark. He had altar instead of alter, as in, "a Schwarzschild kugelblitz can *altar* time." He looks at the time, then downloads the latest amendments into his leather-cuffed Accutron Railroad wristwatch. Clears his throat. Says a silent prayer, crosses himself and heads off to the meeting. He walks into the meeting room, with its burnished mahogany and inlaid pearl table. There are green velvet swivel chairs around it and trays of mustard samples for the guests. He looks around the table of familiar faces in polyester suits and tries not to look like he just sucked on some Mittelscharf when he sees Thomas's son, Conner, occupying Wolfgang's usual chair, to the right of Thomas.

Conner has his boots on the table, laughing at something playing on his personal projection screen. Spiked hair, safety pins in his ear and nose, connected by a chain, wearing a studded black leather jacket. His torn t-shirt has a logo of the band *Anarchist Emperors* on the front. The band's logo is an upside-down king.

"Dolfo!" Thomas says, as Wolfgang sulks into an open chair, at the other end of the table.

"I thought I'd bring Conner in on this one."

Thomas shakes his son's shoulder. Conner scowls as he takes the buds out of his ears and clicks his watch to turn off the display. He looks around, lifts his feet off the table, one boot at a time, nods at Wolfgang and then wipes his nose.

"I thought I would let him observe how we do things, before we get him appointed to the board."

The other board members have mannequin corporate smiles. Wolfgang looks over at the row of half-occupied observer chairs along the wall and then back at Conner.

"Now you were going to tell us about your Klingenstein project or whatever it is." Thomas looks down at his agenda. "Kugelblitz, I mean Kugelblitz-Kugelblitz-Kugelblitz." He nods over to Wolfgang. "Anyway, you-uh have the floor, Dr. Eckhart."

Wolfgang clears his throat, "Well . . . ah . . . the project . . . it's actually called a Sizzle . . . let's start with the presentation."

He presses his watch, but nothing happens. He tries again after checking it. And then again and again, in a series of frantic clicks. Mannequins grin on.

"Um, there seems to be a problem with my link."

"Oh, yeah," Thomas says. "Conner was showing us something funny earlier and it seemed to crash the projection system. He was telling us that we need to upgrade. So, you'll just have to do it the old fashioned way, Dolfo."

"But . . . my notes . . ."

Wolfgang's face turns red and he wipes sweat off his brow with a trembling hand.

"Anytime you're ready, Dolfo."

"Um, the Sizzle project—" Wolfgang coughs.

"Would you like some water?" Thomas offers, reaching for the pitcher.

"No, I'm okay," Wolfgang croaks.

"The Sizzle—Kugelblitz. Kugelblitz is a German word for ball lightning."

Mannequin faces nod.

"You've probably heard about black holes. Black holes are created from collapsed stars, where matter is so dense, gravity so huge, even light cannot escape," Wolfgang says, with his eyes darting around the room.

"So, there's an event horizon, beyond which we cannot see, because no light is escaping. The incredible mass bends space and time and, therefore, time distorts near it. If one could find a way to enter and exit a black hole intact, you'd probably end up in an entirely different space-time or universe.

"We don't know, because no one's made the journey," Wolfgang laughs and coughs.

"Think of Schwarzschild kugelblitz as a tiny black hole, only a few protons large, but one made from energy instead of matter. So much energy in fact, that its density won't allow light to escape. But with the same space-time bending potential as a collapsed star. A very tiny ball of lightning magic.

"We would have to shield ourselves from the Hawking radiation it would emit and hold it in place electromagnetically, because its destruction would cause a release of energy equal to an atomic bomb, but we think we can manage these risks. We will also need a light concentrator such as the world has never seen, but that's a technicality.

"Even though we can't send matter into it, it's theoretically possible to focus other forms of energy into it, like light, or even radio waves, that would cross over the event horizon and exit out in a different time and place in the universe, or even into another universe all together. A universal radio . . . *auf jerden Fall.*

"The potential of a Schwarzschild kugelblitz is enormous, and this kind of one is called a Sizzle. There's no telling what we could do. We could send a signal out across different times, places in the universe or entirely different universes. We could also receive the same signals, potentially bringing us incalculable riches in the form of information.

"Ladies and gentleman, this may be a means for us to create a communication link with the Logos, the Word, reverberating throughout time. It would be like having a hotline to the very essence of the universe, perhaps even the Creator himself. I imagine we'd have lots to say to each other," he snickers.

"The project could be completed within months using our existing facilities in the desert for just under ten billion dollars. That may seem like a lot, but it's a bargain in the scheme of things. Especially with our anticipated revenues from Quadra Code virtual reality games that Thomas is helping to develop."

He nods over at Thomas and everyone else with him.

"But let's face it, money isn't the only issue here, it's . . . *Wertschätzung* . . . prestige." He winks at Thomas. "The value to the standing and reputation of the Church, if we pull this off, cannot be overstated. Ladies and gentleman, your vote today is not just for an important experiment, it may in fact be for the most important scientific discovery of the century."

He sits down, folds his hands together and looks down, trying to suppress a self-satisfied grin.

After a minute, Thomas speaks.

"Very impressive, Dr. Eckhart . . . very impressive. But, as I've been saying for years, we should not be getting involved with projects that don't have clear revenue streams attached to them. The potential profit associated with this venture seems dubious at best. I think I would have been more convinced if you would have done a little more homework on the financial end of things."

Thomas looks around the table and gets several nods.

"I'm sorry, but it's a 'no' for me, Dolfo. What do you think, Conner?"

"I dunno," Conner says, rubbing his finger under his nose and sniffing. "Sounds like a waste of money to me."

"Anyway," Thomas says, "we've got more pressing concerns . . . Conner?"

Wolfgang looks up.

"Yeah," Conner says. "Like, what have you been doing to my dad?"

"What do you mean?"

"Why does he seem so drugged up all the time?"

"What do you mean, drugged up all the time?"

"Like when he's playing that video game. You gave him a pill last time. What was in it?"

"I don't know what . . . everything is . . . there's a safety . . . that he and Cygnus are . . . you love . . ."

Thomas snaps his fingers and guards pour into the room and stand behind Wolfgang while he stammers on like a stuck typewriter.

"I do indeed, but that project is on hold until we run some tests, just to make sure."

"Tests?"

"Show him, Conner."

Conner pulls out a plastic pill bottle and rattles it around with his nose chain sagging from his smirk.

"Those were in my desk! They were supposed to be—"

"I know what they were supposed to be," Thomas stands with a strand of his pompadour falling out. "They were supposed to make me crazy so you could take over ..." Thomas stops to blink several times. "To-uh take over ... you ... you ... Subtractive Loser!"

Guards grab Wolfgang's arms, while Wolfgang bristles at the accusation.

"Get him the fuck out of here!" Thomas yells as Conner laughs and Wolfgang's world turns upside down.

The Review Engagement is about to begin in the Compliance Infirmary in the Church Basement. A three-levels below-ground descent on the confessional booth elevator to a shock show of skinny hallways, white lacquered walls, cement floors, locked rooms, buzzing lights, random shouting and a creepy feeling of constant voyeuristic surveillance by masturbating dirty old men, purulent burger-flipping teens and rotten-toothed pudgy-fingered hags.

Subtractive Loserville.

"You may squeeze the Ankh has hard as you like but keep your hand holding the Orb open."

Wolfgang is across from a man in a white short-sleeved shirt, with sloping shoulders and a black tie. His tag says he's Mathew 13, Review Engagement Officer. The Ankh is a paddle that Wolfgang grasps in his right hand. The Orb is a crystal globe resting on his open left. He's strapped to a chair. Men in black leather overcoats stand behind him with their arms crossed. Behind them, against the wall, leans a tall black man with a toothpick in his mouth. Trimmed mustache and sideburns. A tight afro. Wearing a long toffee-colored leather jacket with lapels as wide as 747 wings. A burnt orange turtleneck. His nametag says he's Moses 1 and that he's Security. So does the butt end of the long-barreled forty-five strapped to his ribs.

"What is your name?" Mathew begins, turning the oscilloscope on with a buzz.

"Wolfgang Eckhart."

Mathew looks at a green screen doubtfully.

"What is your name?"

"Wolfgang Eckhart, like I said."

Mathew looks at the bouncing lines.

"What is your name?"

Wolfgang clears his throat and says, "Wolfgang." Mathew looks at the oscilloscope shakes his head and says, "That's not your name."

"It's the name I was born with."

Mathew shakes his head again, leans back and says, "No, your name is Wolfgang *and* Eckhart."

"Wolfgang and Eckhart?"

"No, your name is Wolfgang *and* Eckhart."

"My name is Wolfgang *and* Eckhart?" Wolfgang answers as sweat beads appear above his lip.

Mathew makes a small tick in a chart. He reads the next question to himself, puts his hands on the desk and straightens. He turns an hourglass on the desk and waits for the sand to run through. He turns it and, after the sand runs through again, he continues.

"Watch the screen, please."

A pop-up screen squeaks up from the table like an old flagpole. It tilts back and plays black and white footage of Wolfgang masturbating to a video feed from an examining room. Wolfgang's eyes flash cherries and his face turns Ferrari red as he tries to look away, but the men force him to watch.

Played front to back, three times over.

On the fourth replay, Mathew stops it halfway and asks, "Why did you slow your hand down at the 3:51 mark?"

Wolfgang clears his throat and squeaks, "What do you mean?"

"Why did you slow down your hand down at the 3:51 mark?" Mathew asks again, replaying the loop and stopping the tape.

"I don't know."

"Why did you slow your hand down at the 3:51 mark?"

"*I don't know*," Wolfgang says. "Maybe there was a lull."

"What do you mean by a *lull?*"

"A lull in what the girl was doing, maybe."

"Lulls in what girls are doing maybe make you slow your hand down?" Mathew asks, turning up the sound.

"*I don't know.*"

"Lulls in what girls are doing maybe make you slow your hand down?" Mathew asks again, watching the Oscilloscope flicker, then replaying the entire sequence.

"Why did you make that sound at the 5:03 mark?"

The door code chimes *beep-beep-beep* and swings open. Moses moves away from the wall and then leans back again.

Mathew snaps to his feet at the entrance of the man.

"Shut it down, Matt. Shut it down. Untie him, Moses," Thomas orders.

Mathew turns off the scope and takes the Ankh and Orb from Wolfgang while Moses unbinds him.

"I got the results back," he says, waiving a printout in his hands. "They were sedatives just like you said. Sedatives. And my blood and urine came back white as a Mormon Christomas."

Wolfgang looks up.

"Anyway, I need your help . . . you, too, Moses."

"What is it?" Wolfgang asks.

"It's Conner."

They're back up in Thomas's opulent penthouse office, from the Compliance Infirmary in the bowels of the Hands of Prayer tower. Thomas scoops mustard, while Wolfgang and Moses sip whiskey. Thomas puts his spoon down, closes his eyes and presses the bridge of his nose between his thumb and finger. Inhales deep and looks up at Wolfgang, snaps his head back, blinks and then blinks again.

"Sir?"

"Sorry, Dolfo. For a second there, it looked like you were wearing a Crusader helmet."

Wolfgang pulls out a handkerchief to clean his pince-nez glasses and then slips them on. He points his nose at Thomas and slowly blinks his eyes with downturned lips.

"That was a bit unpleasant," Wolfgang says. "I have to say . . . to find out that you've been keeping such tapes on me."

"The Church has tapes on everyone, including me. It's how we maintain loyalty. When Conner came forward with those allegations, I had to act on them, even though I didn't believe them."

"What about hanging me out to dry in front of the board?"

"Yeah, I'm sorry about that. But it never went to a vote. We can put it on the agenda again at the next meeting. This time I'll throw my weight behind it, I promise."

Wolfgang's tight lips, short breaths and narrowed eyes go on radiating black, before his shoulders relax and his lips twitch up slightly.

Thomas sighs. "What am I going to do with the kid, Dolfo? He's been given every opportunity and he just keeps fucking up."

"He probably just wants to find his own way in the world, sir. It can be tough on kids living under the shadow of a famous father."

"Yeah, his own way with my big fat trust—," Thomas's phone buzzes. He taps his ear.

"Tucker . . . I'll put you up."

The center screen pops on with Tucker's video feed. Wolfgang and Thomas listen to Tucker's Italian shoes echo off the footway as he walks up to the door of the LPPD Command station. Doors slide open and his footsteps ring off the tiled floor. He looks up at a camera and the door buzzes and swings open as he nears.

"Detective Veracruz, what did he do this time? Urinate on the buffet at the Nugget?"

"Bit more serious this time, counselor."

"Yeah?"

"There's a dead body at the Itercon with his jizz in it." Veracruz turns to look at Tucker. "And cameras off, you know the rules."

When the feed snaps off, Thomas is shaking. "Yeshua Christos," he says through clenched teeth, "I told him to stay on the compound."

"Did he say the Itercon?" Wolfgang asks. "That's Sparzo's."

"I'm on it," Moses says, getting up to leave.

"Call us when you get there," Thomas calls after him.

After he leaves, Tucker calls again. Thomas puts him on the screen. Tucker's in an interview room with Conner, who's shifting around in his plastic chair like a squirrel on meth.

"Anything you want to tell your father?"

"Yeah," Conner says, fidgeting a finger under his nose. "I've been *framed*."

"I have no idea what he told them," Tucker says as Conner gets up to pace around the room, looking for nuts. "But if he keeps talking like this, they're going to loop whatever it is and hang him with it."

"*Framed*," Conner says, sticking his head back into frame, before looking for nuts again, chewing his nails.

"Will they release him?" Thomas asks.

"They haven't indicted him yet, but they're probably typing that up as we speak."

"Well, see what you can do. We need to get him back on the compound where we can control him."

"I will," Tucker says, reaching for his glasses to tap the video feed off.

"How am I supposed to fix this when he was off the compound? Do you think we should wake up Cygnus and ask him to help?" Thomas asks Wolfgang.

"Help . . . as in how?" Wolfgang answers.

"I don't know. Get him to hack into the police lab and spoil the evidence or something?"

"Do you think that's a good idea?"

"Nah, you're right. I suppose not. He'd find a way to get the squeeze on us. He wrote the algorithms for our extortion systems . . . damn!" Thomas says, getting up to pace around with a spoon in his mouth. "What am I going to do?"

Moses calls.

They put his video feed up. He's walking through a casino, all ding-ding-dings, flashing lights and hologram loops. A security guard steps aside to let him through a door. He walks past video monitors into a back office.

"The tapes?" Moses says to a short, bald, fat man wearing an open Hawaiian shirt with chest hair spilling out.

"All here, chief," the man says handing Moses an eight-track tape. "Seven days of footage. You've probably got six hours of sexy time with them before the search warrant shows up."

"Thanks," Moses says.

"I had a quick look."

"Oh?"

"I can see why *you* wouldn't—"

Moses's video feed snaps off. He calls back later to apologize for the dropped call and to say he's got the tape and is coming in.

Thomas paces around the room. "What am I going to do, Dolfo?"

"I might have an idea."

Thomas returns to his seat.

"I'm all ears."

"What if Conner disappears for a while? I mean until Tucker and Moses can do their magic?"

"You mean, go into hiding?"

"Ja."

"Wouldn't that be like admitting guilt?"

"Also consistent with being framed."

"How are we going to do that, when they're going to be watching us?"

"What if I told you that I might be able to get him to Osterbayern without anyone knowing?" asks Wolfgang, taking off his pince-nez to clean them again.

Thomas furrows his brow. "And no one would find him?"

"Nope, it would be as though he walked off the planet," Wolfgang says, fitting his glasses back on his nose.

"You can do this?"

"If the Sizzle project goes through. There will be plenty of scary shipping crates that border inspection officers won't touch."

Thomas blinks to make the Crusader helmet disappear again.

"Sir?"

"Sorry. I just have to get some sleep. I feel like I've been up for a week and now I'm seeing things."

"Crusader helmets?"

"Yeah, and for a moment you were upside down, too."

VIII

STRENGTH.

CHAPTER 14:
TRUE STRENGTH

The first session is with Deidre, who pushes her way past Winston and Oliver wearing a black and gold gi, a black belt and a big freckly smile. They're used to her birth defect by now. But the gi makes her look more like a kid in pajamas than a martial arts instructor. Her gi has an embroidered picture of a woman, subduing a lion without any apparent effort.

She looks everyone over and says, "I'm going to teach y'all a hand-to-hand combat method used by the Irish Republican Army's Special Forces. It's a combination of pressure point Krav Maga, from the Israelis and Irish bar brawling perfected by my uncle," she giggles.

"Now," she smiles while shadow boxing. "Any volunteers? Anyone?" She says, comboing uppercuts and crosses.

"Come on, Winston, why don't you step up?" She waves him up.

Winston is Oliver's personal bodyguard and butler, six foot four and two hundred and fifty pounds, with a flat nose and a square jaw. He grumbles, looks around and walks into the ring with his arms crossed. As soon as he steps in, Deidre shrieks, "*Leprechaun!*," runs a circle around him, slapping him with a series of quick chops that make him laugh, she summersaults, jumps up and motions him toward her with an extended hand.

Winston takes a few wobbly steps and falls over.

Deidre smiles, curtsies and waves her hands with a flourish. To a prone Winston, she says, "Now, don't fret, Cadbury, you'll be as good as new in a minute." To the rest she says, pressing her hands on her hips. "Now, anyone care to guess how I did that?"

"Um, voodoo pressure points?" Andron asks.

"Close . . . but, no. Anyone else?"

"We don't know. Why don't you teach us the Five Fingers of Leprechaun?" answers Lysandra.

"The Five Fingers of Leprechaun," Deidre laughs with her hand on her chest, while Winston gets up slowly, "can be easily taught. In fact, I can teach *you* in a matter of minutes."

Deidre tugs Lysandra along.

After a few minutes, Deidre returns to the center mat, while Lysandra pushes her way between Andron and Dylan. Deidre invites Andron and Lysandra out in front for a demonstration. Lysandra screeches, *"Leprechaun!"* and does the same run-by, quick chops and somersault as Deidre. And just like Winston, Andron takes a few steps and falls over.

Jaws hang open.

"Lysandra, why don't you show everyone the secret ingredient to the Five Fingers of Leprechaun?"

Lysandra holds up her hand to show everyone her ring, with a small needle sticking out of it. They look at it then look back up at Deidre. No one says anything until Winston says, "So, you just scream and then run up and stick someone with a needle?"

"Not exactly. The stick was in before the show, when you all were standing around. Lysandra got Andy when she came back. The leprechaun yell was for show. Look, there's a lesson here. One, that being creative and resourceful is the most important combat technique, way more than strength. Two, that when you're dead or maimed, you don't get to go to a booth review to decide whether the fight was fair. Fights aren't fair. They're 'nasty, brutish and short.' Always have been, always will."

"You've got that right," Dylan says.

"So, for the next lesson, we're going to learn the most efficient way to break a man's neck," she smiles. "Lucky for you, I won't be asking for any volunteers," she laughs. "Instead, I'll be demonstrating on good ole Thomas here." She points her thumb back to a mannequin that looks like Thomas O'Brian, sitting on a chair.

"Now, the idea is to generate sufficient pressure to snap the vertebrae. Fortunately, since we've evolved to stand upright, it takes surprisingly little. There isn't much muscle in our necks because our heads more or less just sit on our shoulders, instead of hanging out like a dog's or a horse's. It's the weak spot in our design.

"I'll show you how to do this at close quarters, like in a chokehold. But I prefer methods that rely more on technique than brute strength. The idea is to build up your kinetic energy and then to transfer that energy to your subject's neck in a few easy steps that you can do practically anywhere." She smirks.

"This one, I like to call . . . *Titty Fuck*."

She ballet hops to the side of the mannequin and rips open her gi, exposing her breasts. She smiles and even the Thomas mannequin seems to be ogling. She casually runs toward it, picking up speed, then lunges to grab the mannequin by the chin, swinging her legs around like a stripper around a pole. The mannequin's neck snaps with a loud *crack*. She walks back toward them, tying on her gi.

"So, as you can see," she says, thumbing back at Thomas's ragdoll head, "I got him to look at my titties . . . now he's fucked."

She tells the mannequin to reset and Thomas's head snaps back up. "Now, anyone care to try?"

Lysandra's arm shoots up.

Jasmin has her array of guns spread out before her and a smile spread across her face. She picks up a replica Uzi RG in her sinewy arms, flicks on the target assist, scans the firing range and then powers it down, satisfied. Looks up.

"Now, honeys, these little barrels of fun may look like museum pieces, but that just gives them some of that old world swagger. They're railguns, so they launch their business electromagnetically. Higher muzzle velocity, no shell casings, more rounds and, boy . . ." She puts her hands on her hips and whistles. "Do they catch fish."

"So, what do we have here?" she says as she picks up a Colt .45 RG. "The gun that won the West or some of that next?" She cocks and uncocks the hammer. "Care to hold it, cowboy?" as she hands the gun to Dylan, who holds the long-barreled gun in his outstretched hands.

"Shit, it doesn't hardly weigh anything."

"That's 'cause it's made out graphene, sugar."

She moves behind Dylan and pulls out a red plastic-looking rip cord from the side of the gun. The barrel flashes green.

"Now hold onto the handle, darling."

Dylan holds the handle until the blinking green barrel turns to solid green.

"Now you're locked in. The gun has mated to you and will only fire in your hands. Push the button on the side."

Dylan does and a heads-up screen pops up above the gun barrel.

"Now use your eyes to set up your preferences."

Dylan blinks through several menus. Leaves it on standard magazine load. Two taps on the side to switch off the safety. He sets the display to blue. Sidewinder voice activation sequence to the word *boots*.

"What does *sidewinder* do?" he asks.

Jasmin moves behind him and nudges him to aim the gun down the firing range.

"Cock it."

Dylan pulls the hammer back and the virtual screen comes pops up. Jasmin leans over Dylan's shoulder and puts her hand on his hip.

"Give the command."

"*Boots.*"

"Now, when I say *pull*, a target will appear. Use the guidance to lock on to it and pull the trigger."

"*Pull.*"

A fat, naked mannequin of Thomas O'Brian pops up. Dylan aims and pulls the trigger.

Nothing happens.

Jasmin shouts *motion* and the mannequin starts to jump and run around randomly.

"Now pull the trigger again. Don't worry that you can't get a target lock. Heck . . . even try to miss."

Dylan fires and a bullet whistles out, twisting in the air and then corkscrewing into the dancing mannequin's bull's eye, tearing it apart on impact. They stare at the smoldering pieces of leg and torso.

"I sure hope they're not going to use these on us."

Jasmin slaps him on the back. "Me, too, sugar. Fortunately, we've got some body armor that'll throw out a decoy. Now let's see what this Winchester RG can do."

They're in the training room, in the latest gym wear. The guys have loose-fitting muscle shirts, ball-hugger shorts, soccer socks and Adidas leather sneakers. The ladies have pink, crotch-plunging spandex one-pieces, with fuzzy socks and white tennis shoes. Winston is explaining the Colossus Iron-Tron 2300 machine to them, an all-in-one fitness system with silver push and pull bars and stacked gravity multipliers made up to look like plastic weights filled with concrete. They even smell like plastic and cement.

"Okay, each station will tax a muscle group to the limit, body dynamic power, aerobic potential and flexibility," he says with a deep voice. "It will score you at the end with a gross number and a sex and age adjustment. You are in a competition with no one other than yourselves, understand?"

There's a dash for the machines and it's game on.

Dylan scores the highest adjusted score, but Andron's isn't far behind—both in the top fraction of a percent for their age. Winston throws up the highest gross number at 2525. Lysandra's test is inconclusive, because of too much variance. The final number—1255—is in line with Deidre's. So, half as strong as Winston.

Oliver, Mike and Jasmin tie at around 1700.

As Winston is about to power down the room, with everyone else anxious to get to their massages and hot tub, Lysandra says that she wants to stay behind.

Mike hangs back and says that he does, too.

After everyone's gone, he walks up to kiss her.

She kisses him back.

"Thought we'd continue on from this morning," he smiles, moving behind her, grabbing her hips and pulling her bottom back to his groin, looking at their reflection in the mirror, with an impish grin.

"I'm not really in the mood right now, Mike," she says, wiggling away.

Mike pushes his erection down and says, "You know, for a . . . for a . . ."

"For a *what?*" she snaps back.

He doesn't answer.

"Finish your fucking sentence. For a *what?*"

He looks away.

"You were going to say whore, weren't you?"

"No I—"

"*Weren't* you?"

"Yeshua Christos, what's your fucking problem?"

"Right now, you. So, why don't you take your 1700 body and get the fuck out?" she says, flipping her hair behind her ear and folding her arms.

"Okay, I'll bite," he says. "I don't get it how you can give it up to anyone with a buck, but with me, it's got to be such a big fucking hassle?"

"My God, GET OUT, you ASSHOLE!" she says as she pushes him and he stumbles back, tripping on a dumbbell.

"Don't worry, bitch," he says, rubbing his elbow before scrambling back on his feet and heading for the door. "I'm so out of here! I liked you better as a blonde, anyway."

The door slam reverberates in the workout room. She picks up a few plastic gravity weights and tries a few curls. Stops and puts her face in her towel, before tossing it aside. She looks up at the Colossus with narrowed eyes and a clenched jaw. She marches over, wiping away a tear. Jabs the red *test* button, then moves from station to station, red-faced and straining. Rests with her head in her hands panting, then climbs back on the stair climber and swipes for the results. She wipes sweat off her face with her towel and drinks from her water bottle.

Every category returns a #DIV/0! result, except the last, her gross score rating. She blinks at the result: 3005.

"So, I'm stronger than Winston, am I?" she says out loud.

"*Pour sûr.*"

She pads to the exit in fluid steps, then effortlessly flips her water bottle at the bucket across the room.

"Asshole," she says, as it kerplunks straight in.

CHAPTER 15:
THE MUSTARD SEED

"I don't know, Cygnus. I think there should be more inter-action with Yeshua in the Judea loop, 'cause that's what's going to sell."

Thomas samples another glob of his specially prepared mustard with an ornate crucifix sampler spoon that he now wears around his neck at all times.

"I mean, I think our customers aren't just going to be gamers looking for a thrill, but video pilgrims looking to tour the Holy Lands and meet Yeshua."

They're back in the room with the overgrown white shag-grass. Thomas looks like a walrus in his skin-tight neoprene suit. A walrus with a pompadour and a red-brick mustache. Wolfgang has a tweed suit jacket, vest and brown tie, fat-knotted into a double Windsor. Cygnus wears a smoking jacket with his thicket of side-burns and walnut calabash professor pipe. The black half-moons are still there and he's relaxed, but his eyes are bulged awake like a strangled fish. Moses is standing by the door with a toothpick and the butt end of his forty-five glinting in the electric lights.

"Duly noted," Cygnus replies. "Any luck finding the magic mustard sauce, guv'nor?"

"They're getting close, but still not there," Thomas says, smacking his lips. "So, this next one is about escape?"

"Yup, your synapses will be blooming dancing in this one, guv. Id, ego and super-ego all firing at once. The game will throw you into some sticky dogs and lay down a Burlington Bertie that your mind can't find its way out of."

"What if it can't?"

"Not a chance. Daft escape-fu is coded in our DNA, because only the best Houdinis made it to the ball."

"I understand survival of the fittest. I don't understand how it relates to the game."

"Your sub-cee will come up with escape artistry while the game tries to paint it in. The better the artistry, the better the paint-ins. The game and brain will dance like that to make something glorious and personal. But the survival instinct always wins out in the end."

"I get it. So, I'm going to be the author of my own traps and secret doors?"

"In a word, guv. In a word. And you can tap your avatar's abilities, too. So, if your avatar can fight, you can fight. Your mind influences the plotlines and rescues. So, with a chimneysweep, you get shite like a ladder dropping out of the sky. With you, it's going to be an Oscar for best original screenplay."

Thomas grins.

"I'm telling you, mate, you might as well start working on your Oscar speech. That is . . ."

"That is, what?"

"You have to be willing to try the pill again because it doesn't work with the hypnotizers."

"I dunno, Cygnus, I had them checked out, along with the safety override, and they came back clean, but my doctor's worried that I might have had an allergic reaction that last time."

"So, you want to go back to staring at knives, droning monks and jet turbines?"

"No."

"Well?"

"I dunno, just a little nervous, I guess."

"What if we upped the ante?"

"What do you mean, upped the ante?"

"You wanted more gameplay in the Judea loop?"

"Yeah."

"We can step up the level of difficulty. Make the Six-Day loop a cakewalk, the Crusader, a minger. And then go balls-to-the-wall in Judea?"

"I'd still have the kill switch, though, right? I mean, in case things got too wild?"

"Quite. And you already know that it's foolproof."

"What do you think, Dolfo?"

"I don't know, sir. You're always pushing yourself too hard. Maybe you should take it easy this time."

"Ah, fuck it," Thomas says, shaking out a pill into his pudgy hand. "Put me in, coach."

"That's the spirit, Tommy boy, that's the spirit."

"Would you like me to get some water for you, sir?" Wolfgang asks.

Thomas nods.

Wolfgang whirl-walks through the shag to the bar sink, pulls out a paper cup from the dispenser, looks up and smiles as he runs the water. Behind the bar, he quickly pulls out an eyedropper and squeezes a few drops of a faint brown liquid into the cup. Looks up again, smiles and then squeezes out a few more. He returns with the paper cup that Thomas takes from him, pops the pill into his mouth and gulps it down with the water, crushing the cup, tossing it aside while saying, "Pitter patter."

"Indubitably," Cygnus replies, drawing on his calabash. "Pitter patter."

"Where is everyone?" Thomas asks as they walk into the sphere center.

"I put them on standby, sir, since I've mastered this invigilator thing. I also thought that their services could be better deployed in the research sector, helping with the mustard and beer projects. I can recall them if you wish?"

"No, that'll be fine, Dolfo, good thinking. I know you've got my back," Thomas says back-slapping Wolfgang and throwing him off kilter, then looking back at Moses, "and I gots my nigga, too, right, Moses?"

Moses picks up the diver's helmet and mumbles, "Sure thing, massa," lifts it over Thomas's head and snaps it into place. Thomas laughs. "Hey, don't be frontin' on me, I was just playin'... we cool?" Moses grins and helps Wolfgang connect the wire harnesses. "Yeah, we cool." Wolfgang winches Thomas's shoulder straps with a hard tug. Cygnus stands behind his turntables and mixing board, with its rows of dials and toggle switches. He looks up and says, "Ready?" Thomas adjusts his helmet slightly, bites down on his mouthpiece and gives the frog a wave.

Wait a minute.

Frog?

Zap

Thomas is slumped over while the machine goes into its plunk-plunk-buzz sub-routine. Wolfgang looks up at the display and sees Thomas looking down at his avatar and flopping his arms. He reaches into the Sphere, to the kill button switch, feels for the wires, follows them to the wall.

And yanks them out.

Moses watches with raised eyebrows. Slow rolls his eyes over Thomas and Cygnus, reaches in his overcoat where he keeps his forty-five and pulls out a silver toothpick case instead. Plucks a toothpick out with his teeth and presses his hand on the door pad. The door clicks open and he steps out.

Wolfgang looks at Cygnus, who is listening with a hand over his earphone and walks over to the Convulse-ES machine. "Now, when I give the signal... *Verdoppeln die juice.*"

"What's that going to do?"

"Give his short-term memory a proper wash when we pop him into certain sequences."

"Ah, zo," Wolfgang says, pauses, then adds, "I still don't get why it was so important that we get him to swallow the placebo when we were slipping him LSD in his water anyway?"

"Because," Cygnus grins, "the game's psyche-scramblers are like vampires."

"How's so?" Wolfgang asks.

"They can do a lot more damage if you invite them in."

Plunk... plunk... buzzzzz... flash.

First, it's the breathing—the feel of his oxygen mask on his face. Then the vision—looking through his visor at the front of his Mirage. Then the feel—the joystick in his right hand, throttle in his left, feet on the pedals and his G-suit squeezing his legs. Then the sound—the steady whine of the engine.

And the recording.

Stall . . . Stall . . . Stall . . .

Then the rush.

He throws switches, watches needles spin, trying to relight his engine. Three seconds to impact . . . *three . . . two . . .* he yanks the ejection handle. There's a bang and his face slams into a wall of wind. He closes his eyes and winces while he spins strapped to his seat. His chute snaps open, the horizon jitters and then levels. There's a moment of ease with the wind whistling by, where it's just him and the desert coming toward him. But then heartbreak when he sees his Mirage fireball in the distance. The MiG crashes and burns soon after. Barak peels off and thunders away.

On his own now.

He thinks about his Beretta, tucked into his safety vest. He tries to reach for it but can't reach behind far enough. His parachute flaps in the wind, then falls gently to the ground after he crashes on the Mars-like surface. He hears the grinding gears and engine whine of a fast-approaching jeep. He throws off his helmet and unlatches his shoulder harness. Unzips his canvas survival bag to grab his Beretta. Looks up and there's a rifle butt slamming toward his face. He reflexively bobs out of the way, while counter-slapping the rifle to the side, then grabbing it. He yanks the gun and the soldier holding it forward and stabs him in the throat with his Ka-Bar.

He sweeps and side-kicks the other soldier in the knee, reaches back into his survival bag again and this time finds the Beretta. Flicks off the safety and brings it down at the collapsed soldier waiving his hands for mercy . . . *pop-pop.* Aims at the other soldier with the gurgling throat, but doesn't fire. Bait. The air cracks by his ears, and he runs and dives behind a rock and comes up with his Beretta. He hears other jeeps roll up. The gunfire stops and he knows the drill. They want him alive. Then it's the swinging lightbulb, the jumper cables gripping his balls and the fingernail puller. He senses something near and knows he has less time than he did in the Mirage.

He runs and fires on a hunch. Empties his clip and makes it back to his ejection seat. Dives as sniper fire divots kick up near his legs. He stays down behind a slight bluff trying to reach for it in the back of his ejector seat, but the dust kicks up around him and bullets crack by. He senses something near again, makes a desperation dive and manages to grab the handle this time. The handle to his flare gun. He shoots it and the flare rockets up, fizz-lighting the sky. He hugs the ground.

He hears it before they do. Because he was born to hear it. To know it. A faint whistle that grows into a battle shriek that turns into thunder. He knows it's Barak without looking. A flyby, twenty feet over deck, tearing a strip off the desert in its wake. They waste ammo firing after it. They should be running.

He hears it bank and knows what's next.

Sand splashes up fast to where the jeeps are. Flaming hot metal slamming into metal, explosions, flames.

Then the choppers.

He is saved.

On the chopper, his chest constricts and he turns pale. The delayed terror comes like hurt after serious injury. Hands that were surgeon steady on the battlefield are shaking like a Hitler handshake. The chest pain is deeper than the present, triggering an internal to plea to a forgotten person.

"You okay?" the lieutenant shouts over the whirling blades as they approach Jerusalem.

"Yeah, a little rattled is all."

"Understandable. They're calling it the Six-Day War now and you're going to be one of its heroes."

"I don't feel like one."

There is nothing but the turbines and steady thumping of the blades, then the lieutenant taps him on the shoulder, points and smiles.

His eyes widen at the sight.

An Israeli flag above the Western Wall.

There's a *hiss* and a kind computer lady's voice.

Level one complete.

["Now!" Cygnus hollers to Wolfgang]

ZAPPPPPPPPP

Thomas is looking at the Western Wall inside the city gates. Peter the Hermit is laughing and tugging on his sleeve. Thomas looks at him through his metal faceguard, smelling a wooden city on fire.

"*Dues vult, Dues vult*, can you believe it, Stephan?" You must come with me at once, to the lay the relic at the foot of the true cross in the Sepulchre."

Avatar memories strobe in. Another hi-res data dump that smells, tingles and breathes.

Of mockingly being called Lord Vassal of the Spear after Peter Bartholomew's trial by ordeal, where Peter walked through piles of burning wood, clad only in his tunic, hoisting the Lance. Seeing Peter horribly burned and dying twelve days later.

Of having made it to the gates of Jerusalem to begin their siege and starving themselves instead. Of seeing the black dome of the mosque on the Temple Mount invite them in the morning and mock them at dusk.

Of hitting into a large cache of timber in Samaria from which they could make siege towers. Being harried by the winds of a sirocco that sandblasted their faces while they struggled to build.

Of parading around the city walls barefoot and chanting, led by the Hermit.

Of looking up the stars while climbing up the siege tower and over the walls. Hearing the bloodcurdling screams as Crusaders invaded homes, hacked civilians, gorged on their food and raped their children.

The thought both sickens and excites him.

"Sorry, Father," Thomas says, breaking from the Hermit's grip. Shouts back, "*I'll be there soon . . . but I have to help secure the city.*"

He spies a woman looking back at him with frightened blue-brown eyes and running. He races after her down a cobblestone lane, hearing footfall ring off the ancient walls, shaking out screams of the dead to join the living. He runs head-long into the chainmail mitt of a white ghost knight and skids to a stop.

The knight speaks.

He says . . . *don't.*

Thomas blinks at the apparition, pulls out his sword and slices it. He must find her, he thinks, she is the key.

The ghost knight mists away.

He searches for her with boiling eyes and hungry jowls, opening doors and running down alleys. Looking through homes, raising his sword at frightened occupants. Asking, "Where is the Magdalene?" to confused and terrified eyes. No one speaks. Nobody understands.

He decides to go back to where he started and begin again.

Then he sees her.

Blue-brown eyes at the end of the lane and then disappearing behind a corner. He runs after her, a wolf in armor after a rabbit. He reaches the end and pivots around the corner, running faster than he did in Antioch after the Turks, when the battle turned and the enemy was on the run.

A wooden plank swings toward his face.

["Now!"]

ZAPPPPPPPPP

His head is pounding. He reaches for his temples and discovers that his Crusader helmet is gone. So is his chainmail. So is the spear. She must have made off with Stephan, too, because he's no longer in him. Instead, he's back in the body he was in by the river. He tries to get up and realizes it's the crippled river body.

He limps down the road with a curled hand, hoping to find someone to help him, maybe Peter the Hermit, who he thinks will recognize him. He thinks that he should try to make it to the Holy Sepulchre. He concentrates on his walking, trying not to catch his sandal on a high cobblestone. He smiles when he sees a mounted Godfrey of Bouillon, holding his sword and steadying his horse, while shouting orders to the group of infantrymen with him. He limps toward him and cries, "Godfrey, thank God. It's me, Stephan. I have been accosted. In the name of the cross, please help me!"

Something's wrong. He thought the words in French, but spoke them with the barbarous tongue of the Ishmaelites.

"Godfrey, it's me!"

What curse is this? Still babbling. Godfrey and his men stare at him, then Godfrey says something to them in French. He recognizes that it's French, but no longer understands it. He tries to say *Dues vult* over and over, but it comes out as *Allahu akbar* instead.

One of Godfrey's men pushes him. He tries to keep his balance but stumbles to the ground. Another he recognizes as Lambert, boots him in the chest. He feels a rib crack and tightness across his chest. He tries saying *spear*, but it comes out as *harba* instead.

Lambert and another infantryman march him down the street. Lambert rams him forward with the shaft of his battle ax. Thomas looks up at the Dome of the Rock and knows that he'll be slaughtered there. He has to escape. But how? He can hardly walk and there're two armed Crusaders marching him. He remembers the other body by the river, the agile one, and wishes he had it instead. But how can he make the switch? The white knight was a warning and he ignored it, once again going down alleys he shouldn't. When he knew it was wrong. The knight was his inner voice. And he hacked it away with his sword. Like he's always done. The maiden was someone he was supposed to protect instead of defile. How could he be so stupid? How could he keep repeating the same mistakes and reaping the same bitter harvests? Now he's marching to the dome of his doom and he's so very sorry.

So . . . so . . . very . . . *sorry?* His hand slightly unbinds.

Because he begs forgiveness. His knee bends less to the inside.

Sorry for all his sins. His back straightens.

He has it now.

The path.

"My Lord, I seek forgiveness." And the switch is complete.

"Shut up," says Lambert, jabbing him in the back.

He continues to limp, but it's an act.

He slows and waits for the jab in his back. Slows and waits for the jab. Slows and waits for the jab. Slows and waits then . . . *ducks*.

Lambert stumbles while Thomas spins and grabs Lambert's chest plate, steps back with Lambert's forward movement, mashes his sandal's heel into Lambert's hipbone, slides his lower leg under him and tosses him, grabbing his battle ax as Lambert flies over. He comes up and swings the ax at the other Crusader. The blade whistles in the air and slams into the Crusader's helmet. A dented helmet flies off and the Crusader drops, spurting blood from a gash in his head. Thomas swings around to block Lambert's sword, but the shaft breaks. Lambert raises his sword again. Thomas makes an arm block and closes his eyes.

He opens them to see Lambert with a spear sticking out his chest, a spreading blood stain, saucer eyes and a noiseless scream. It's the Holy Lance. Lambert has been run through by the Lance. He falls over, gurgling blood. Behind him stands a small Crusader with sagging chainmail and low hanging armor. The Crusader's helmet slips down over the Crusader's eyes and the Crusader pushes it up again.

The blue-brown eyes are unmistakable. It's the maiden.

"You should come with me if you want to escape," she says, pointing to a small group of frightened refugees.

"Where are you going?"

"To the hills."

"With the other Muslims?"

"We're Christians. They're slaughtering us, too."

"I'm sure you'll be safe in the Sepulchre, if I brought you. If you give me back my armor, that—"

He doubles over, resting his hands on his knees.

"Are you okay?" she asks.

"Yeah, just give me a sec."

He puts on his chainmail and armor again, nods for the troupe of refugees to follow him and leads them to the Holy Sepulchre. He hands them over to the care of the Hermit and then takes off his helmet.

There's a *hiss* and he waits for the cheery computer lady's voice before making his move.

He needs out. He can do the Judea loop another time. His chest pain is too real.

Level two complete.

He pushes the kill switch. Pushes and pushes it, but nothing happens.

What the—?

["Now!"]

ZAPPPPPPPPP

Smells come to him in thousand watt wafts of body odor, straw and urine. Then chest pains, confusion and ringing in his ears. He adjusts his jaw. He doesn't know who he is or how he got there. His memory comes back in fuzzy drops. He looks at the prison walls and imagines that he can escape, if he speaks the words, only.

"Speaks the word, only."

The words reverberate. He said them out loud.

"What words?" The prisoner, who he remembers is named Peter, laughs. "If I say them, will you be my slave girl?" his head cocked.

"Hold your tongue, you piece of shit . . . or I'll cut it out for you," Judas says. Peter blows him a kiss.

He tries to get up, but there's a crushing weight across his chest. He remembers being slammed in the ribs with the blunt end of a spear by Longinus, the centurion who captured them with a detail of soldiers. They didn't even make it to the bottom of the Temple stairs, thanks to Judas's stupidity.

He looks around the cell and wishes he was alone. Whenever men are together, there's always airs to put on, jokes to be made. This is not a time for airs or jokes. They're waiting for Pilate, the Procurator, to show up from Caesarea. And they're facing death for their crimes.

He has to find a way out.

The door clanks, opens and soldiers shove a man in, who stumbles and falls. He stays face down on the stone floor with his chest heaving, then struggles to stand, hopping on a leg. He wipes blood from his nose with the back of his hand and looks at them with swollen eyes.

"And who might you be?" Peter asks.

The man replies, "I am Jesus bar Abbas."

Peter's sooty face cracks into a grin. "Well, peace be with you, son of your father, Jesus Barabbas, I'm Peter bar Abbas. And these two," he snorts, pointing over to Thomas and Judas, "are Simon and Judas . . . bar Samarian whores."

"You shut your filthy mouth, or I'll do it for you," a red-faced Judas spits, lunging for Peter.

"Stop," says Jesus, stepping between them, with uncovered hair swinging across his face. "Must we do the work of our persecutors?" His voice singsong yet sure.

Judas and Peter grunt and go off to their corners, while Jesus slides down against the wall next to Thomas and sits with his legs up and forearms resting on his knees. "I know who you are," Thomas says to him. "You're the one they call the Nazarene, I saw you at the Temple, overturning tables. Do you think your followers will be able to save us?"

Jesus looks over at him. "My followers are talented fishermen, but poor soldiers," he laughs. "Put your faith in the Lord instead."

"The easy road of forgiveness and the hard road of redemption, right?"

Jesus nods.

"I get it, but what value is the path of redemption if it led us here?"

Jesus answers, "A man can control what he sows, not whether it rains."

"Thanks, but I'd rather have escape plans rooted in something a bit more solid than hoping it rains."

Jesus says, "What does it profit a man to gain his freedom but lose his salvation?"

Thomas's face wrinkles.

"What does that—"

Zap

He's tied to Judas and Jesus as they are pulled along up the street. He sees an old man pull back his mason jar, nod toward a young boy up the street, who looks and runs. Thomas smiles. That's it, he thinks . . . the signal. He tugs on his rope to get Jesus's attention. Jesus looks back with an eye swollen shut. Thomas nods, looks up the street and winks. Jesus shrugs his shoulders, half-smiles and continues walking.

Brethren sicarii must be planning to attack the small detail of soldiers and the lone centurion escorting them. He scans the street looking for likely places for his dagger-mates to ambush and free them. Free them so they can make their way north, to Galilee, where they'll earn wages as day laborers in the vineyards. Live with the people. Where they'll send word to Jesus's followers and slowly build their numbers. She'll be there, too. The Magdalene. He imagines that she'll be impressed when she finds out about their daring escape, that he's about to lead. They'll want revenge right away, but he'll counsel them to plan more carefully this time. Jesus will nod in agreement, to his trusted friend and adviser.

He tenses as they pass an alley, certain that this is where his brothers will strike. But nothing happens. Nor does it at the next intersection. Or the next two after that. Instead, the street widens as they near Herod's palace, guarded by a contubernium of straight-nosed praetorians with silver and gold helmets and bright crimson plumes. He sees the boy he saw earlier whispering to Caiaphas, who is standing with a delegation of the Sanhedrin. Caiaphas stiffens when they walk by, strokes his long black beard, sniffs the air at them and wrinkles up his nose. His gold breastplate glitters in the sun over his blue linen vestments and rainbow sashes.

They walk up marble steps to the palace, on Persian carpets toward the inner courtyard. The gateway is fragrant with flowers, frankincense and spring water. They're forced to their knees before a throne. Soldiers straighten while a slight, bald man with blotchy skin, a pointy nose and yellow eyes, wearing a white robe and a red sash, breezes past them and climbs up the throne. The Imperial horn line sounds and Longinus shouts in Latin that court is in session. They're made to stand as Pilate says, "Hail Caesar," with a nasally voice. Jesus is the first to be brought before him.

"And who is this . . . *rag*?" Pilate asks in Greek.

"Jesus of Nazareth," Longinus answers.

"And what charges have you brought against him?" asks Pilate, eying the delegation from the Sanhedrin.

Caiaphas speaks with a deep priestly voice. "Our council has convicted him of blasphemy. We bring him before you for acts of treason."

"Blasphemy?" Pilate spits. "It's not a crime against Rome to deny a non-existent god. If his crime is blasphemy, then don't the laws of your backward cult allow you to stone him to death?"

No one answers.

"So, start throwing stones. How is this any concern of mine?"

"He claims to be the messiah, the chosen one, our king. Only Caesar has the power to appoint kings. Therefore, he is an affront to Caesar's rule."

"This man … a king? You have got to be joking. Should I be concerned if an ant wishes to appoint himself king of the cockroaches? You … rapscallion … what do you have to say for yourself; are you claiming to be king of these people?"

Jesus looks up and says, "My kingdom is not of this world."

"See, there you have it. This nobody is claiming to be king of nowhere. You can have him back to stone to death."

This time, Ananus, Caiaphas's father-in-law, answers, "But your eminence," he pleads, "the man caused a riot at the Temple. He breached Rome's peace. He—"

"I know what he did. He undermined your authority, not Rome's. I'm not here to do your dirty work. I shouldn't be here at all, in fact. I should be in Caesarea enjoying wine by the sea instead of this latrine. I haven't decided what to do with this one, yet," he says, popping grapes into his mouth.

"What about these other two?" he asks, chewing.

"Sir, my men and I caught them fleeing the Temple with stolen coins and we found these daggers on them," Longinus announces, holding up the weapons. "They're cut-throats and thieves."

"If there's anything I despise," says Pilate, spitting grape seeds, "it's cut-throats and thieves. They shall be scourged and crucified. How much did they steal?"

"Thirty silver Tyrian shekels, sir."

"How much is that worth?"

"About a hundred and twenty drachmae, sir."

Pilate whistles. "Good, I order that the coins be forfeited to me for the cost of these proceedings."

"And what about the Nazarene?"

"May I speak?" Judas asks. Longinus moves to slam Judas with the butt of his sword, but Pilate waves him off.

Thomas breathes easier, thinking that Judas is about to profess Simon's innocence. To tell the procurator that he acted of his own accord in the temple theft. Certain that he is about to be freed, he plans a speech to ask for clemency for Judas and Jesus. He waits anxiously, with a tear welling up and a lump in his throat, for Judas's expected great act of sacrifice and love.

"This man," Judas continues, "the *Nazarene*, said that he would tear down Roman eagles if any were put up in the Temple. If it wasn't for his turning over the moneychanger's tables and distracting the guards, we wouldn't have been able to rob the Temple. I am but a lowly thief, sir. I pray that you spare me for this information."

"Well, that settles it," Pilate says while Thomas's stomach churns and his chest tightens. "We can't have rioters, and I'll put up eagles anywhere I want. He shall be scourged and crucified as well. For this brigand's information, he shall be spared being scourged. On second thought, scourge him anyway. Nobody likes a snitch."

"So be it, sir. And what shall be recorded as their crimes?"

"These two shall be inscribed as brigands and this one . . ." he looks over at the satisfied faces of the Sanhedrin and say, "King of the Jews."

The soldiers, centurions and court officials burst into laughter, while Pilate breaks into a smug smile and the faces of the Sanhedrin sour.

"Please, sir," Ananus protests. "Make it *claimed to be king of the Jews* instead. It will be as though Rome appointed this man our king and then crucified him."

"What I have written, I have written."

Thomas steps forward, "Sir, if I may?" All eyes are on him. "You're making a mistake. A huge mistake. I'm a minister from the future and this man is a prophet, God's only begotten son. Your deeds shall burn around your necks for eternity if you harm him, I'm warning you. I demand at once that you set us free, or at least allow us proper legal representation."

There's a long silence, after which Pilate laughs. "What language was that?" then nods at Longinus, standing behind Thomas.

["Now!"]

ZAPPPPPPPPP

He opens his eyes and he's back in Antonia's Praetorium, stripped naked and tied to a whipping post that smells of cedar and blood. A soldier practice-cracks his leather whip with its imbedded iron balls and sheep bones. It feels like he's been up for days. His eyes sting and he can't think straight. Judas is on the ground, in a heap of torn flesh. They've put Jesus in a cloak, pounded a crown of thorns on his head and have given him a reed to hold. They're chanting, *all hail, King of the Jews*, while taking turns punching him in the face. Jesus stumbles around like a wounded deer, hounded by hyenas.

"*No, no, no ... time out. Tech support. I want out,*" pleads Thomas, with a parched mouth, desperately trying to push a kill button in his hand that isn't there and doesn't work.

Whip-Crack

Leather, metal and jagged bones rip into his skin. His head explodes with pain. He tries to pull himself out of Simon, but only manages an even crueler state where he is both experiencing everything and looking down from above.

Whip-Crack

He tries praying but nothing happens. He thinks of the woman. Nothing.

Whip-Crack

"God, no ... *please ... ladders-coming-down ... ladders-coming-down ... ladders-coming-down ...*"

Whip-Crack

"For Christos sake! I am the leader of the Church you piece of—"

Whip-Crack

Pieces of flesh strip off his back each time. The greater the injury, the more painfully he screams, the more he pleads, the more viciously he is whipped.

Whip-Crack

He's all tears, snot and blood.

Whip-Crack

His mother doesn't scoop him up. The cavalry doesn't arrive, helicopters don't swoop in and the marines don't climb over the walls. There's no love, forgiveness, mercy, justice or God in the world. Only . . .

Whip-Crack

Whip-Crack

Whip-Crack

Thirty more and he's floating above looking at the raw meat on his back. He can't focus his eyes. His head feels like it's filled with stone. He can't form words. He babbles something that he doesn't understand. He can't remember his name. Or any name. His vision is split between looking from above and out his eyes. He hears Longinus say that he should be grateful. "With such a fine scourging, you'll suffer less on the cross."

But the words make no sense.

["Now!"]

ZAPPPPPPPPP

He watches himself from above being marched out of the fortress toward Golgotha with a heavy crossbeam strapped across his neck. Jesus and Judas are stumbling under their burdens in front. He catches glimpses of normal life in the city, without any hope of rescue. He only wants it to end.

Pilgrims mock them. The wooden crossbeam digs into the wounds on his shoulders. The grinning hyenas that escort them are lost in reveries, no doubt thinking about their homelands or their plans for the evening. Jesus stumbles and cannot continue in spite of being ruthlessly kicked.

He breathes in burning air past parched swollen lips.

Longinus stops a pilgrim and orders him to help Jesus carry his crossbeam. They are soon walking again on the narrow cobblestone streets, out the city gates. He sees the crucifixion poles up ahead. It's near noon and the sun has joined in the torment. A crowd has gathered around. A shout goes out when they near. He realizes now that they have not come for rescue. They have come for the show. He spots the Magdalene wailing for Jesus. No one cries for him.

They're unbound from their crossbeams that soldiers take to lay on the ground. Longinus hands him a wineskin and says, "It will numb your pain." He gulps down the wine and myrrh, and wheezes, "Thanks."

Longinus nods.

"You have to help me."

Longinus raises an eyebrow.

"Get word to . . . get word to . . ." He can't think of the word or concept. "Get word to . . . *Caesar*. Tell him I'm having trouble with my heart, real trouble, and this has to stop. Has to right away . . . *okay?*"

Longinus regards him and nods understandingly. Waves over to his soldiers. Thomas looks up, with hope in his eyes. Longinus says, "Hail Caesar," while solders grab Thomas and drag him kicking to his crossbeam.

"Please," he says while they drag him along. "You don't understand. I can't go up there or I could die. I'm serious. *This has to stop.* I'm *serious.*"

He looks down from above and feels a soldier kneeling on his arm while another pounds a spike through his wrist. Fire burns up his arm and his fingers curl. They nail the other spike and it hurts worse. The crossbeam's hitched to the top of the pole. A cheer rings as *Brigand* is affixed to the top. They drive spikes through his feet.

Spikes. *Through my fucking feet.*

A small wooden plank serves as a chair and cruelly digs into his tailbone. He can hardly breathe. Pulling up on his wrists or pushing up on his feet allows a few deeper breaths, but it's too painful to keep up, a choice between increasingly painful options and diminishing returns.

The crowd cheers when Jesus's titulus is affixed—*Jesus of Nazareth, King of the Jews.*

An hour later, he's given vinegar to drink from a sponge fixed to a pole. His moans and cries are mocked by the crowd. It hurts too much to push against his spikes. It hurts too much not to. He soon won't be able to push at all.

A raven lands on his crossbeam and pecks at his wounds.

It hops over to peck at his face, but he's able to shoo it away.

He turns to Jesus and says, "This kingdom of which you speak, is it real?"

Jesus doesn't answer, just groans in pain. Another hour and he's mostly watching from above while the raven plucks at his wounds. He feels an intense tightness across his chest as he breathes quick, shallow breaths. He hears Jesus mutter, "Father, forgive them, they do not know what they are doing," which spurs Judas to taunt, "If you're the Messiah, why don't you save yourself—and us?"

Thomas calls over, "You deserve to die, but this man is innocent."

Speaking weakens him. He feels death coming. He no longer tries to fight the raven as it tears flesh from his ears.

He gives up. Quits.

A memory dump of his own floods in.

Of when he first started out as a preacher and actually believed. When he actually ministered. How he adored his wife, when they were young. How he perverted everything he once believed. How he became a wicked man, gladly serving the beast. How he enjoyed making others squirm. How he defiled himself and others. Told lies. How he lusted for power, extorted and murdered.

How he deserves to die.

He thinks of the tiny seed within him, trampled under long ago. A hardy seed that survived stony ground, stayed dormant for years and now is ready to bloom.

He has the answer. The key to his release.

With all his heart and focus, he wills himself *into* Simon's body rather than out. Fully and completely. No longer Thomas. No longer caring about saving his life but about something of far greater value. He tries to make Simon speak but is too weak to make words. He pushes again, knowing that the effort will kill him.

The words come out in spurts.

"Remember . . . me . . . when you come into . . . your kingdom," he gasps.

Jesus looks over. No longer the face of the man in the game, but the face of the man reflected in the cloth that he looked up at for so many years. The suffering God. The God of loss.

Yeshua asks, "What is it thou seek, Thomas?"

"My Lord," Thomas replies with a broken voice and a parched mouth, "I seek *salvation*."

"Then," Yeshua answers, "truly I say to you, today you shall be with me in Paradise."

Longinus swings a mallet and cracks Thomas's shins. Without being able to lift himself, he's no longer able to breathe. His chest constricts and a board shoots through his arms.

No longer in pain.

His breathing slows to shallow gasps. Gasps and he's back in the Sphere, looking out his diver's helmet at Wolfgang's uncaring raven eyes. Gasps and he's back on the cross with a raven picking at his wounds.

Gasp (sphere)

Gasp (cross)

Ga—

And he's . . .

(never more).

"Is he dead?" asks Wolfgang, after a few minutes of studying Thomas's dead eyes and listening to the flat tone of his heart monitor.

"Indubitably."

Cygnus is seated, bent over, breathing heavy and pressing his palms into his eyes. There's smoke coming out of his turntables and his mixing board is sparking.

"I have nothing left."

"What the hell happened? You were supposed to raise his hopes with the first two loops and then crush them in the third. Throw your frog face in at the end and tell him to go to hell, so that his last seconds would be pure terror, not some preacher's fantasy of salvation."

"I couldn't help it. His psyche fought back, overpowered the game. I completely lost control at the end. That was all him. He won in the end, in spite of what I threw at him."

"Well, at least he's dead," Wolfgang says, studying Thomas's limp body, before turning back to Cygnus. "I suppose I should sound the . . . Cygnus?"

Cygnus is slumped over in his chair, fast asleep. The hologram pops out and Wolfgang is alone with Thomas's body.

"You should have treated me with more respect, you should have . . ."

Wolfgang takes off his pince-nez and wipes away tears.

"You should have ..."

Thomas's silent eyes stare on.

CHAPTER 16: MATEUS AND CHOCOLATE STRAWBERRIES

There's a 1977 Mateus Rosé between them on an oak kitchen table. There's a stained glass lamp swaying slightly to the Leonard Cohen music, throwing off dimmed ultra-spectrum light. They're dipping strawberries, bananas and apple slices in an apricot-colored chocolate fondue pot and chewing on pieces of Beaufort d'été cheese.

Oliver leans back with his glass of wine, pulling on his blue cardigan and mustard-colored turtleneck. Jasmin's long nails sparkle as she soaks a strawberry into bubbling chocolate with her fondue fork. Lysandra's silver bracelets jingle as she cuts small pieces of cheese and her blue-brown eyes deepen, looking into the blue plasma flames.

"So, what happened?" Jasmin asks.

"What happened when?" Lysandra asks back, brushing a strand of her chestnut hair aside.

"With you and Mike?"

"Why . . . *did he say something?*"

"Relax, girl, he didn't have to. I saw him walking back to his room, like a kid with a popped balloon," Jasmin says, while holding one hand under a chocolate-covered strawberry and bringing it to her mouth with the other. Then moaning and chewing slowly.

"It was nothing, just the usual you're-a-dancer-must-be-a-ho type of thing," Lysandra says, then biting her lip.

Jasmin snaps her head back. "Oh no, that ain't right."

"Zero tolerance for that sort of thing," Oliver says, getting up. "Zero tolerance."

"Don't," Lysandra replies. "Like I said, I'm used to it. I'll handle it," she sighs, throwing Oliver a willful look until he sits back down.

"You sure?" Jasmin asks. "A few minutes with Dylan and he'll be singing a different tune."

"Yes," Lysandra laughs. "I can handle Mike. You don't need to sic your dog. He just does all these inconsistent things, like gathering daisies for me in the morning and calling me a ho in the afternoon."

"That's easy," Jasmin says.

"Why?"

"Someone has a bad case of *amour fou*."

"Pourquoi les garçons ne peuvent-ils pas gérer leurs émotions?" Lysandra sighs.

"Plus ça change," Jasmin replies. "Plus ça change."

Lysandra chews on her cheese, drinks her Mateus.

"And what about Andron? How was his *citrouille* this morning after last night?" Jasmin asks.

"Not too good. He'll be okay. I worry about him, though."

"Oh, he'll be all right, darling," Jasmin says, her glass of wine arcing around. "He's been through a lot, being tortured like that, spending all that time on the streets and then in prison. And then losing everyone. I think he's worried about losing you."

"He risked everything and lost everything for—" Oliver adds.

"I know. I admire him, too. It's just that my dad drank a lot . . . and then ended up killing himself, so I guess this kind of thing bothers me."

"Just because other folks had too many parties, don't mean you ain't entitled to yours, girl," Jasmin says, leaning in to splash some more Mateus into Lysandra's glass.

"Do you know for sure that he," Oliver says, softening his voice, "killed himself? I mean, did he leave a note?"

"No," Lysandra says looking down.

"Did he ever talk about killing himself?"

"No."

"Well—?"

"Those Church freaks probably did it," Jasmin adds.

Lysandra looks into Jasmin's eyes, switching from one eye to the other.

"Wasn't there a maid who said she saw two strange men on the floor that evening?" Oliver asks.

"Yeah, but I thought she couldn't say which room they came from?" Lysandra answers.

"Couldn't say or was told not to say?" Oliver answers back.

"Then there was that stuff about the blood test being faked that showed he was drunker than an uncle at a wedding," Jasmin adds.

Lysandra's chest flushes red and she stiffens. Jasmin pats her hand on her shoulder.

"So, did you read any of the *No Limits* book?" Oliver asks after a minute, chewing on a piece of cheese. "Winston says that you were interested in it."

"A few pages," Lysandra says with her jumpy smile. "I don't understand a lot of it. I guess I have to be shown things rather than reading them from a book."

Oliver laughs, "I knew Henri for over fifteen years and even I don't understand most of what he wrote."

"You must miss him."

"With every breath," Oliver's voices catches. "It would be a dream of a lifetime for him to have met you. There's parts in the book that I swear—"

"I dunno, my book's gone anyway," Lysandra says.

"What do you mean, it's gone?" Oliver asks.

"I dunno," her smile jumps. "I left it on the table on my balcony this morning, went over to talk to Andron and, when I came back, it was gone."

"That's weird," Oliver says. "I'll have Winston bring you up another and look into it."

"That's okay," Lysandra says, "I'm not sure I should read any more of it. I mean, it had all this underlining in it and it kinda made me feel uncomfortable."

There's a long silence, after which Jasmin says, "Underlining? ... *Oliver?*" noticing Oliver's sheepish look.

"Okay, I'll cop to the underlining, but I never took it," Oliver says and then looks at Jasmin. "What? I can't help it if I think she's the one he was describing."

"I told you that pushing that stuff on her would weird her out," Jasmin says.

"It's just as well. I may not know much, but I know I'm not that person in the book. So, sorry to disappoint. My parents are dead. I killed my mother by being born, my father drank himself to death. Or was pushed off a balcony because of me. And a church owns me and wants me dead, *apparently.*"

Lysandra runs her hands through her hair and rests her elbows on the table.

"I don't even know who I am. There's all these expectations on me that I can't even hope ..."

Jasmin rubs Lysandra's back and glares at Oliver. Then puts her hand around Lysandra's shoulders and pulls her near. "Girl, don't you worry about any of that. You have to be what you want to be, not what someone expects of you. Look at me," she says as she slides her hands up and down her white poufy shirt and high-waisted polyester bell-bottoms.

"I'm living proof."

Lysandra and Oliver laugh, chew on pieces of cheese absentmindedly and sip from their wine glasses.

"He used to drag me along on all these trips, you know," Oliver says finally.

Lysandra and Jasmin look over at him.

"When he was writing, I mean. His eyes would burn with this intensity, so you just knew. When he wrote *No Limits*, he insisted that we go to Wien to look at the Spear of Destiny. Or to Constantinople, to pray in the Hagia Sophia."

"The Hagia Sophia?"

"It's this huge ancient church, with a giant dome. Incredibly beautiful. The Ottomans turned it into a mosque, and now it's a museum. Hagia Sophia means 'Holy Wisdom.' That's what Henri believed in. The feminine Holy Spirit."

"Did you ever experience anything like he writes about?" Lysandra asks.

"Not really. I just followed him around like a puppy. I don't know. I don't know anything about this stuff, actually. This isn't about what colors go well together or owning the runway. I wish God would send me a sign or something. Tell me what I'm supposed to do, because I have no friggin idea."

"He already did," Lysandra says, putting her hand on Oliver's arm and looking straight into his eyes.

"He gave you Henri."

<hr/>

Later that night, Jasmin and Lysandra walk quietly to their rooms. Jasmin stops at Dylan's door, turns to Lysandra and whispers, "Don't judge me."

Lysandra smiles and runs up to give her a hug before going off to her own room.

Before closing off the lights, she scrolls through her messages on her intraweb. Deidre's video "5 Fingers" is there of her laughing about Lysandra's line earlier. She clicks on "this morning" from Andron and a text pops up.

"I hope you're feeling better. I forgot to tell you that in that room, I heard your mother call you a tiger. So, goodnight, tiger, I um ... oh, what the heck ... you probably know already :-)."

She hovers over Mike's video, "I'm sorry," then presses it and sees that it's him in a string of confessional booth outtakes trying to apologize.

"Okay, I'm trying to draw up a formula to explain why I can't stop myself from saying stupid things around you and all I got is F equals M A and I'm equally ef'n sorry. Yeesh, like that's going to—"

He spins to the camera and says, "Okay, here's the deal," trying to hold a serious face, then bursting out laughing. Cut.

"I don't know, I've gone over it and can't understand why my brain can't check my mouth, but I do. . . . I . . . fuckkkkk—"

"What I said was stupid. And wrong. And I'm sorry."

Lysandra smiles at that last one and puts her com down, then quickly picks it up and loops the videos back again, pausing to look in the background of Mike's room. She enlarges the image. There's a *No Limits* book on his credenza, but it's too blurry to tell if it's hers and there's no second book in any of the scenes.

She clicks off, sighs and looks over at the daisies. Snaps the lights off and blinks up at the darkness. Closes her eyes, then opens them again.

Closes them and her face relaxes.

A tigress asleep in the savanna.

CHAPTER 17:
ALL HAIL THE MUSTARD KING

The cadets are dressed in mustard-colored robes, with a raven insignia on their red armbands. They line the front rows of the assembly hall replica cathedral in the Pecado Hands of Prayer tower, wailing and crying with outstretched arms. Some sport pompadours. Heads of state, celebrities and major donors line the rows behind them. The Holy Books now include the *Four Pillars of Ecumenical Reform* that Thomas wrote to increase Church revenues, part of the *Gospel of Leader Thomas*. Fourth Pillar—Celebrity Endorsements.

Thomas would be pleased, Wolfgang thinks, jerkily stepping on the stage to a tsunami of raw emotion. He pauses before the hologram poster of Thomas with a giant smile and mustard spoon in his mouth. Snaps his hand to his forehead and holds the salute for a full minute while the hall thunders. Dabs his brow with his handkerchief, turns and walks to the gold and crystal rostrum with a raven insignia in front. He motions for them to sit, folds an arm, grabs his chin, studies his notes and then the crowd with unblinking eyes. Steps back from the rostrum, then back up again.

"Cadets, distinguished guests, parishioner-shareholders," he says with a shrill voice that rings off the walls over coughs and creaking pews.

"Today, we celebrate the phase-passing, the transfiguration, the glorification of our beloved Leader, chairman and friend, Thomas O'Brian. We mourn him not. We mourn him not, for we know he's merely become afterburner vapor. His loving vapor surrounds us. We *breathe* of it and partake of him."

Wolfgang breathes in deeply and so does the entire assembly.

"O Savior Vapor," he says with closed eyes, "suffer us not one second of the void without your word to guide us. You were a prince among men. You could better any pro at golf, satisfy any woman, you had more money than anyone, the smartest in any room. You were a man of impeccable taste, piety and humility.

"A man to lead us. Wonder counselor. Most reverent. Most wise.

"The King is dead.

"Long live the Mustard King!"

The hall shakes. A few cadets throw themselves on the floor and spasm with rapture.

"The Leader did not leave our cupboards bare, as unworthy as we are. He left us with his unfinished work that he's entrusted to our feeble hands. The most important projects mankind has ever devised. We must not fail him," he says, shaking a finger.

"We must not fail him because his dying wish whispered in my ear after he suffered the passion with Yeshua was that I do everything in my power to complete..." He curls his fists, looks up and shudders, "...*der Sizzle Project!*"

The hall shakes with his clenched fists.

"Balled lightning in our control. A black hole of energy through which the Logos, the Word, can reach us. A communication medium to distant worlds in the universe, blossoming into the past and into the future. Stretching even to parallel universes. In short, in actuality and, in the name of our Thomas," he says to the rapt faces, "a telephone line to God."

He brushes his hair back and paces behind the rostrum with folded arms, regarding the sea of faces and then inhaling them. He continues, stridently.

"Think of what marvels this wunderbar fireball can bring to us. Thank you," he clasps his hands to Thomas's image. "Thank you." He wipes a tear from his eye. "Thank you, my beloved friend, for honoring us with this sacred responsibility in your name. But, there's more." He waves a finger, his shrill voice rising.

"The love of the Mustard King has no bounds." More finger waving.

"He has bestowed upon us another sacred trust. A project that we have been working on in secret, but now, on this glorious day of our Leader's transfiguration, we share with the world.

"My loyal cadets.

"My friends.

"We have from the very spear that pierced Christos, the Spear of Destiny, a blood sample from Christos that we have cloned and from which will come the son of Man. Yeshua Christos reincarnated shall pick up the spear himself and lead us into communion with the Word through der *Sizzle*."

Wolfgang pauses and scans across the sea of slack jaws.

"The well of the Mustard King's love for us is deeper still. As has been widely reported, our glorious Leader died helping to develop a virtual reality game like no other. A game so real that it allows us to slip into the skin of an assassin in the time of Yeshua, a Crusader in the First Crusade, a fighter pilot in the Six-Day War.

"Ladies and gentleman, I give you the greatest entertainment experience mankind has ever devised.

"I give you . . . Jerusalem 4C, the world's first taste of Quadra Code."

The lights darken. A 3D hologram pops up showing Thomas donning his diver's helmet, watching Jesus overturning the tables at the Temple, raising the Spear and shouting *Dues vult* over and over, inverting his fighter jet, starting his bombing run and then Jesus saying to him, "Truly I say to you, today you shall be with me in Paradise." It finishes with Thomas slumped over in the sphere while Mozart's "Requiem" thunders through the hall. Cadets tear their robes.

The hologram disappears and the music stops. Thomas's coffin moves and shakes. Stunned looks are exchanged. Wolfgang looks around in alarm. Praetorians rush up to whisk him away. A cadet screams, "It's Armageddon!" Another, "He's coming awake, he's coming awake!"

Thomas's coffin shakes faster and moves out toward the audience. A curtain appears in front of it and then is torn in two. The coffin flashes kaleidoscope colors. Flashing faster and faster until the coffin pops open.

It's empty.

The lights go out. There's a lone spotlight.

A door in the coffin hisses and a platform slides out with a black cube and gaming helmet on it.

Then a sign in huge burning letters flashes.

JERUSALEM 4C

WITH QUADRA CODE ™

ON SALE NOW

CHAPTER 18:
THE CRAZY 8S AND THE
ALTAMONT—A—GO—GO

Mike pants as he jackrabbits into Lysandra. He freezes on "FUK!" collapses, kisses her cheek, rolls off and then reaches for his inhaler. "Sorry, sweetheart," he says, gasping. "It's just <puff> that you're so <puff> fucking gorgeous."

"It's okay," she says.

"I think if we did it more, I'd get better."

Lysandra rolls on her side to look at him. "More than twice a day?"

Mike stares at the ceiling while his breathing subsides, then says, "I blame the Church."

"*The Church?*"

"Were you ever a cadet?"

"No, we went to the services, but I never enlisted. Why, what was it like? Did you have to wear those robes all the time?" she teases, poking his arm.

"Not once I became an officer," Mike stiffens, then relaxes. "It was the sex they made us have."

Lysandra looks back at him with soft eyes and still lips.

"It was great at first," Mike says turning to face her. "I mean when you joined. There'd be pizza, beer, mescaline and sex for the new recruits. Whatever you wanted."

Lysandra nods slightly, looking into his blue eyes, switching from one to the other.

"Then you'd have to go over everything with your Spiritual Review Engagers right after and they'd start asking you why you did this or why you did that, because they recorded everything. Then they'd make the engagement sessions longer and you'd try to make the sex shorter, so there'd be less to talk about."

Lysandra's lips twitch, fighting a smile.

"The stuff they'd ask you about was totally weird, too. Like, what were you thinking about when you closed your eyes or why you itched your nose during oral and what made your nose itch. After a while you tried to avoid sex, so you could skip the engagement sessions altogether. If you had any, you'd try and get it over with as quickly as possible."

"I can see why you'd want to escape."

"Yeah, that and other reasons."

"Is that how you got this?" she asks, tracing her fingers over a scar on his arm.

He flexes a ropy bicep and says, "Yeah, I got it in the van, when they…" before turning on his back to look at the ceiling again.

"You don't like talking about it?"

"No," he sighs, "I don't mind."

"When they dropped the canister in?"

"Yeah."

"It almost looks like an animal scratch."

Mike turns his head to look over his shoulder at it. "No, I think I scraped it on a wire going for my puffer."

"That must have been horrible… with your friend in there?"

"There wasn't enough …" He turns to look at the clock. "Hey, we're supposed to go to that club tonight, we should get ready."

"Why, what time is it?"

"Just about eight," he says, sliding out of bed.

She watches his pizza back and chalky butt walk into the bathroom. Sighs, sits up on her elbows and looks around his room… and spots it. The *No Limits* book she saw in the videos on his credenza. She slips on a robe, looks over at the bathroom and tiptoes over while water snaps on in the bathroom.

She picks up the book and starts thumbing through it. Casually turning the pages and cocking an ear toward the bathroom.

"*What are you doing?*"

The voice makes her jump and sends shivers down her spine.

She spins to see Mike in a bathrobe staring at her unsmilingly. She puts the book down and says, "I was just going to do some reading while you showered, since mine's been missing for months."

"Missing?"

"Yeah."

"That's weird . . . Sooo, you think I took it?"

"No. It's just that mine had some weird underlining in it and I was wondering if yours did, too."

"So, why don't you look?"

"No, it's okay it—"

"No, if you need to look, you should look," he says as he walks over and picks up the book. "Where was the underlining?" She looks over his shoulder as he flips through it from beginning to end.

"Happy?"

"Yes."

He puts his hands on her shoulders. "Look, Lysandra, I know that you've been through a lot, but you're just going to have to get used the fact that I love you and would never hurt you."

"I know," she says, kissing him.

"Now come on, the shower's ready," he says, taking her hand.

On the way, she glances at something by his bar that might be a book but looks away and follows him instead.

Andron strikes the throwback matchstick. The sulfur stings his nostrils. The fizzing reminds him of a fuse he lit a long time ago. A fuse that ended his life as he knew it. He draws the flame and watches it singe the fluorescent green leaves.

Whips the matchstick around to put it out before it burns his fingertips, then stokes the embers with quick puffs.

All the wonders of the world cannot match that sweet smoke, he thinks. Or the visceral pleasure of a printed book. Especially a book as fine as his frayed copy of *No Limits*. He's sitting on his bed with his ankles crossed. A heavy cloud of smoke envelops him. He reads a passage:

> The backstabbers came in like locusts and harassed us for a year. O children of the light. O children, guard the light. Avoid their sharpened knifes. Avoid the shadows where they breed. Endure. Endure. Know that this plague will pass. That the blood from our backs will flower our gardens. Themselves will devour and in their passing, a new kingdom ...a queendom, begun.

He stares at his open hand, wiggling his fingers, and wonders if his life is real.

If he is, right now, trapped in a virtual reality game. Or if the game in which he is trapped is also of his own making. Year after year. Was he sane? Did grief cause this? Was Earth real and Terra a game? And what of our ends? Are they burned in chambers and forgotten as smoke? Is this our life? Is this our doing?

Deidre bursts into his room, all freckle-faced and smiling like a cricket.

"Yeshua Christos, Andron, are you getting high in your room again?"

He squints at her. Inhales deeply and disappears behind another puff of smoke. With a squeaky voice, he says, "I was just getting caught up on my reading."

"Well, we're leaving right away. So, time to vamoose, goose."

The itinerary on his nightstand has them celebrating the last day of their training with a night on the town. They've been at it for months, training, drilling and planning. Now they're chording like a Nashville guitar. The hour is upon them. Their time come. With Thomas's fascist successor, there is none to waste.

"I dunno, I thought I might sit this one out, old as I am."

"Dylan's going. And he's an old boot, just like you."

"That's because Jasmin's been," he rests his book on his chest, lowers his chin and looks over his reading glasses and says, "...fueling him."

"Ha-ha, you stone-aged stoner . . . come on," she says, running up to pull on his hand like a granddaughter. "We're supposed to be pretending to be our characters . . . It'll be fun . . . we're going to the Altamont-a-Go-Go."

Deidre's right, he thinks. They should practice their high wire act a few times before going without nets. It's been drilled into them that their raid's going to be done with safeties off. People are going to die, including a few of their own.

"Leave now if you ain't got the stones," Jasmin said.

Andron allows himself to be dragged along.

They're in the rapid transfer van. A '75 Ford E-series shaggin' wagon doing a hundred and twenty miles per hour. Oliver had eight-ball murals painted on the sides because that's what he's calling their gang: the Crazy 8s. Riffraff mercenaries, social flotsam, cons and cowboys. Eight renegades taking the fight to the jackboot Church's lair, defended by its legion of praetorians.

He wonders if they're ready. If they stand a chance. But Mike's right. They don't have a choice. If they don't fight, they'll likely be barbequed in a drone strike. If they do fight, well, maybe they might live. Maybe.

A delayed wave of THC hits, and he's thinking about playing high school football again. He was a third-stringer, who never got on the field, except in warmups. He couldn't understand why he stuck it out. The practices were mostly jumping jacks, stretches and sit-ups, in smelly hand-me-down equipment and grass-stained uniforms. It wasn't for the jacket, either. He never wore it. It wasn't to be part of a team. He had enough friends. It was for . . . he doesn't know.

He thinks about altered states and whether he created this one to make up for being shitty at sports except for a couple of glory years in hockey. An altered reality where he's somehow a first-stringer on a rebel combat team. But he has no illusions in this illusion. If this is one. His value rested on his knowledge of the monster. He knew its twisted ways, its punky inclinations. Maybe he's Dr. Frankenstein, who's joined the villagers to kill his own creation.

Maybe he should ease up on the pot.

At least he isn't drinking. Back when he was in virtual Berlin, Dr. Schweisser diagnosed him as an addict chameleon, who threw off old addictions for new ones. Maybe he just happens to like altered states. Maybe he catches glimpses of how things really are when he's completely zonked.

He's decided to go with Frank Manz again, for his false identity. It worked like a charm last time. Wonders if he's got other false identities. Identities that are so deep, he's not even aware of them. Is this really him? Is this his group? He looks around at the other Crazy 8s.

"You guys mind if I light one up?"

They grab a table near the stage. Dishwater flavored coffee sits in front of him. A Rolling Stones tribute band plays "Honky Tonk Woman." Mick Jagger's surrogate is convulsing and preening. The Keith Richards guy is leaning back, ripping out bluesy riffs on his Fender with a cigarette dangling out of his mouth. The Charlie Watts fellow purses his lips while rolling around the drums, before tapping on the high-hat and snare. Mick Taylor's guy's fretting hard, the world on his strings. Out to prove he's as good as the man he's replacing, and that that guy was better than the guy he replaced (Jones) and the guy who replaced him (Wood). Bouncers in leather vests with *Hells Angels* patches on the back are parked around the stage. They're drinking beer and brandishing sawed-off pool cues.

Legend has it that the real band liked to do gigs here, a long time ago. So, when the tribute band plays, it's kind of a big deal. Andron thinks that he has a soundboard imbedded his brain that allows him to key in on individual sounds. Follow them to their origins. Jagger guy's voice a cappella. Keith's unamplified guitar strings. Distortions, imperfections. These are the bumps along the wall he used to run his fingers over in his prison cell. Distortions, imperfections, pimples on your face. That's what makes things real. That's how Andron was able to settle the question about whether he's in a real world. These subtle imperfections can't be found in Cygnus's worlds. Worlds without true beauty.

Cygnus.

He'll soon be meeting the *dude* again. Fittingly, "Sympathy for the Devil" is playing. Andron peers down into his black coffee and reckons he doesn't have any. "They don't make music like they used to," he shouts over to Jasmin, who nods and sways. Even Dylan doesn't seem to mind, taking swigs from his longneck. Mike's hovering around Lysandra like a smitten moth. Oliver and Winston are head-bobbing to the music. Deidre is next to him, tapping her feet. When fake Mick and the boys saunter off the stage for a break, he decides he might as well have one, too.

The retro bathroom is a nice touch. But he's pretty sure there weren't ads for STD spray-ons while using an urinal back then. Nor was urine recycled and reused for subsequent flushes— a beer perpetual motion machine. Zipping up, he walks over to counter and sticks his hands in the All-Clean, another modern invention. Looks up into his eyes and feels dizzy. Club chatter pulsates like a slow-motion chopper blade over the drone of the electric lights.

On the way back to his table, he decides to pick up some more joe. So, he squeezes up to the bar to order a cup. He smells strawberry shampoo before he sees her. Like she just stepped out of a shower. Curly hair, cougar-aged, but a mere kitten to him. Notices that she's drinking coffee. Licks his lips.

"Either you're a cop or you're a pathetic drunk like me."

Her eyes flash over him. "I guess I'm a pathetic drunk, then," she says, ". . . like you."

"One of whatever she's having. And bring her another while you're at it," he calls over to the bartender, holding up his wrist-pay.

"Coming right up, chief," says the bearded female bartender.

"Oooh, big spender. Thank you."

"No problem . . . it's the least I can do for a fellow degenerate, before they engineer us out of the gene pool."

Their coffees arrive and they clink mugs.

"Name's Frank, beer sales rep," he says, extending a hand.

"Patty, and I'm with the band." She lightly squeezes his.

"The Stones?"

"Uh-huh."

"So, which one's yours?"

She smiles. "All of them . . . I manage them."

"Ahh, you manage their groupies, too?"

"Nope," she laughs. "They're in charge of cleaning up after their own messes."

"Well, that hardly seems fair?"

She shakes her hair and looks at him.

"That they get groupies and you don't."

She smiles. "So, beer rep, did you get too high on your own supp—"

A man in a green suit, black shirt and loosened tie barges in between them. He puts his arm around Patty and sticks his tongue down her throat. Andron keeps on grinning and leans back. When you can't bluff, check or bet, take the kick to the balls and fold. He nods to the man, reaches for his coffee and plans to fold.

"Honey, this is Frank. Frank, this is Murdock."

"Frank?" Murdock wobbles, does a double take. "That ain't no Frank. That's Andron Varga."

"Um, nope. I'm Frank."

"Ah, okay, I get it . . . shhh," he says, blowing on his finger off-center. "I know you, 'cause I played you in a movie."

"Movie? What movie?" Patty says, leaning forward between them.

Murdock sways around glowering at Andron and says, "Private production, can't talk about it. But I basically had to deliver a one-liner. It was more like a commercial. What was it? Oh, yeah," he steps back, swishing his drink over its sides.

"I'm asking you and this empty room, surely, there must be someone somewhere to love me."

He stumbles forward, smiles.

Andron feels like he just got caught masturbating in a confessional booth. He reaches for his coffee, with fingers that feel like they have toilet paper stuck on them.

"Like I said, you've got the wrong guy."

"Nope, don't think so, bud." Murdoch rolls up his sleeve, stumbles forward and tries to tap his wristwatch holo up proof.

"Heyyyy, what's the big idea, leaving me out?" Deidre bursts in, bumping into Murdock.

"Nichole!" Deidre and Andron high five.

"Um, this is Patty and Murdock," Andron says.

"I'm Murdock and that's Patty. You might be Nichole," he says, gawking at her forehead, "but that sure in the fuck ain't Frank." Murdock sways and lifts his watch again.

"Oh my God, you've been lying about your name all these years, Frank? How could you?" Deidre giggles.

The band comes back on the stage and the place starts jumping. Deidre shouts, "Come on, let's go dancing." She grabs Patty by the hand and Murdoch by the sleeve and tugs them out to the dance floor with Andron following. The band reopens with "Under My Thumb" and the four of them dance. Which, for Murdoch, means stumbling forward and back with his arms bent while Deidre bumps into him, spins, shakes her hips and puts her arms in the air. He stops to look at his watch again, then rubs his shoulder. His eyes roll as he falls forward, clutching his chest and slams into Andron, who goes sprawling into a frizzy blonde in tight leather pants and a bikini top.

She gets up holding her leg. "*Watch where the fuck you're dancing, asshole.*"

"Sorry, I was pushed."

"I don't give a fuck," she snaps back.

"I don't know what you're smokin', old man, but that's my girl." A tall angel wearing a raccoon hat shuffles up to him, wonky and menacing, like an ataxic mountain man.

"He said he was sorry," Deidre says.

"*I wasn't talking to you, bitch!*" the biker chick shrieks, lunging for Deidre while one of her gang yanks Deidre sideways by the hair. Andron steps toward them, but there's a crack in the back of his head, and the next moment he's on the floor being thumped by sawed-off pool cues and stomped on by biker boots.

He turtles and blocks his ears. A bottle crashes behind him and one of the bikers tumbles forward, cross-eyed. He catches a silver-toothed grin, a flash of fist and another biker is launched back, Fosbury-flop style.

Dylan's in the fight.

Andron jumps back up to his feet and arm-blocks a swinging pool cue from Raccoon Hat.

He flashes back to his training.

Deidre told him there was no point in learning anything new cause he'd just revert to hockey once he got punched in the face. So, he spent hours upon hours doing knuckle pushups, inverted palmers and punching the Makiwara board until his fists were corded wood and his wrists rebar.

The cue swings for him again, but this time he blocks it with his forearm and yanks the raccoon hat over the biker's eyes, grabs him by the scruff of his jersey and tilt-a-whirls Tie Domi bombers into his face, welcoming him to the faceoff circle.

He side-glances at the other Crazy 8s.

A red-faced Dylan breaks out of a chokehold by breaking a fat, hairy arm. Winston's piston-punching another biker who he's got by his tattooed throat and Oliver's blond hair is swooping over his face while his platform shoes are tap dancing on noses, knees and cheekbones.

And there's Lysandra, Deidre and Jasmin, standing with their arms crossed looking bored while biker chicks with bloody noses and swollen faces carry each other off the dance floor. Deidre catches Andron's eye, yawns and looks at her watch. He lets go of Raccoon Hat and the biker crumples to the floor.

Meanwhile, Mick Jagger's surrogate is pleading with the audience to, "cool out . . . everyone just cool out."

Patty screams, "*Someone please help, I can't feel his heart*," as Murdock's mouth foams. A shot rings out and panicked human cattle moo for the exits. Deidre grabs Andron and pulls him toward the door with the fleeing cattle. Out in the parking lot, they all dive into the shaggin' wagon that's firing up its turbine-electric engine.

"Wait, where's Mike?" Lysandra shouts as they're about to slide the door.

They catch him sprinting for the van, arms bent and hands pumping. Oliver yells, "We gotta go!" and the van starts to roll away. Dylan and Winston grab Mike's arms and pull him in just as the van doors slide shut. The van goes into the rapid lane, whirling up to a hundred and twenty miles per hour. Mike takes a puff, then reaches into his jacket and waves an eight-track around.

"I hacked into their security and got all the tapes."

They all applaud.

"Okay, everyone, group photo," Oliver says, setting up his cam and starting its projected thirty-second countdown.

"What do you want to take our pictures for?" the girls protest, trying to fix themselves up.

"An idea for a new mural," Oliver replies as the timer counts to zero and they huddle together. It flashes and they're all mangled faces, rapper poses and smiles.

Yeah, Andron thinks, rubbing his fingers over the rapidly growing welt on the side of his face.

They're ready.

CHAPTER 19:
DER SIZZLE

"**B**ring them to me."

Wolfgang is in his Pecado office with a giant raven insignia behind him. A door opens and three bound cadets are frogmarched in by guards dressed as Roman praetorians with red plumes. The girl is crying and shaking. The boys have ashen faces, their eyes riveted straight ahead.

"Can I ask you three a question?" Wolfgang starts off. The cadets look down.

"Was there something about the service honoring our beloved leader that you found ... *Ich weiß es nicht* ... boring?"

The three cadets shake their heads.

"Did it fail to meet your standards for amusement?"

They shake their hands again.

"Something lacking, perhaps!?" he shouts and spits.

"No, Über Raven, we all loved it," the girl answers, fearfully.

"Then," he says as he pushes a button showing footage of the three of them at the monthly mustard service with less over-the-top enthusiasm than their fellow cadets, "why do you look so bored?"

The three cadets look down.

"Do you know what *Senfgeist* means?" he asks them.

They shake their heads.

"No?"

They continue staring at the ground.

"It means Mustard Spirit," he says. "Now get these three *arsch*-violins out of my sight and throw them in the Basement, where hopefully they'll learn to show a little more *Senfgeist!*"

They march the cadets past Wolfgang's personal assistant, Dr. Franz Oppenberg, a tall man in shorts, lederhosen, suspenders and a green hat, who is waiting at the door.

"Mein Über Raven?"

"Yes, Franz, come in, sit down."

"I had the orders prepared, mein Über Raven," Franz says, presenting the executive order in a leather folder to Wolfgang.

"Ah zo," says Wolfgang, reading over the order revising the Code of Conduct to abolish review engagements for sexual activity, while at the same time abolishing sexual and psychedelic exploration altogether, except for those aspirants who have achieved the uppermost levels or paid their way in. He looks at Franz and signs the air. Franz responds by handing him a Mont Blanc. Wolfgang signs the order with a flourish and then holds the folder up for the cameras before waving them away.

"Now, how is the Minotaur Project coming along?" Wolfgang asks.

"Super fantastic, mein Über Raven. We found the perfect cadet volunteer. Nearly two meters tall with," he leans in to whisper, "*ein großer Schwanz.*"

Both men snicker.

"And with the LSD-2, the connection is wunderschön."

"Wunderbar, Franz. Wunderbar. Herr Cygnus will be pleased. Now . . . what's next?"

"Mein Über Raven, you're giving President Sparzo a tour of the facility and then there's the communication experiment with der Sizzle."

"Ah yes," Wolfgang says getting up. "Let's go meet our Nützlicher Idiot."

Wolfgang whirl-steps down the hallway of Bastille's B-wing with its lacquered floors, walls and exposed HVAC pipes, with his arms behind his back and his chin poked forward. White-robed cadets line the halls. Wolfgang does not look at them. President Sparzo smiles and nods, rubbing his arthritic hand.

Wolfgang slides open doors to the brightly lit Plenary Nursery, guarded by the Church's elite Praetorians. The nursery is mostly stainless steel, with twelve clear plastic incubator cribs and twelve preemie babies in them. Twelve frowny-faced, genetically engineered babies fidget around, still smarting from the fresh beatings they took exiting their surrogate mothers.

Nurses in white duty uniforms patrol the rows, like amateur actors on a stage for the benefit of the president. A demonstration of neonatal fascist efficiency. They check the diaper drains and tweak the feeding tubes with furrowed brows. Carpeted robotic arms comfort any crying babies, of which there are few.

"So, this room is the Plenary Nursery. The plumbing alone cost a fortune. The refresh rate on the HVAC takes milliseconds and the temperature system—"

"So, these are all baby Yeshuas?"

"All twelve of them. So, as I was saying, the temperature can be perfectly maintained at a fraction of a degree. A fraction," Wolfgang says pressing his thumb and forefinger together.

"Twelve? As in twelve disciples?"

"Nope, only one will make it. The climate is ideal for early human incubating."

"What happens to the others?"

"We will pick the best one to lead the Church. Any unused genetic material will be incinerated to prevent accidental environmental release."

"Incinerated?"

"After being humanely given a needle, of course," Wolfgang says. "We are not monsters around here." He snickers.

"How do you decide between them?"

"We figure by age two, the right one should have risen to the top. Meanwhile, we can spot a few for early elimination. Weaklings and so forth."

"Ah."

"We are aiming to cultivate only the strongest Yeshua strains here," Wolfgang says, looking up at Sparzo with his pince-nez.

"I see," Sparzo nods, as they walk between the incubation chambers. They stop at the last one. He looks into the crib and asks about Specimen 12, who seems a bit darker-skinned than the rest. *"Hi there, little fellah,"* he says, as he reaches in to tickle Specimen 12's chest.

"Please, Mr. President, we discourage such interactions . . . Anyway, that one is slated for early elimination."

"Sorry," Sparzo says, pulling back his hand, "I guess attachments would be an unfortunate thing in this line of work."

"Indeed."

"So, what happens once you pick the winner?"

"We will pair him with two of our elite cadet corps, those with the highest accumulated game scores."

"Do you have them picked out already?"

"We have."

"Is it possible to meet them?"

"They are on a mission right now."

"Ah," Sparzo says, as they walk toward the door. "That's funny."

Wolfgang looks over at Sparzo with his pince-nez.

"My arthritis seems a lot better."

"Ah, no doubt due to the hyperbaric chamber, Herr President," Wolfgang says pointing up at the overhead pipes. "The installation costs for those were through the roof. We went through three contractors installing them. Three!"

Wolfgang and Sparzo stand with several others in front of a concrete-encased sapphire glass viewing window, looking into a large chamber. A hologram video with a bright orange fiery ball dances beside them. They are wearing welder helmets, radiation jumpsuits and mittens. Wolfgang's jumpsuit has a red Über Raven patch. Sparzo's says *Visitor*.

"So, is that the Sizzle?" Sparzo asks through his com, while pointing a mitt at the hologram display.

"Not exactly. That's an outer shield that formed around it that we don't quite understand."

"So, the Sizzle is inside?"

"Ja."

"What does it look like?"

"Like nothing. It's so dense that light cannot escape from it. It's also very tiny, atomic, yet weighs more than a cruise ship."

"Wow, so how did you make it?"

"With a lot of light. A lot. Have you heard about Einstein's equation: E equals M C squared?"

"Uh-huh."

"Well, it's a two-way street."

"Meaning?"

"Meaning, where a tiny amount of mass can produce a huge amount of energy, like an atomic bomb, a huge amount of energy, such as light, can make a tiny amount of mass."

"Ah, and thus the rolling power outages."

"Yes, the Church is forever in your debt, Herr President."

"So, the Sizzle is inside the fireball?"

"Yes, the temperatures within are many times hotter than the sun's core, but outside, it is strangely cool. We don't quite understand."

"So, are you still feeding it electricity?"

"Not anymore. It will bleed Hawking radiation but will last about four years before completely breaking down."

"That sounds rather dangerous. How do you contain it?"

"Not to worry, Herr President, it's radiation shielded and held in place by powerful electromagnets."

"So, what are we doing today?"

"We're going to fire a digital signal into it and see what comes out the other side."

"A digital signal of what?"

"We thought we'd start with the Beatles."

"Which song?"

"Across the Universe."

———————◆◆◆◆———————

Sparzo's behind a panelboard with his hand on a lever with a ceremonial bow tied to it. He looks back at Wolfgang, nods to him and throws the switch. A sweeping analog watch pops up, that spins in tenth-of-a-second sweeps.

Ten ... nine ... eight ...

The transmitter initializes and the room shakes.

seven ... six ... five ...

The transmitter starts to glow red.

five ... four ... three ...

The phonograph recording crackles and George Harrison's opening riff begins.

two ... one ...

There's a flash.

The song plays out and then nothing.

Sparzo turns to shrug his shoulders at Wolfgang, then steps back in alarm. The Sizzle starts to grow then flashes a bright white light that fractures the sapphire observation window. The hologram display snaps off. The lights flicker. Praetorians rush in to form a circle around Sparzo and Wolfgang with their crossbows drawn. Sparzo is handed over to Secret Service agents who whisk him away in a helicopter. They carry Wolfgang to the Bunker. Bright blue alarm lights flash and an ear-piercing alarm pulses out beeps.

———————◆◆◆◆———————

In the Bunker, Wolfgang sits on his beanbag swivel chair wringing his hands. Research cadets in white robes pore over their portable computers. A lady cadet brings in an espresso, which Wolfgang sips. A hologram Cygnus scratches his sideburns and cracks his neck looking over several virtual readouts.

"Can anyone tell me what in the hell just happened?" Wolfgang asks, putting his espresso down and adjusting his pince-nez.

"Mein Über Raven, everything is fine. Der Sizzle has shrunk back down in size. When it flashed, it sent out a signal that we're still analyzing," Franz says, looking over a tablet computer.

"What kind of signal?"

"Sir?"

"What kind of signal?"

Franz hesitates. "An amplitude modulated radio carrier wave, sir."

"A what?"

"AM radio signal, sir."

"An AM radio?"

"Yes, sir."

"From where?"

"We don't know. It's a human, though, and in English."

"Is it one of our own?"

"Doubtful, since it came from within the Sizzle."

"So, the Sizzle sent us an AM radio signal of someone talking and we don't know where from?"

"Not at this point."

"Any ideas, Cygnus?"

"Yes and no," Cygnus says, squinting over a few readouts.

"Care to explain?"

Cygnus looks up and swipes away the display screens in front of him. "It could have been from my planet, but there is no way of knowing. I don't have a databank of every radio broadcast. But it does sound like it was from our Texas."

"I wish to hear it." Wolfgang says.

"Of course, guv, here it is," Cygnus says, starting a countdown on his fingers. Cygnus has created a radio studio room in his hologram display. When his countdown ends, an *On Air* light snaps on.

There is only radio crackle at first, and then a solitary voice:

… two avengers …

… ahem …

Two avengers prayed for deliverance.

They were on a boat, on an ocean, sinking in a storm.

One spoke.

"For it is written, 'Ye may be the children of your Father which is in heaven: for he maketh his sun to rise on the evil and on the good, and sendeth rain on the just and on the unjust.'

"Lord," the first avenger's drowning voice pleaded. "I thought that my good deeds might have purchased me a little rain insurance here?"

The other avenger did not speak.

He had gray whiskers and a jiggly jowl.

He could not ache, he just looked up into the rain.

Both men drowned and from their bones I made you.

O

I

am

the

dirty

traveler

communicating

disestablishmentarian

supercalifragilisticexpialidocious

fafafafafafafafafafafafafafafafafafafafafafafeeling

. . .

Wolfgang listens to the end of the crackle. His breathing is shallow with annoyance at the disconcerting sounds around him. He wishes to hear the message again, alone, with no interruptions. He folds his arms and unfolds them. Scowls at everyone, until they look down.

"Ten billion dollars," he shakes his head and raises his voice, "TEN BILLION . . . and for *this*?"

"Can someone please tell me . . . *what . . . in the fuck* . . . was that supposed to mean?"

"It could be a koan," Cygnus offers.

"Was ist ein koan?"

"A koan is a paradox or riddle used by Zen Buddhists to provoke enlightenment by forcing out logic."

"What sound does one hand make clapping together? That type of thing?"

"Exactly—"

"There may be other explanations," Franz says.

"Such as?"

"It may be a code, a riddle or mathematical formula."

"Any idea?"

"Not yet, sir. But that last bit was actually a Fibonacci sequence, if you count the letters in the words."

"Meaning?

"We don't know yet, Herr Raven."

"Fine," Wolfgang says, getting up to leave. "Let's go with the koan idea for now. We'll let our enlightenment seekers hear it . . . only after they've sunk millions with us for spiritual development."

Wolfgang smiles at his idea as he leaves the room. The alarms are off and cadets are trickling back to their stations.

"Herr Über Raven," Franz says, catching up to him.

"Yes?"

"During the alarm, we received a report that the actor, Murdoch Hunter, died of a heart attack at a nightclub in Kanada."

"So?"

"So, he was an actor in the Cygnus Virus project."

"Ah . . . are they suspecting foul play?"

"No."

"Did he leave anyone?"

"A wife, sir, Patty Brantson."

"Do you think he talked to her about anything?"

"We don't know, sir."

"Hmm, send her flowers and a card with our condolences."

"Yes, sir."

Wolfgang stops to adjust his pince-nez.

"And then have her killed."

"*Killed*?"

"Yes. Make it look like a suicide."

Franz nods.

"We can't have any leaks here, Franz. We're running a tight ship."

THE TOWER.

CHAPTER 20:
THE TOWER CARD

The officers tap off their neuro implants as CAM-DI looks up at them with her azure eyes. Waits for their attention, then deals out a virtual tarot card that lands upright and slowly turns on a corner axis. On one side is the Tower, on the other, Judgment.

"Just two more to unpack," she explains. "The Tower's crown being blown off by a lightning bolt can mean what it suggests—upheaval, destruction and sudden change. It can also be a liberating jolt of inspiration that topples doctrines built on false ideas, freeing the mind. Judgment is the final outcome here."

"So, what happens?" Commander Penny asks.

"Only one way to find out," CAM-DI replies, flashing a glossy smile as she twirls her finger above the card, making it spin faster and faster until it's a blur.

They tap their implants on again.

CHAPTER 21:
THE CHARGE OF THE CRAZY 8S

There's a desert.

There's a blacktop highway cutting through it.

There's a frescoed school bus shifting gears, with a cartoon photo of eight warriors and a bolt of lightning blowing the top off a tower.

The anti-drone falcon, Festus the Just, circles above.

It spies its prey, swoops down and sinks its talons into it. Seconds later, the predator drone's higher brain functions are scrambled. A screen snaps to snow at the Predator Command Center. The display on Jasmin's laptop blinks from red to green.

"Signal acquired," she says.

Mike flips a hand up from the steering wheel and signals, *five minutes*.

Graphene shields slam over the windows. Andron taps his six-T shooter RG, tells it to arm, as do the others. Helmets go on. They're all wearing combat fatigues and matching *No Limits* shirts beneath their flak jackets. He double-puffs and exhales.

Double-puffs and exhales.

The bus twists around a corner, redlining in low gear. At Checkpoint Charlie, a praetorian guard steps out, laughing. Jasmin flicks a toggle and a hellfire zips off the predator. Five seconds later, it slams into the guard tower, shattering it into chunks of rebar, concrete and embers. The bus crunches over debris and crashes through the gate. A rooftop SAM and machine-gun nest starts firing. The predator's second hellfire fireballs into it, turning it into rubble. Festus the Just releases its grip and the drone loops down peacefully then slams into the doors of the Bastille's front entrance.

The bus takes a hard left, teeters, creaks, then tips over, crashing on its side, skidding to a stop in a cloud of dust and crunching gravel.

Silence settles as the wind carries the dust cloud away from the overturned bus.

Seconds later, there's a loud hydraulic whirl as a ramp lowers from the bus's undercarriage and *thumps* to the ground. A graphene shield wings out to the side in loud *clanks*, creating a trench wall. The Crazy 8s spill out and deploy behind it. Deidre sets up a cover-fire position with her Winchester. Mike stays in the bus in a swivel chair, with its fifty-one-millimeter RG pointed out of a bubble turret popped out on the top, aimed at the Bastille. He swivels around, looking for targets. Swivels around.

An alarm sounds, red lights flash and two pillboxes pop out in front of them like giant lawn sprinklers, spraying bullets. Mike pulls on the trigger and his RG *fizz-zurls* red-hot lead. The pillboxes hammer the bus. There's a crack in the bubble glass and an explosion that Mike narrowly misses by diving out. Bullets crack above their heads and slam into the shelter wall in jackhammer bursts. Deidre fires back, joined by Mike. The other 8s cower behind the shelter wall, with their guns drawn, panicked eyes and frozen limbs. Andron's heart thumps and rolls like an eighties drum solo. He can't swallow. He feels sick, his mouth full of sand.

"We've got no grenade launchers," Jasmin's voice screeches over the com, "and none of us is going to be able to get close enough to throw one into one of those pillboxes before getting cut down. It's too hot, honeys. I'm calling for extract." She presses her com again. "Charlie-Romeo-Alpha-Zulu-Yankee, this—Whatthafuk?" she screams.

Andron looks back and sees that Lysandra is no longer at his side. He looks through his periscope and blinks. She's in no-man's-land, zigzagging with cheetah speed toward a pillbox, spraying her Uzi RG and juking bullets.

Like nobody's business. Like nothing he's seen.

She whips out a grenade from her vest, pulls the pin with her teeth and hurls it at the pillbox, a ninety-mile-per-hour fastball. It flies through a narrow slit, flashes, and then there's nothing but smoke billowing out. It cripples the pillbox next to it, too, so that it's aimed in the wrong direction. Praetorians anthill out and take up firing positions.

"*Ah, fuck it, we're going over,*" Jasmin shrieks, dashing out from behind the bus. "*Come on, motherfuckers, let's go,*" she screams, fixing them with her wild eyes, pumping her RG with one hand before climbing over the wall, Dylan right behind her.

An adrenaline dump thaws Andron's feet and he climbs over, running with Oliver and Winston. Mike and Deidre blast their RGs in rapid-fire *fizz-zurl fizz-zurl fiz-zurls*. Andron shrieks as he runs toward the guard positions, spraying bullets without aiming. In the corner of his eye, he catches Dylan go down, clutching his chest. Jasmin grabs Dylan with one arm and takes aim with the other. One guard drops, then two, then three, as she picks them off one by one with her deadeye aim.

Lysandra's first to the other pillbox. Guards soon have their arms in the air. Andron, Oliver and Winston roll up right after. They aim their guns at the wincing faces, while Winston and Oliver ziptie them. Another guard bleeds over a machine gun, then slides off in a wet hump. Andron turns to see Dylan's cowboy boots pointing skyward with Jasmin kneeling beside him, compressing his chest. Mike and Deidre scan the horizon with their RGs. The rest have their guns drawn, backs against the building. Andron tries to run toward Dylan, but Winston grabs his flak jacket and yanks him back.

"We have to keep moving or we won't be able to help anyone, you hear me, motherfucker?"

Andron tries to run again, but Winston yanks him back and then pushes him forward.

They creep along the wall toward the entrance, using a camera to periscope around corners. They fan out behind the burning hull of the drone, directed by Oliver's hand signals. Winston runs up to the entrance, slaps a plasticine charge on it, then ducks for cover as the blast blows the doors open with a metallic *thunk*.

Winston and Oliver advance, with Andron and Lysandra taking up rear cover positions. Winston and Oliver spin through the doors, guns pointed. Seconds pass, then Winston blips *clear* over the com, and Lysandra and Andron rush in.

Winston and Oliver are positioned behind a marble desk in the grand hall with its black granite floor. There are over a hundred Church cadets in white robes with raven insignias, kneeling with their hands behind their heads. A door swings open and Wolfgang enters, flanked by Moses and Franz. Wolfgang has his hands in the air, whirl-walking toward them. "Please, no more bloodshed," he pleads, his boots ringing off the granite. Winston runs up to grab him, pressing his gun against his chest. Wolfgang says, "We're pacifists. Can you please tell me what is the meaning of your raid?"

Wolfgang looks around for an answer.

Winston frisks him for weapons and then taps his com. "*The Bastille has fallen . . . repeat . . . the Bastille has fallen.*"

"*Roger that,*" Mike says, tapping his com and nodding over to Deidre.

They sling their Winchesters over their shoulders and lazily walk out from behind the wall toward Jasmin and Dylan. Jasmin is pressing a bloodied bandage over Dylan's chest. She's taken off her flak jacket and has put it under his head. Jasmin spots Mike and Deidre. "We have to get him out of here!" she shouts, looking up at them and back. Dylan's burbling blood out of his mouth, while Jasmin presses down.

"I need to get back on my feet," he coughs.

"Oh, honey, you have to stay down—What are you two standing around for? . . . Get help!" Her frantic eyes look up.

Mike and Deidre look around and nod to each other. Deidre drops her Winchester and casually points it at Dylan's chest. Jasmin slaps the gun aside and shouts, "What the fuck are you doing?" but Deidre slowly brings it around again and aims it at Dylan. Jasmin's eyes flash with horror and realization as she desperately tries to throw herself over Dylan to shield him, while Mike aims and blasts a smoldering hole in her back. She slumps over, covering Dylan with her limp body, wheezing, "I *lovvvvv . . .*" in his ear with her last breath.

Mike kicks Jasmin's lifeless body aside, uncovering a shallow-breathing Dylan, who tries to raise his gun with a shaky hand and fire it, but Mike fires a round into his chest. Dylan tries to raise his gun and shoot a second time, mouthing, "Why?" This time Mike aims at Dylan's head. There's a *fizz-zurl*, then blood splatter and spaghetti on the barren ground.

"Because," Mike says to Dylan's caved-in face and shocked eyes, "I fuckin' hate cowboys."

Deidre and Mike sling their Winchesters over their shoulders and head toward the entrance.

"What took you so long?" Andron shouts, looking at them up and down as they walk up. "Where's Jasmin and Dylan?"

Deidre and Mike snap their RGs off their shoulders. Deidre points hers at Andron and says, "They're dead. You will be, too, if you don't shut up." Andron blinks, unable to comprehend the horrifying turn.

"Deidre?" he says weakly as she avoids his eyes.

"I said, shut up."

Lysandra slings her Uzi down, points it at Wolfgang and squeezes the trigger, but it doesn't do anything but make a series of electric *clicks*. Winston tries firing his and it doesn't work, either.

"I'm afraid your railguns won't work in this," Wolfgang says, waving his arms around, "house of God," and laughs.

Winston tries slapping his RG on the side, but it still doesn't fire. He throws it on the ground and reaches for his knife. A shot rings out and Winston falls backward. Eyes turn to Moses, his long-barreled forty-five with smoke coming out of it and his long brown jacket flowing in the AC.

"Moses prefers the Old Testament when it comes to bibles and guns," Wolfgang says. "Anyone else care to test the waters of Babylon? . . . Anyone?"

Oliver drops his gun and runs over to Winston while praetorian guards run up and jab spear guns in Andron and Lysandra's backs. Oliver gets to Winston and cradles him in his arms. Winston looks up, has a few shallow breaths, forces a weak smile and then goes still.

"Um ... *Überraschung!*" Wolfgang howls. He looks around at the confused faces and then snorts, "*Surrr*-PRIZE!"

CHAPTER 22: THE MONSTER

Andron, Oliver and Lysandra are tied to chairs in the sphere room in their combat pants and *No Limits* shirts. Wolfgang's sitting on a golden throne, the Spear of Destiny resting in his lap, wearing brown baggy pants tucked into black polished riding boots and a brown topcoat with a bloodred raven armband. His dark hair is buzzed short on the sides, long on top and parted to the side. His eyes glower like black pearls. Cygnus stands nearby in a hologram beam. He's added a black bowler hat, an athletic protector, fake eyelashes and a walking stick to his thicket of chops. Deidre and Mike are seated on either side of Wolfgang, wearing red robes and pointy hats, like open-faced Klansman wizards. Franz stands beside Wolfgang in his green hat, suspenders and lederhosen, holding a tablet computer. There are six praetorians standing guard in front of the throne, with red plumes on their helmets, silver and golden plating, and armed with spear guns.

There's a large cube in the middle of the room, seemingly made of light, with a fireball floating in the middle that pulses like a heartbeat. When it's not buzz-crackling like a snapped high-voltage power line, it barks out random broadcasts, like Adolf Hitler's incendiary monologue at the 1934 Nuremberg rally.

Wolfgang steps off his throne and whirl-steps back and forth in front of Oliver, Andron and Lysandra, sniffing the air and making lemon-faces while tapping the Spear in his hand. His boots finally scrape to a stop in front of Oliver. He uses the tip of the Spear to force Oliver's chin up.

"Oliver Mancer, I presume," he says over his pince-nez.

"Please, don't harm my friends. I can pay whatever you want, just name it."

Wolfgang looks over to Cygnus and says calmly, "What do you think, Cygnus, should we accept silver pieces for destroying one of our drones, damaging our building?" Then he shakes and spits, "*Plotting to kill us, bankrolling the entire operation and killing ten of our guards?*"

"I think we should smash-smashy his head in with a silver hammer, guv'nor, if you ask me."

"Please, Cygnus, we are a Christosian Church. Would Yeshua do that? I don't think so." Wolfgang whirl-steps to a side table, lays down the Spear and returns with his arms behind his back. "Yeshua would forgive Oliver of his transgressions and would set him and his friends free, with a mild request that they sin no more."

He whirl-steps back to Oliver.

"But we're not so forgiving. And Lord knows we could do with a large charitable contribution from the husband of that penny-a-liner, that hack, that fool with a pen, Henri Charlevoix." Wolfgang stands with his groin inches away from Oliver's face and his hands behind his back, rocking on his boot heels.

"Now, can you imagine what a coup that would be, Cygnus? To have Oliver donate his vast fortune to the Church, after his beloved husband devoted his entire life to trying to destroy it?"

"I suppose it would be a big biggy, guv. An ultra-spectacular jobber for one and all."

"Indeed, Cygnus, but there should be some humiliation to go along with it, don't you think? After all, we can't just let him buy his way out of problems. What example would that set for our kinder?"

"Would only be fair, guv, and would teach the wee ones a valuable lesson."

"Genau," Wolfgang says, "I agree," as he grabs Oliver by the hair and makes him look up. "What do you say, Herr Mancer to . . . let me think . . . for you and your friends' freedom . . . five hundred million dollars and a nice, juicy suck off?" he asks, stroking Oliver's cheeks with his leather-smelling hand.

"Yes, I'll do it, if you let us go," Oliver's voice cracks.

"Do what?"

"I'll transfer five hundred million to the Church and . . . I'll do it, if you let us go."

"You'll do what?" Wolfgang asks, cupping his ear.

"I'll give you a . . . a . . . blowjob."

"The deal wasn't for a blowjob, Herr Mancer. It was for a *nice, juicy suck off*," he says, slapping Oliver across the face with the back of his hand.

"Then I'll do it," Oliver cries, with a bleeding lip.

"Do what?"

"Give you a . . . give you a . . . *a nice, juicy suck off*," he whimpers.

"No, thanks, I prefer a different kind of head," Wolfgang blurts, baring his teeth, while pulling a silver hammer from behind his back and raising it.

It gleams in the light.

Then smashes down on Oliver's head, followed by several wild hammer swings that land with wet fish *twacks*, spraying blood, skull and brain parts. TWACK TWACK TWACK TWACK TWACK until Oliver is a dead fish with a cratered skull.

Cygnus laughs as everyone else winces and looks away.

Lysandra pulls at her restraints as a praetorian jabs a needle in her arm and she slumps over. Andron sobs with sudden memories. The boyish smile, blue eyes and flowing hair. The generosity and kindness. Fighting side by side with him in the Go-Go. The fragile kid he first met in the derelict park. Another casualty. Andron's eyes are wild, looking down, puffing through clenched teeth.

Wolfgang whistles as he walks up to Andron with a crooked smile. His uniform covered with Oliver's blood, skull and brain pieces.

"What about this one, you suppose he'd like to get hammered with his friend?" Wolfgang asks as he practice swings the hammer, stopping it right before hitting Andron, then leaving it resting on the top of his head with his arm extended.

"I don't know, guv? He did fetch the bitch for us, so we owe him a little for that."

"What are you thinking, Cygnus?" Wolfgang asks, turning back to look.

"Let me have some fun with him first, guv. Turn his brain into mush-mushy, before giving it the ole' smash-smashy."

"Wunderbar idea, Cygnus," Wolfgang says, as cadets run up to take the bloody hammer from him, hold a bowl for him to wash in and hand him a warm damp towel to wipe his face and hands. "Guards, put him in the suit and stick his head in Cygnus's world."

Praetorians rope an electric cord around Andron's neck, before unbinding his hands. They force him to stand, while they strip him and make him put on the neoprene suit. "Jesus, Andron, you've really let yourself go," Cygnus laughs, seeing Andron naked. They force him to the chair, strap him in and lock the helmet in place. Cygnus puts records on his turntables, listening to each in turn with a headphone that he holds over his ear. "Any last words, Andi-o, before I stick you in the blender?" he asks, while praetorians winch Andron's shoulder straps and wire in the back of his helmet and suit with quick connects.

"Yeah, I do," Andron puffs. "I killed you before, you fucking sonofabitch, and I'm going to do it a—"

"Oh, Andron," Cygnus says, after making Andron's body go limp. "You're so butch."

"Wach auf, Liebling, your coming out Zeremonie is about to begin," Wolfgang whispers, gently stroking Lysandra's cheeks.

She's on a gold-leafed altar bed with winged gargoyles for legs that are shaped to look like they're holding silver bedposts in their claws. She's on satin sheets with scattered rose petals and is wearing a snowy charmeuse robe. Her arms and legs are spread apart, bound to each post with brown leather straps.

Wolfgang taps her cheek and says, "Wakey-wakey."

"I'm awake, asshole," Lysandra says, looking around the stage and room. She sees Andron twitching in the sphere, Deidre and Mike sitting beside Wolfgang's throne, sipping coke from silver chalices and eating popcorn, while Franz taps away on his tablet. She pulls on her leather bindings.

The Sizzle plays another broadcast:

Crashing, oh! Four- or five-hundred feet into the sky and it . . . it's a terrific crash, ladies and gentlemen. It's smoke, and it's in flames now; and the frame is crashing to the ground, not quite to the mooring mast. Oh, the *humanity*! And all the passengers screaming around here. I told you; it—I can't even talk to people, their friends are on there! Ah! It's . . . it . . . it's a . . . ah! I . . . I can't talk, ladies and gentlemen. Honest: it's just laying there, a mass of smoking wreckage.

"*You asshole, Judas*!" Lysandra screams over to Mike from her bed. "*How could you?*"

"I was just following orders. Anyway, you're the GMO with bootleg genetics. So, you're the asshole around here, methinks, *Subtractive Loser*," he shouts back, then pops some popcorn in his mouth.

"You said you loved me."

"What can I say?" he says while chewing. "You was played. You were a dead lay anyway. Very subpar for a stripper." He pops some more popcorn in his mouth.

"*You* took my book."

"Nah, that was me," Deidre says.

"Huh-why?"

"Just fucking with your head so you'd distrust the others, maybe give my hubby a better shot at your crab-infested panties."

"Your hubby?"

"Enough!" Wolfgang shouts. "This is a religious ceremony, not a soap opera." He slides the Spear between Lysandra's breasts, cutting her dress while licking his lips. Lysandra looks away in disgust. He stands and whirl-walks to the Sizzle platform and kneels before it, holding up the Spear with both hands.

"Sophia, we shall defile and impale the Magdalene for your glory. By this sacrifice and by our possession of the Holy Spear, we will bring about the rightful order through your Holy Church, amen."

The Sizzle crackles out:

For it is written, Job 38:

Where were you when I laid the earth's foundation?

Tell me, if you understand.

Who marked off its dimensions? Surely you know!

Who stretched a measuring line across it?

On what were its footings set,

or who laid its cornerstone—

while the morning stars sang together

and all the angels shouted for joy?

The doors open and a procession of celebrities in Klansmen-like red robes parade in with upside-down crucifixes and fake beards, chanting *Sanguineum Maria*. Those up front wave around golden thuribles that waft out clouds of hashish while the rest clutch red candles. The procession splits to form a semicircle around the stage.

Wolfgang walks out to front center with Franz beside him. A floodlight snaps on him while the bottom-lit bed glows red. Lysandra shakes her head back and forth, pulling on her bindings. A silver speaker-box microphone squeaks down from above and Wolfgang puts his fists on his hips and speaks into it.

"Aspirants of the sacred brotherhood, so sprach Nietzsche, *if you stare into the abyss, the abyss stares back at you*. For the first time, instead of looking into virtual reality games, virtual reality games are going to look into us.

"Using one of our strapping cadet volunteers wearing a specially designed helmet and silicone sensing hair, Cygnus will experience our world and provide 4-code data stimulus for our latest game, *Bloody Mary*."

He raises his hand and the assembled start chanting, *Sanguineum Maria*. He nods to Franz, who presses his tablet and a stage door swings open.

There's the sound of hooves and a caterwaul that rattles the walls. The hooded men step back and up-tempo their *Sanguineum Marias* with shrill voices.

HRROONNH-snort

The Minotaur steps into view. The audience gasps. Head of a bull, body of a large chiseled man, covered in black silicon hair and a giant erection poking through its loin cloth. It looks to the side and bellows *HRROONNH-snort* again before clopping across the stage in its hoof-boots. It stops and coughs, "*Hrroonnh*," in a nasal voice.

"Sorry," Franz says to a frowning Wolfgang. "Bad Wi-Fi."

He taps on his tablet and the Minotaur starts clomping forward again, bellowing *HRROONNH-snort*.

It clops to a stop at the foot of the altar bed, drops on all fours and crawls up, sniffing and snorting the bottom of Lysandra's feet and then moving up her body with gooey snorts to the nape of her neck. It crawls up until it nudges Lysandra's legs apart with its knees. It pulls off its loincloth and puts its hands on its hips, exposing its hairy, throbbing monster.

It runs its hand over Lysandra's knee and up her inner thigh. She stops struggling, becomes strangely still and then mumbles something.

"What did she say?" Wolfgang asks Franz.

"I don't know, something French," Franz replies.

She says it again. The words ring this time, with a voice ancient and pure.

Libère-moiiiiiii!

She yanks on a strap and this time it pulls a bedpost clean out of a gargoyle's hand. The gargoyle breaks and the altar bed collapses on its side with a heavy thud. The Minotaur loses its balance and tumbles off. It rears up on its hooves, bellows out an *HRROONNH-snort* and clops back to the collapsed bed. Lysandra frantically fumbles with the buckle strap on her other wrist, with her back to the Minotaur. Fumbles as the Minotaur climbs on the bed. Then thrusts her free hand out toward it, turning to face it, unable to free her other hand.

"Stop," she says.

The Minotaur stops and snorts.

"T'as une clope?" she asks, flicking her thumb as though she's holding a lighter.

"Une clope? . . . a smoke?"

The Minotaur grunts and snorts.

She turns and, this time, manages to unbuckle her other hand. She grabs the silver bedpost and swings it around and smashes it into the Minotaur, connecting with his jaw and dropping him like a slaughterhouse bull.

She unbinds her legs, rolls off the bed and comes up holding the bedpost like a katana.

"What are you waiting for? *Kill the bitch!*" Wolfgang screams at the praetorian guards who are staring at her, gap-mouthed.

The fireball crackles "Ride of the Valkyries."

One takes aim and fires. Lysandra deflects the spear with a wrist-flick of the bedpost and then baton-twirls it as she rushes them. She spins and kicks one in his helmet, denting it and sending him flying. Grabs another's spear gun and forces him to shoot it into the throat of the man next to him.

Her punches, kicks and cracks of the bedpost are Wagner in triple-speed. Her arms blur into a multi-armed cyclone Kali from which praetorians fly unconscious, dead or grievously injured. Kicks a spear gun out of one of their hands. As it flies up, she thrusts the blunt end of the bedpost into another one's face. The spear gun lands in her hands just as Mike stands and aims his RG at her. She zings a spear that twangs into his chest and his RG drops out of his hand along with his popcorn. He clutches the spear shaft with a confused look, his life bleeding away.

"Oops," she says, covering her mouth. "Did I fire that off too soon? I blame the Church."

She aims the spear gun at Deidre. Deidre extends her RG out beside her, slowly lowers it, maintaining eye contact. Springs to her feet, does a few warm-up punches, cracks her neck and then snarls at Lysandra.

Lysandra frowns back, then smiles and drills her with a spear.

"*No fairrrr...*" Deidre wheezes, as she collapses, staring quizzically at the spear jutting out from between her breasts.

"That was for Rachy," Lysandra says. "Indiana Jones'd ya."

The Sizzle, which had been slowly growing larger and brighter the whole time, drifts out of its containment unit, causing a huge spark and killing the power. Backup power snaps on with a loud chirping alarm, flashing blue lights and repeating:

Attention, core containment loss, everyone must evacuate the building immediately.
Attention, core containment loss, everyone must evacuate the building immediately.

There's a stampede for the exits, with Wolfgang in the rear, whirl-walking as fast as his robot-assisted legs can carry him. Lysandra picks up the bloodied silver bedpost and helicopters it at him. It smashes into his legs, shatters his robotics and sends him sprawling. He tries to keep going by pulling himself arm-over-arm on the tiled floor.

She picks up the Spear and runs up to him, watches him slither along the ground and then squishes her foot into his back. He turns over to look up at her with outstretched arms.

"Please, I can give you anything you want."

"I have it all, right here, right now," she says, raising the Spear over her head with both hands.

"Please, I have a family," he says shielding his face.

"So did I, asshole," she says, as she plunges the Spear into his ribcage and twists it.

"Um ... *Überraschung!*" she says, as the life drains from Wolfgang's black eyes, "*surrr*-PRIZE!"

CHAPTER 23:
THE FIFTH FORCE

"You okay? . . . *Andron?*"

Lysandra has the helmet off and is undoing his shoulder harness and bindings. Bright blue LCD lights are still flashing, but the alarm is only screeching in the hallways.

"*Andron!*" She shakes him again.

"What have you done to him?" She spins to glare at Cygnus's hologram, who had been slumped over in his chair before and is now rubbing the side of his head.

"Nothing, Birdie, he'll come to in a moment," Cygnus says, suddenly following the Sizzle with alarm.

Andron snaps awake with a gasp of air.

"You all right?"

"Yeah," Andron says, looking around at all the dead bodies and the Sizzle hovering around the room. "What happened?"

"I get triggered when I hear chanting, I guess. How about you?" she says, helping him to his feet.

Andron raises his eyebrows at her, then scratches his head. "I think that thing messed up what was supposed to be happening in the game and then things really went strange," he says, looking at the fallen Minotaur.

"So, what do we do now?"

"Are there any more guards?"

"Everyone ran for the exits when the alarm started going off."

"Has he been bothering you?" Andron asks, thumbing back at Cygnus.

"Nah, he's been mostly offline since he game-overed as the bullshit ass-clown from suck lagoon."

Cygnus half-smiles but doesn't say anything.

"Listen," Andron says as he puts his hands on her shoulders. "Let me deal with him. I want you to get out of here and run. Don't stop running until you get to the evacuation point. Then get yourself back to the compound and start telling everyone everything. And I mean, *everything*. Understand?"

"No ... I *don't* understand," she says with a quivering lip, looking into his eyes.

"Lysandra, I saw it," Andron says with a glint in his eye. "In the game I mean. With that thing bending things. The fifth force." He puts his hands on her shoulders. "You were worried so much about who you were and I was worried about why I was, when all along the problem wasn't with who or why we are, but with where-when we are."

"I'm so glad you worked that all out, but what happened to *in this together*, huh?" she says, pushing him.

Andron walks up, wraps his arm around her, and she cries into his neoprene chest.

"I love you," he says. "I always have and always will, but you already know that this has to be. That this has always been."

She looks up at him, blinking away tears. "But you're the only one I have left."

"You have to go now. It's the only way, or all this will be for nothing and we all will have died in vain. The Confederacy. I saw it. It's important. Do you understand?"

She nods.

"I also know how to end this, but you have to run as fast as you can. *Understand?*"

She looks in his eyes for the longest time. Stands on her toes and kisses him on the cheek. The kiss lingers like a daughter's from long ago. She turns and heads to the door, picking up her Uzi RG. She checks it and sees that it's back online. She turns to look at him one last time, wipes away a tear, then runs out.

She jogs down empty corridors and grand hallways. Lights flash and the alarm is fingers-on-chalkboard chirping, but there is also the faint sound of babies crying. She keeps going, making it all the way to the exit, stops, bites her lip and then runs back. Looks into several rooms, pointing her Uzi RG around, but they're all empty. Looks up at the lights, checks a watch that isn't there and starts to run again, but freezes after running by the plenary nursing room.

"Are they making more babies like me?" she whispers, as she crouches down and moves slowly to the window. She slides up against the wall and peeks in. Blinks at the sight of Franz moving from crib to crib injecting babies with a large needle.

"What the fuck are you doing?" she shouts, as she bursts through the door.

Franz looks up at her and then down at the baby he's just put down. "We're in IP abort protocol. All Yeshua strains must be terminated under strict orders of the Über Raven."

"But you're killing babies . . . you monster!"

"I have my orders," Franz answers and then says, "Heil, Raven," before moving to the last crib.

"Heil, fuck you!" Lysandra says, as she fires a burst of her Uzi RG into Franz and he drops dead, clutching his death needle.

Lysandra checks the cribs. Each one has a cold dead baby in it, except the twelfth one. The child Franz was about to murder. Lysandra looks down at the child, who's not crying but moving slowly. She picks him up, holds him against her sheer dress, lowers her head to smell him and smiles.

She stares at him and then brings him up to kiss. He touches her cheek with his tiny hand.

The touch warms her cheek and grows within her.

The blessed and everlasting hand of peace.

She feels love and hope in the middle of the carnage. Feels forgiveness. All the weight she'd been carrying, the loss of her mother, father, Cookie, Rachel, Jasmin, Dylan, Winston, Oliver, Mike's betrayal, Deidre's backstab, leaving Andron. All this loss and, in the middle of it, from that child's fingertips, light. Light, bursting forth where there was a black hole before. A peace settles over her unease, a peace that surpasses all understanding. She looks at the child and speaks to him in French. She says a phrase that means not "free me," but one that means, "we are one, we are free."

"*Nous sommes un, nous sommes libres,*" she says as she tickles his cheek, before running back out into the hall with baby Yeshua in one arm and her Uzi RG in the other.

Runs.

Into the long barrel of a forty-five, pointed by Moses Jones.

"Sorry, sugar," Moses says. "You and that baby are Church property. I can't let you just walk out of here."

"Then pull the trigger," she says looking from one his eyes to the other and rocking the baby, with no trace of fear.

"Do you have any idea what a forty-five would do to your pretty face at this close range?"

"I think, actually, I do," she says calmly. "But do you have any idea what firing it will do to you?"

The barrel wavers.

Wavers.

Then Moses pulls the trigger.

Pulls it again.

Two praetorians slump over at the other end of the hallway, their spear guns falling out of their hands. Moses looks back at Lysandra.

"I know how to get us out of here," he says, turning to run. "...*Follow me if you want to live.*"

Andron walks over to Wolfgang's corpse, puts his foot on his stomach and pulls the Spear out of his chest. Walks over to the throbbing fireball, shielding his eyes with one hand and brandishing the bloody Spear with the other. Raises it above his shoulders as he nears.

"Don't do it, Andron. You'll kill us all."

Andron turns to look at Cygnus, who is dressed like old Cygnus, when they visited his planet together, such a long time ago. "That's kind of the idea," Andron says.

"Why?"

"What do you mean, why?"

"I don't think you want to end your life so flippantly."

"Why not? Didn't you teach me about the eternal recurrence? Aren't I fated to come back in a better world?"

"That was bullshit I fed you at the time. The universe and our lives are bubbles that pop and never come back again."

Andron stares at Cygnus without answering.

"Andi-o, you'll have to trust me on this one. I offer you your only chance at eternal life. There is no one to perpetuate our existence but us. This is all fixable. This entire mess. Fixable. Come on. You know me and what I can do. I can make it so you can take over the entire Church. All of it. Think of what we could accomplish."

"Oh, yeah. And how are you going to do that?"

"I can make this all look like an attempted coup orchestrated by Mike that you foiled at the last minute, saving the Church. Let's just say I have some leverage with the directors and Thomas's son, who we can squeeze to do what we want."

"I'm familiar with your methods, Cygnus. I don't particularly want to be the head of an evil empire."

"Andron, it doesn't have to be that way. You can introduce reforms. All sorts of reforms. Anything you like."

"What's in it for you?"

"This may seem funny to you, but I've changed. I don't have a Yeshua complex anymore. In fact, I've grown tired of this planet. I don't belong here. I just want your help to send me home. For all I know, they've figured out how to regenerate it by now."

"What about Lysandra?"

"She can go, even though she makes me weak. It won't be so bad if she moved far away. I'll leave her alone. You have my word."

"The word of the prince of lies?"

"Andron, I have always done right by you. All my moves have been driven by necessity. For survival. That's all there is in this universe. There's no God. There's only the choice to become one. To rise above good and evil. You have a chance to evolve into the next phase, to become a god, like me."

Andron's grip on the Spear loosens. He looks at the ground, confused.

"Did you ever stop to think, Andron, that we were meant to meet each other? To survive? That you were meant for something more? To transcend your limitations? To evolve?"

"I don't know, Cygnus, you paint such a bleak picture of the universe. That there's nothing in it but an empty struggle to adapt and survive. That there are no morals, no right or wrong, no human decency, except that which serves a selfish purpose."

"I'm sorry, Andron. But, in my three thousand years of existence, that's all I've found, a meaningless dance of the four fundamental forces of the universe— gravity, electromagnetism, the strong nuclear force and the weak one. And I'm offering you a golden ticket. Come on, it's always been about us, from the very beginning . . . *us*."

"You see . . . that's where I think you're wrong, Cygnus. There's a fifth force, a fifth fundamental interaction that's as old as the universe, extends to every particle, never weakens and can move objects over vast distances."

"What fifth force?"

Andon straightens, holding the Spear in his hand.

"I've thought about this. A higher love . . . something you know nothing about, but I began to theorize about in—"

He looks over at Cygnus, but his hologram has snapped off. There's rushing hoof steps and he's tackled from behind by the Minotaur. The Spear flies out of his hand.

He spins on his back, but the Minotaur has him pinned with its enormous weight. It looks up and roars, *HRROONNH-snort*, then savagely beats Andron in the face and head with its hairy fists. Andron is knocked into a dizzy half-consciousness. He sees himself from above. Sees himself fading.

Sees himself grab the beast by its balls and squeezing them with his nutcracker grip.

The Minotaur yelps and tries to pull away while Andron reaches for the Spear and thrusts it into its throat. The Minotaur gurgles and its helmet tumbles off and thuds on the ground sparking and buzzing, revealing the man underneath, covered in silicon hair.

He walks toward the Sizzle, shielding an eye. His other is swollen shut, his nose pointing the wrong way, his ears are ringing. As he nears, his face burns like it's been splashed with battery acid as he's pelted with radiation. He's weak. He drops to his knees and throws up. He wipes his mouth, looks up and sees the ghosts of Astrid and Naomi telling him, "it's time" and to "see it through."

He puffs through clenched teeth and gets up on one foot, then the other.

Catches himself before falling over.

Hops on one foot.

He brings the Spear next to his ear, reaches way back with it. Hops forward.

Then drills it into the heart of the Sizzle in a giant explosion of light.

Followed by a mushroom cloud.

JUDGEMENT.

CHAPTER 24:
JUDGMENT

The picture becomes a postage stamp.

The one with Lysandra, torn white dress, breast exposed, running with a baby in one arm and an Uzi in the other. An exploding building behind her, taking up the entire sky. Moses sprinting beside her with his long brown jacket flowing behind, forty-five in hand.

The icon of the *No Limits* revolution.

Lysandra makes it back to the compound with the baby, unharmed by the blast and its fallout. She's adopted by Oliver's family and leads the *No Limits* revolution. A revolution that spreads like mustard sown on fertile ground.

Some call her Magdalene. Others, Joan of Arc. Very few know that the child she carried out of that building that day is a genetic clone of Yeshua. A baby damaged by its birth and time in the Church's soulless nursery, but an exact match just the same.

There's an investigation and arrests. Moses turns state's evidence. Most of the Church's hierarchy end up wearing orange. All except Conner, who beats the murder rap only to become the battered face of the Church as it's bludgeoned to death by lawsuits.

The Church disbands, its assets sold for fines and reparations. A victims' trust is awarded the rights to *Jerusalem 4C*, which crests at a billion users a day. The Authentic Yeshua mustard and beer brands are sold in ballparks.

Sparzo is impeached and the *Domestic Terrorism Act* is repealed. The skies no longer have killer drones flying around, controlled by bounty hunters, licensed to kill political outlaws. Lysandra even ends up on the presidential ticket.

Oliver symbolically rests next to Henri Charlevoix. The lineups to visit the graves stretch for blocks. Many bring dog-eared copies of *No Limits* with them.

The Hall of the Revolutionaries in the Nevado desert is a national monument, with large marble statues of Dylan, Jasmin, Winston, Oliver and Andron.

Indeed, the fifteen years following the Storming of the Bastille are marked by prosperity and peace. Nobody sees the shit that goes down once our ship arrives.

The feed stops.

The crew members each tap their neuro implants.

The spinning card slows and then falls, Judgment side up.

They all stare down at the archangel Gabriel blowing on her trumpet, calling up the faithful.

"What shit goes down when our ship arrives?" Commander Penny Armstrong asks as Carlos and Aiden look at CAM-DI with alarm.

"I don't know. The rest is white."

"What do you mean, the rest is white?"

"It's subject to an HFL."

"HFL?"

"Heisenberg Feedback Loop."

"Heisenberg Feedback Loop?"

"It's what happens when the predictor is part of the prediction, if you will."

"So, it's white because we're part of it?"

"Exactly."

"But you know that shit goes down?"

"Yes."

"Why not anything else?"

"Let me explain it with a story."

"Is it a long one?" Penny groans.

"Ha-ha, no, it's short.

"A man walks into a fortuneteller, wanting desperately to know his future. So the fortuneteller looks into her crystal globe and sees that he gets killed crossing the road leaving her building."

"So, she tells him?"

"She can't."

"Why not?"

"Because she'd see an entirely different future, one where she warns him about crossing the road and he avoids dying, but then she doesn't see him getting killed crossing the road to begin with, so he gets killed anyway because she doesn't warn him—"

"Ah, it gets stuck in a loop, I get it. So, what does she tell him?"

"She can't tell him anything about his future, because her globe is white. So she tells him the only thing she can."

"Which is what?"

"Choose your paths carefully and hope for the best."

There is long pause, after which Penny says, "Sorry, CAM-DI, not meaning to be rude, but after all that . . . the mustard seed and everything . . . the best you can come up with is, *choose your paths carefully and hope for the best?*"

"CAM-DI . . . are you okay?"

CAM-DI waits for a wave of nausea to pass.

"Yes, Commander, I'm fine, just a little played out. Anyway, whatever I come up with really doesn't matter . . . it's what you come up with that matters. That's what the card's about, coming to your own realization. But only you can take that step."

"Are we any closer to knowing how Cygnus got on our ship, at least?"

"Commander," CAM-DI says, looking at Penny with her bright blue eyes. "I think you already know the answer."

"Does it have something to do with the Sizzle?"

"Yes. I mean ramming the Spear of Destiny into a Sizzle was bound to cause some freaky shit to happen with where-when things end up. But there's more behind it that you're not seeing, but I think you're close. Don't think so hard about what happened that sent Cygnus here, think about why. The Hermit card."

"You mean why Andron threw the Spear into it?"

CAM-DI nods.

Penny rubs her chin. Her jade eyes narrow as she looks down with a furrowed brow. After a minute of staring at the same spot, her face brightens and her eyes lift up to look at CAM-DI with the answer.

"It's because of the . . ." she bites her lower lip to begin to say the two words.

THE END

ACKNOWLEDGMENTS

Ratings matter! Please leave one at your favorite place.

For Judea in the time of Jesus, Edmund Stapfer's, *Palestine in the Time of Christ* (Hodder and Stoughton, London (1886)), was a rare find and highly illuminating.

To learn about the true heroes of the Six Days War whose exploits inspired Thomas' adventure, you must read Steven Pressfield's, *The Lion's Gate: On the Front Lines of the Six Day War* (Sentinel (2014)).

Steven Runciman's, *The First Crusade* (Cambridge University Press (2005)), was a great resource and a good read on all things crusader related.

I am once again greatly indebted to Dan Zakreski and Val Nicholson for their editing and guidance. Further editing was provided by Kelly Lamb, who I highly recommend. The cover art and layout were created by bookstylings.com who did great work on my first book and on this one.

This one goes out to my father, Peter, a rock of a man who set me on the path of righteousness and tolerated my wanderings.